Fiona knew she should leave.

*I*t didn't help that when Holburn stood this close, her brain lost its ability to reason. She caught the scent of his shaving soap. The smell of it didn't just make her knees weak, it created a yearning deep inside her that urged Fiona to move closer . . .

"I should go," she murmured without conviction. Her feet stayed planted right where they were.

He poured more wine, filling a glass for her this time. "Then have a drink before you leave."

She took the glass, more to give her something to consider other than *him*. His anger was gone and in its place was a sensual intensity that she had best avoid—but feared she wouldn't. It had been a long time since she'd felt this attraction to a man. She gulped the wine. It went down the wrong way and she started coughing.

"Steady," Holburn urged, his voice low, seductive. He lightly rubbed a hand between her shoulder blades. His touch felt good. Too good. "Who are you?" he asked quietly. "Let me have a name."

Fiona had honed a good sense of self-preservation over the past year. This man meant to seduce her, and if she wasn't careful, she was going to let him.

By Cathy Maxwell

Cathy Maxwell

A SEDUCTION AT CHRISTMAS

AVON

An Imprint of HarperCollins*Publishers*

This is a work of fiction. Names, characters, places, and incidents are products of the author's imagination or are used fictitiously and are not to be construed as real. Any resemblance to actual events, locales, organizations, or persons, living or dead, is entirely coincidental.

AVON BOOKS
An Imprint of HarperCollins*Publishers*
10 East 53rd Street
New York, New York 10022-5299

First Avon Books paperback printing: November 2008

Avon Trademark Reg. U.S. Pat. Off. and in Other Countries, Marca Registrada, Hecho en U.S.A.
HarperCollins® is a registered trademark of HarperCollins Publishers.

Printed in the U.S.A.

10 9 8 7 6 5 4 3 2 1

This book is dedicated to Powhatan, Virginia—

to my friends and neighbors,
to the Y and the yoga studio
and the yarn shop and the restaurants
and Oakdale Stables and St. John Neumann's
and all the churches and
to everyone who makes this a fulfilling place to live.

I'd also like to thank Sara Saavedra
for her help with the translations
and hope she will be available
when Andres has his own story.
Gracias!

As always, I am wealthy in my friends.

The Prophecy
Whose hand guides our destiny?

1800

*I*t was hell being the family black sheep.

Usually, Dominic Lynsted—Nick to his friends—weathered the role well, even took pride in it. He enjoyed defying his overbearing uncles by pushing every boundary. After all, what good was there to being a young duke if you didn't have some fun with the title? At one and twenty, Nick had held the title Duke of Holburn for eleven years, but only since he'd recently wrestled control of his estates from his uncles' guardianship was he really beginning to enjoy himself.

However last night had been one of inspired debauchery.

Memories, snippets really, made their appearance

between the hammerlike pounding of his brain against his skull. He recalled beautiful, sloe-eyed women, music, and dancing. Nick couldn't remember ever experiencing such exuberance. Of course, now as he came to wakefulness, his eyelids felt glued to his cheeks, his body lacked the strength and the will to move even a hair's distance, and his mouth tasted of soured wine and the licorice-flavored liquor the locals made. The good news was he *could* feel his legs. At one point during the night before, he hadn't been certain he would walk again. He'd taken a step and fallen. He'd hit the ground hard.

Nick remembered being picked up and shouting that from hence forward he wanted to be carried by lovely Greek women everywhere he went, even into Parliament. In response, he had been carried, but Nick couldn't remember by whom or why—nor did he care.

First, he had to survive the anguish of over-indulgence. Later, he would atone for his sins. He'd apologize to the deadly dull Lord Livermore, his chaperone on his Grand Tour, for bailing out on any of the previous evenings' plans—wait!

Had it been yesterday when he'd met Andres? Or two, three, four days ago?

Nick could no longer remember.

Well, there was naught he could do now but

return to Lord Livermore and face his uncles' wrath when he returned to England. He knew they'd hear of this and any other transgressions since his cousin Richard was also making the Grand Tour of Greece and Italy with him. Richard would tell. He always did.

One thing was certain: his new-found friend Andres Ramigio Peiró, Barón de Vasconia, knew how to enjoy Greece.

He wondered if he could convince the silver-eyed Spaniard to accompany them to Rome?

"But I'm not going to drink anymore, I'm not going to drink anymore, I'm not going to drink anymore," Nick vowed in a litany under his breath, until he realized he wasn't wearing his boots.

Nick opened one eye to stare at his stockinged feet and was almost blinded by the Greek sun.

And the reason his bed was so hard was because he wasn't in it. He was lying on rock-solid earth, surrounded by ruins.

"What the devil—?"

He had no idea where he was. And it was quiet. Too quiet.

"Andres?" His voice was little more than a frog's croak.

There was no answer other than the annoying buzz of insects in the distance.

His head feeling as heavy as an anvil, Nick

gingerly came to his feet. That's when he noticed
the plump sheepskin flask leaning up against
the stone wall where he would see it. Greedily, he
stumbled toward it, uncorked it, and drank. The
water was already warm from the sun's heat but
his swollen tongue needed the liquid.

Nick drank until the flask was dry. Some of the
water had spilled out of his mouth and onto his
shirt. His neck cloth and jacket were long gone.
He didn't remember taking them off. He wiped
his mouth on his shirt and took stock of his surroundings.

He'd seen enough ruins to know he stood on
the foundation of what had once been a temple
built into the side of a mountain. No, there wasn't
one temple here, but dozens. The ruins seemed to
go on forever. At one time, this had been a powerful, sacred site—suddenly he knew where he was.
Delphi.

At one point, he and Andres had talked about
Delphi, the place the ancients had believed to be
the center of the earth. Nick remembered Andres
telling him at the taverna that they weren't far
from that once-holy site where the High Priestess
of the Oracle prophesized a man's fate. It had been
one of the few sober moments between them.
Nick had said he wished he knew his destiny and

Andres had laughingly promised to bring him to Delphi.

Well, here he was.

Nick turned in place. A road, a ribbon of dull gold amongst the dusty green of the trees, snaked down the mountainside into a valley but no one traveled it. The mountain's craggy peak rose above him. The path around the ruins of numerous small temples was blocked by fallen stone walls and other debris that had gathered over the decades. The sky was a bold, clear, blue, the sun merciless. The buzzing became pronounced. Locusts.

He wondered where his boots were . . . and the horses . . . and Andres—

A sense of foreboding settled over him. His money purse had been in the inside pocket of his missing coat. The idea that Andres would rob him didn't make sense. Nick had freely paid their expenses and there was really very little coin left in the purse, not that there had been that much to begin with. His late father's expensive tastes and gambling losses had emptied most of what was in the Holburn coffers. The cost of maintaining numerous estates was running through the rest. His uncles were financing his Grand Tour.

No, there was only one thing Nick owned that

was valuable—his signet ring, the gold emblem of the House of Holburn. The ring had been a gift from Charles II and priceless in the eyes of the family.

His uncles had coveted the ring even more than they did the title. They made it clear they thought Nick unworthy to be duke. They were both self-made men who hadn't stood in the shadow of their ducal brother but had earned titles of their own, Lord Maven and Lord Brandt.

Meanwhile, Nick's father had scandalized society by marrying his mistress, an opera dancer. As far as the uncles were concerned, the marriage had tainted the bloodlines. They'd told Nick as much a month ago when he'd successfully demanded the ring along with control of his estates. They had wanted him to continue to let them control his affairs, but Nick had turned one and twenty and the law was on his side.

They'd given him what he'd wanted, but not before predicting he was irresponsible enough to lose the ring—and now he'd fulfilled that prediction.

Nick stared at his bare hand in disbelief. Andres had been his friend. He'd *trusted* him—

A sound of pebbles tumbling over the rocks coming from the far side of a huge block of marble caught Nick's attention. "There you are," he said, relief overcoming his anger as he moved through the ruins toward the sound. "You are not going to believe what I thought you'd done—"

His voice broke off at the sight of a crone squatting in the shade of the marble. She was dressed in dusty, brown muslin, her bare feet as dark and leathery as his boots. She didn't look at him but rocked back and forth, humming as she sifted through the stones around her, letting them drop through her fingers into a basket beside her.

Nick wasn't superstitious but there was something not right here. It was too odd, too eerie. He took a step back, aware of how ancient and desolate a place this was.

The singing of the locusts was louder now and he realized with a start that the sound was coming from her. Her voice grew until it echoed off every rock and every tree on the mountain above them.

He whirled on the woman, his patience gone with the loss of his ring. *"Who are you?"*

She didn't answer. Didn't even turn toward him but continued sifting through the dirt.

His head was clear now, but the air around him had grown thick, sulfurous. Breathing became difficult . . . and was it his imagination or was the sky darkening? It was still the same blue but a veil of darkness seemed to rise all around him.

Nick tugged at the neck of his shirt, craving fresh air. The locust chorus filled his head and he knew something evil lurked here. Something sane men avoided—

The crone raised her veiled head and looked right at him. *She was deformed.* Her eyes were sightless, milky membranes. Her nose was nothing more than holes in her face and her mouth full of black, rotting stubs of teeth. The thin, gray braids around her face began curling like snakes.

Nick staggered back in horror. He lost his footing and was sent head over heels down a hill to land on the marble foundation of another temple below. He hit the ground hard. For a second, the air was knocked out of his chest, paralyzing him.

The crone came to stand where he'd just fallen. She spread her skinny arms and her body began to lengthen and grow stronger. Her muslin robes turned to snowy silk. Her skin became smooth and took on the glow of youth. The braids changed from snakes to curls of the rich, glowing red of the setting sun.

Gasping for breath, Nick wanted to believe his mind played tricks—and yet the ground felt firm and real beneath him, the marble warm from the sun.

Her face became the sky. Rosy lips formed around teeth that were suddenly white as pearls.

Her veil floated in the air around her, its shadow shielding those terrible eyes.

"What do you ask of me?"

He didn't know if he *heard* her as much as sensed her speak. She spoke a language he did not know and yet he understood.

If this was madness, so be it. Slowly, Nick came to his feet. The apparition didn't fade but hovered before him.

What did he want?

There was only one thing. "I want my ring."

A light seemed to go through her, causing the vision to waver, and then she said, "Beware innocence."

Nick waited. There had to be more. What sort of a prophecy was that?

The vision's lips curved into a secret smile. She was done.

But *he* wasn't. *"What the devil do you mean?"*

Her head bowed. She was fading.

"I want *more*," he shouted. Didn't she understand? He had to have his ring back. It was his heritage, his right. Worse, his uncles would never forgive him. He'd never be a man in their eyes— and Nick realized he wanted that. As much as he pretended not to care, as often as he flouted their authority—they were the only father he had.

He would never be forgiven if he lost it.

He'd never forgive himself.

The vision didn't care. She vanished, fading into the relentlessly blue Mediterranean sky. The air was filled with silence.

Nick felt as if all energy had been drained from him, and then he heard a sound. He turned and found the crone once again sitting in the shade of the ruins, her fingers running through the stones in her basket.

Nick took a step up the hill toward her, and then caught himself. She was no help to him. What had been was no longer.

And then he realized it didn't matter.

Beware innocence.

What sort of prophecy was that? *He* could have predicted the same thing. Nothing good came of trusting. Hadn't Andres brutally borne that point home?

Sooner or later, every man had to stand on his own.

But first, he had to find Andres before the bastard sold his ring. He would start in Athens with a visit to the jewelers. If Andres was wise, he would have the ring melted down. Nick planned on reaching him before he could do such a thing.

He turned his back on the crone and began walking down the steep, stony path. It was hours before he met a traveler on the road and two days before he arrived in Athens.

Ignoring Livermore and his cousin Richard's questions, Nick started going through every haunt he and Andres had visited before the night in Delphi. But he didn't find the Spaniard or his ring. Not even a search along the docks turned up anyone who had even seen Andres leave Greece.

In the end, Nick had no choice but to return to London and confess he'd lost the ring.

Of course, Richard had already told the uncles of Nick's disappearance and Livermore had added his own complaints about Nick's "rakehell behavior."

For once, his uncles did not openly chastise him. No, their disapproval would run through the months and years ahead. But their opinion couldn't be lower than the one he held of himself.

A search for Andres had to be set aside as the business affairs of the Holburn estates took over. Nick had demanded control of his affairs from his uncles and now was to learn that the expenses of a duke with a large, extensive family were many . . . and his uncles' stewardship during the years of his minority had not served him well. For all their arrogant pride, they hadn't paid close attention to their guardianship of his affairs as they should have. Nick was closer to ruin than he could have ever imagined.

In desperation, he turned to gaming tables and that's when something strange began to happen.

Like his father before him, Nick's luck at cards had never been good. He'd wasted more money than he cared to admit on chance. However, since his fateful meeting with the Oracle, his luck seemed to have changed. It was as if he could *not* lose. That didn't mean he didn't suffer losses. The cards sometimes did turn on him. His horse sometimes did come in last. But overall, through the course of an evening, Nick always ended up ahead. Sometimes by great sums, sometimes by small ones.

Fearing he was being fanciful, he tested his theory by trying to lose. He couldn't. By the end of the night, fortune always came his way.

He attempted to transfer this strange good fortune to other ventures—cargo ships or investing in the funds or planting new crops. Those ventures always failed and it wasn't only Nick who suffered but also those investors who had joined him in the scheme.

Guilt drove Nick to recoup his losses. He began playing for higher stakes. Gambling lost all amusement. It became survival. His companions became the habitués of the gaming world, the roués, rakes, and scoundrels. His dueling skills with both pistols and swords became both legendary and necessary. In time, Nick's soul became as hardened as theirs . . . or so he feared.

Beware innocence.

He obeyed those words, secretly fearing what special door in hell they could unlock.

Not for him was the comfort of wife and children. He saw to the well-being of those relatives dependent upon him, but kept his own company lest they also be tainted by the dark prophecy that had been cast over him.

His only hope of salvation was to find the ring his foolishness had lost.

He sent men in search of it, but it was gone. Both the emblem of his ancestry and Andres Ramigio, Barón de Vasconia, had disappeared.

But Nick knew that someday their paths would cross again, and when they did, he'd make the silver-eyed Spaniard pay for his treachery—and maybe then the Oracle's prophecy would be broken.

PART I
Chance

Three goddesses spin a man's fate:
Lachesis sings of the things that were,
Clotho those that are, and Atropos the
things that are to be.

Of the three, fear Atropos . . .

Chapter One

December 1809

*F*iona Lachlan draped her shawl over her head as she pushed her way through the narrow, crowded street. The damp coldness of the December evening air cut right through the thin muslin of her dress. She tried not to shiver as she moved toward a hired coach waiting for her at the corner.

Well, it didn't actually wait for *her*. The woman who had hired the hack, Hester Bowen, was expecting Annie Jenkins to come. It was up to Fiona to convince Hester to take her in Annie's place.

The hack driver saw her coming and jumped from the box to open the door. Careful to keep her head down, Fiona climbed inside.

"You're *late*," Hester complained. She rapped on

the ceiling. *"Drive,"* she snapped at the coachman who shut the door behind Fiona.

"I said *eight*," Hester continued as the driver set the coach in motion, "You've left me waiting a full *ten* minutes. I'll tell you, Annie, my time is more valuable than yours . . ." Her voice trailed off into a beat of suspicious silence.

Fiona kept her head bowed, her hands clasped tightly in her lap. Every turn of the coach wheel was in her favor.

Hester ripped the shawl away. *"You aren't Annie Jenkins."*

Caught, Fiona quickly confessed, "No, I'm not. She couldn't come this evening and asked me if I would. My name is Fiona. I'm her neighbor. We let rooms next door to each other—*please,*" she beseeched, reaching for Hester's arm to stop her from throwing up the window and shouting for the coachman to stop. "Annie sent me. She said it would be all right. She assured me you wouldn't mind."

Hester's eyes were alive with anger. "You are *Scottish.*" She curled her lips and pretended to gag.

"I am, but my accent isn't thick," Fiona answered, almost choking on the words. She hated having to defend her heritage, something she seemed to have to do daily in London. "And I do speak well."

Better than you, she wanted to add. "Whatever errand you wished Annie to perform, I can do it."

"Annie and I are friends," Hester countered. Her voice had a hard edge.

She was a bit older than Fiona's own three and twenty years. In the coach's flickering light, her blond hair seemed almost white. Beneath her fur-lined velvet cape, she wore a beaded and lace gown of the darkest blue. Its bodice was so tight, she appeared to have cleavage up to her neck. All in all, she appeared exactly what she was—the most infamous courtesan in London. "We go back a long way," Hester said. "I *trust* her."

"Well, Annie and I are friends, too," Fiona answered. Necessity made for strange bedfellows. "She knew you needed her and asked me to help."

Hester sat back against the hard leather seat with a snort of disdain. "So what has happened to Annie this time? Has she deviled herself with gin or fallen in love—again?"

"She eloped," Fiona answered. "This morning. Her last act before she left was to knock on my door and beg me to help you."

"Who did she run off with now?" Hester asked without sympathy.

"A soldier. She is in love."

"Annie is *always* in love." Hester gave a heavy sigh. "Why are we all such fools when it comes to love?" Her words were laced with the irony of self knowledge. She looked at Fiona, studying her now and then nodding as if in approval. "What did Annie tell you about the task?"

"She said for me to dress well—"

Hester's keen gaze ran over the white muslin Fiona was wearing, seemingly taking in every detail. There had been a time when Fiona had owned a closet full of the finest dresses. This dress and her dog Tad were all that was left of that former life.

"You look presentable enough," the courtesan decided. She reached over and picked one of Tad's dog hairs off Fiona's shawl, rubbing her fingers and releasing it to the floor.

Fiona gathered her courage. "You offered Annie twenty pounds for this favor. Will you pay me as well?"

Hester's lips curved into a sly smile. "Desperate for money, are we?"

"Of course. Isn't everyone?"

"In London," Hester agreed.

Fiona had been earning her money as a dressmaker but last month Madame Sophie had let her go. Madame's cousin had arrived from Belgium and took Fiona's place in the sewing room. As talented as Fiona felt she was with a needle, she was discovering few wanted to hire a Scotswoman, especially one who had the air of "Quality." They preferred their seamstresses without ambition or intelligence, the better to do as they were bid without questions. They didn't trust Fiona's knowledge or her manner.

Meanwhile, she needed money. Her landlord, Mr. Simon, threatened to turn her and Tad out into the streets. Fiona had already discovered how hard it was to find rooms that would let her keep Tad. She didn't want to lose these.

Of course, with twenty pounds, she might even be able to *leave* London. When her parents were alive, she'd dreamed of having her coming out here, of meeting a gallant gentleman, being swept off her feet. As a well-known magistrate's daughter, she could have hoped for a brilliant match. Now, she couldn't wait to kick the dust of this godforsaken place from her heels, and her longings were for a small cottage in the country where the air was free of soot and she could live in peace.

"Annie said it was not—" Fiona stopped, feeling heat rush to her cheeks. She forced herself to be blunt. "She said I'd not have to please a man."

Hester's sly, lazy smile vanished. Her gloved hand curled into a fist. "You'd best not. I'll slice your face so no one would want to look at you if you spread your legs for this one."

The brutal threat didn't intimidate Fiona. She'd learned that manners and fine clothes often masked evil in London. "You needn't worry," she said stiffly. "I don't do that."

Hester's gaze narrowed in disbelief. " 'Don't do that?' " She snorted. "We *all* do *that* if it is to our advantage. 'Tis not much work. You close your eyes and let them have it."

Bile rose in Fiona's throat. Memories she hated clouded her mind with images she struggled to forget—

"Are you all right?" Hester demanded. "You've gone pale. You aren't going to swoon on me, are you?"

Fiona shook her head, fighting the darkness. It had been a long time since she'd let this fear grip her—

"Then *breathe*," Hester ordered, something Fiona didn't think she could do until Hester reached over and slapped her.

The memories were replaced by shock. Fiona lifted a hand to her cheek. The slap had not been hard, but it had been effective.

Hester settled back into her corner of the hack, her expression thoughtful. "When were you raped?"

"A year ago." Fiona didn't even think to not answer. Tears threatened. She forced them back. Those men had ruined her, robbed her of her chance of a decent man—

"You'll overcome it," Hester said. "You are strong. We all are when we must be." She paused. Speculation gleamed in her eye before she said, "You know, you've the face and the body to earn fifty pounds in an hour if you've a mind to. You could do very well for yourself."

"I'd rather starve," Fiona returned, aware that she was close to doing that right now. Since her rape by a party of soldiers hunting for her rebel brother, there had been only one man who had caught her slightest interest—the Duke of Holburn. She'd seen him at a party almost a year ago when she'd been wearing this same dress. Their gazes had met, held. He'd even followed across the ballroom, but then she'd had to leave the dance to help her brother and his wife escape London before they could be captured.

Since then, she'd learned the duke had a dangerous reputation. Decent women avoided him, not that she was worried. He didn't travel in the same circles as seamstresses and she doubted if he would remember her even if they should meet again.

"What do you want me to do for the money?" Fiona asked.

Hester lifted a fur muff that matched her cape from the seat beside her and pulled from it a small vial. "I want you to pour this into a man's drink."

"What is it?" Fiona wondered, fearing the worst.

"Not poison," Hester assured her, "although he will wish it was once this starts to act." She turned the vial toward the light. "It will make him puke his guts out and think twice before betraying me again."

"Betray?"

Hester's smile turned bitter. "What? You think I couldn't fall in love? He thinks I will skulk away like a dog. He's wrong."

"Who is *he*?" Fiona asked.

"Lord Belkins," Hester announced as if Fiona should know him. "He's been my lover for years."

"But no more," Fiona hazarded.

"No," Hester said, sucking in the word as if she had a physical pain in her chest. But then her gaze turned malevolent. "He said I was growing too old for him. He didn't even trouble himself with a parting gift. Well, he's about to receive a parting gift from me. You see, I faked a letter to him. Signed it from a 'feminine admirer.' He loves that sort of thing. Fancies all the women adore him." She smiled at her cleverness. "I suggested a secret meeting. That's where we are going now."

"And I'm to be his feminine admirer?"

"Of course. He'll like you. He likes redheads. His mother was a redhead." Seeing the look on Fiona's face, she said, "Don't think too closely about it, dear. Men are odd."

Fiona didn't doubt that. "But I thought you said I wouldn't be called upon to—" She paused, not wanting to say the words.

Hester understood. She waved Fiona's concerns away. "Not if you pour this into his wine before matters reach that point. I was told it would act quickly."

"Won't he see me?"

"Not if you distract him," Hester answered as if she was talking to a simpleton. "Be clever. You can't tell me you don't know how to be coy."

She did. Fiona had been the belle of the kirk back home in Scotland. She used to lead many lads on. Those days seemed so long ago. She took the vial from Hester. It seemed a simple thing to do for twenty pounds.

"I've hired a private supper room," Hester continued, "and the wine is already ordered. For all his fine manners, Belkie guzzles like an oarsman. When the contents in that vial start to effect, come for me. I want to watch it work and let him know that I set this whole ruse up. That will teach him not to cross me."

"But won't he be angry?"

Hester laughed. "What is in that vial will make him harmless quick enough. Oh, don't look at me that way. It won't last long or have a permanent effect. He'll recover."

At that moment, the coach pulled to a stop. "We are here," Hester said with a note of excitement.

Fiona felt the shape of the vial in her gloved hand. Her conscience troubled her. It was a cruel trick she was being asked to play. "I'd like my money now," she dared to say.

Hester shook her head. "I'll pay once the deed is done."

"What if something goes wrong? I should still receive my money."

The courtesan tilted back her head and laughed. "Nothing will go wrong. Belkie will be like clay in your hands. We'll be on our way home within the hour—and you'll be holding your money in your hand."

The door to the hack opened. The driver waited to help her down. Fiona hesitated. "Where are we?"

"The Swan's Nest. It's a cozy little inn, tucked in close to the city and the perfect place for a lover's tryst. The host's name is Mr. Denby. He's expecting you but under Annie's name."

"Annie's name? What if something goes wrong?"

With a lift of one eyebrow, Hester explained, "Well, that won't bother either of us now, will it? Annie's long gone from here."

"How long will I have to wait for Lord Belkins?"

Hester gave a half laugh. "He's here," she said with complete assurance. "Belkie was never one to miss an appointment."

Fiona drew her fringed shawl around her shoulders and climbed out. The ground was damp and soft beneath the kid slippers she had borrowed from Annie that morning before she left. They were a bit too small for her and obviously very worn since the wet seemed to seep into them.

A rising fog gave the Swan's Nest the appearance of complete isolation. Fiona would be hard pressed if asked to describe exactly where she was.

She slipped the vial into a hidden pocket sewn into the seam of her dress and walked toward the torch-lit front door. It opened before she could reach for the handle.

A balding man with the jovial appearance of someone's favorite uncle gave her a bow. "Mrs. Jenkins?"

Fiona nodded, resisting an urge to glance back where Hester waited in the hack. "Are you Mr. Denby?"

"I am. Your guest is waiting."

Her heart leapt to her throat, making it difficult to speak. "Thank you," she managed to say.

He shut the door. "This way, please." He led her through an empty tap room.

"You don't have much custom tonight," Fiona observed as he led her down a narrow hallway.

"We are a very private establishment."

"So there aren't other guests?" she wondered.

"We *always* have guests." He stopped mid-way down the hall. "Your room is the last door on the right," he informed her in a low voice. "The table inside is set for dinner as you instructed. There is a scarf on the other side of the door. When you are ready for us to serve, hang it out in the hall."

"Thank you," Fiona murmured. As he stepped aside to let her pass, a new idea struck her. "If I need help, would someone come if I gave a shout?"

"We usually don't interfere in the guests' games," he told her. "However, if you are concerned then I'll keep my ears open for you."

"Yes, please," Fiona said, gathering her courage. She went down the hall, checking to be certain the vial was in her pocket as she moved.

At the door, she stopped in indecision. Should she knock? Or enter without any announcement? What did men expect from unknown lovers?

Mr. Denby still stood in the hallway, watching her.

Fiona gave a knock. One light rap to the door. There was no answer from inside. "Belkie" must have assumed she was an idiot for knocking on a door for a room she hired.

She smiled at Mr. Denby.

He smiled back.

Reminding herself of the twenty pounds waiting for her, Fiona turned the handle, and opened the door.

The candlelit room was designed for seduction with sound-muffling draperies covering the walls and a linen-covered table intimately set for two. But what made her stomach twist into a knot of apprehension was the four-poster bed that dominated the majority of the room, its bedcovers turned down in open invitation. A welcoming fire burned in the grate.

However, something was wrong.

The room was empty. Hadn't Mr. Denby said Lord Belkins had already arrived?

A chair had been pulled from the table. A glass of wine poured. Perhaps Lord Belkins had stepped out for a moment?

After all the stewing she'd been doing over entering this room, to find herself alone seemed a bit of a disappointment.

Then again, his absence could work in her favor. She could pour the vial into his wine now.

But just as Fiona moved forward to do the deed, a strong hand came out from behind the door and grabbed her. It clamped over her mouth, preventing her from shouting an alarm, while another hand jerked her up against a hard, muscular body.

Panic ripped through Fiona as Lord Belkins kicked shut the door, holding her prisoner with his body, his hand covering her breast—

"You aren't the Spaniard," he said with angry surprise. He released his hold as if scalded, sending Fiona toward the table.

She caught herself before she could fall and reached for the closest weapon she could find—a fork. She whirled to face him—and then it was her turn to freeze in shock.

Her attacker was none other than the wickedly handsome, dark-haired Duke of Holburn.

How many times had she *thought* of him? *Dreamed* of him? *Hoped* that someday they would meet again?

Now, here he was, larger than life, furiously angry, and the only thing she could think to say was, "You aren't Lord Belkins."

"And *you* aren't Andres Ramigio," the Duke of Holburn shot back—and she realized he didn't recall meeting her. Not one flicker of recognition crossed his face.

The man of her dreams didn't remember her.

It was a humiliating moment.

He frowned at her fork, dusting off some imaginary piece of lint from his sleeve. "What are you going to do with that? Prick me to death?"

"The idea has merit."

She meant the words.

Chapter Two

*T*he tart's cool response to his comment caught Nick's attention.

At last, he troubled himself to give her a good hard look and then almost dropped his jaw in stunned surprise.

The resemblance between her and the Oracle he'd met nine years ago in the ruins at Delphi was uncanny. Almost frightening. And yet there were differences.

The Oracle had been a spirit, a glowing, ethereal vision whose eyes had been hidden from him. This woman was flesh and blood and her eyes snapped with insult. He could well imagine her skewering him with her fork, but he didn't

understand why. He really hadn't been that rough with her.

What she did share with the Oracle was beauty. Her cheekbones were high, her red hair a dark auburn that tumbled becomingly down around her shoulders, the pins having been knocked loose when he'd grabbed her. She was of average height, her waist trim, her breasts full. It was almost the perfect figure for a woman, except there was a leanness to her as if she'd missed more than her share of meals. It was a look common amongst London's lower classes.

A memory floated in his consciousness. "We've met before," he said, speaking his thoughts aloud.

He knew he was right because her shoulders straightened and her gaze grew wary. "Where was it?" he asked.

"Where is Lord Belkins?" she countered. She had courage. Few spoke to him in that manner.

Nick spread his arms to show he hid no tricks. "I don't know."

"He was supposed to be here."

"He sent me instead," Nick answered and decided to lay all his cards on the table. Then perhaps she would relax to tell him her purpose and he could gain a clue to the mystery of Ramigio.

"Lord Belkins owes me money. A gambling debt." It was no news that Belkins was done up.

He'd lost huge sums to men all over town and the rumor was he had little chance of meeting those obligations. "He came to me yesterday with an offer. He said he could arrange a meeting with Andres Ramigio, Barón de Vasconia, if I would forgive the debt, something I was willing to do. The barón took something from me once that I want back. I've been searching for years for him. You can imagine I leapt at the opportunity. I was expecting the barón to walk through the door, not you."

His explanation obviously did nothing to ease her fears. She kept her fork pointed at him.

"What of yourself?" he prompted. "Why are you here?" And why did she expect to meet Belkins when he so obviously hadn't planned on being here himself? If Belkins had passed up an assignation with this beauty, he was a fool.

A small worry line appeared between her brows. Her glance drifted to the door behind him and he knew she wanted to escape.

He wouldn't let her do that. Not until he knew more about her. It had to be more than a coincidence that she, who looked so much like his vision at Delphi, should appear at the same time he'd been approached about Ramigio.

He tried charm, albeit his was rusty from disuse. In fact, his smile stretched his face in wa

he'd not felt for quite some time. "I know I gave you a scare when you first came into the room. That wasn't my intention. I beg you to accept my apology, Miss—" He paused, waiting for her to fill in the answer.

She hesitated, reluctant to relax her guard, but at last said, "Bowen. Miss Bowen."

"Like in Hester Bowen?" he hazarded. "The woman who paid for this room?"

"Yes, that's me."

"Liar."

Her eyes widened at the accusation. Nick almost laughed at having caught her in the fib. "Hester Bowen is known by every gentleman of my acquaintance. She makes certain it is that way. You are no Hester Bowen." He flicked his gaze over her person in an appreciative way. "And you should be thankful of that."

Risking that she wouldn't bolt for the door, and undecided of what he'd do if she did, Nick walked to the table. He pulled his coin purse out of his pocket and held it up for her to see before dropping it on the table. "What is your name and why are you here?"

It is to her credit that she stood in indecision a moment. She didn't trust him, and she shouldn't. Her gaze dropped to the purse.

"Hester Bowen hired me to come here and

deliver a message to Lord Belk... He jilted her and she's very angry. I don't believe she knew anything about this Ramigio you keep talking about, Your Grace."

Her lilting Scot's accent didn't detract from the culture and intelligence in her voice. She held her head high and her movements had a natural grace. This was not the sort of woman a man associated with Hester Bowen and her kind.

He moved the purse an inch across the table toward her, prompting her, "And your name?"

She swallowed, and then said, "Fiona." She reached for the purse with her free hand, her shawl falling off her shoulder to hang loosely over one arm.

Nick snatched up the purse. "One second," he warned. "You haven't answered *all* my questions yet. Besides, I find myself hungry. Aren't you?"

"No," she said, even as her stomach rumbled loudly.

Color flooded her cheeks. Nick almost laughed until he saw the flash of irritation in her eyes. "I answered the questions that were important," she informed him. "You are changing the bargain."

"It's my bargain to change," he said. "And it is a long ride back to London." As if to punctuate his words, a cold blast of air came down the chimney, making the flames in the fire dance. "A quick bite," he urged soothingly, "and then you can be on your way." He didn't wait for her response but left the room, leaving the door open as he stood in the hall and called, "Denby, we want our supper."

"I was supposed to hang the scarf from the inside door handle to the outside," Fiona said. "That was the signal we wished to be served." She raised a hand to self-consciously push a stray lock of her hair back in place.

He had her. He'd seduced enough women to know he'd crossed an important hurdle. Nick turned to give her a smile—and then was riveted in place by the memory of exactly when and where he'd seen her.

"Lady Viner's ball," he said. "You were even wearing the same dress." Amazing that he could remember even that detail.

Her sudden stillness told him he was correct.

Nick walked back into the room, shutting the door. He leaned his back against it. "My mother had arranged a match for me to a young woman the Duke of Colster was trying to rid himself of."

Her gaze narrowed. He'd touched a nerve. "He wasn't trying to be rid of her. He'd thought to arrange a decent match."

With a shrug, Nick told her it didn't matter to

him one way or the other. "Mother had made the arrangements on her own, asking a hefty price for her services. Mother has a greedy nature."

"As I remember you weren't very interested in meeting the young woman." And then, almost as if her pride couldn't stop her, she said, "Who is my sister-in-marriage now. She's a fine woman and a good wife to my brother."

"Then we wouldn't have suited," Nick surmised lightly. He wasn't interested in the other woman or his mother's misplaced avarice.

"She married my brother that night," Fiona informed him proudly. "They are very happy together."

Nick nodded, barely paying attention. She was so very lovely. "Fiona," he said, wanting to test her name. "It fits you. There is a gracefulness to it."

He wanted her.

The need was primal, instinctive.

It had been a long time since he'd desired a woman so much.

"I saw you in the ballroom," he said. "I followed. You knew I was there."

She didn't deny the charge. Resting her fingers on the back of the chair as if needing to steady herself, she said, "You didn't remember me when I first came into this room."

The universal feminine complaint.

Nick let a slow, easy smile cross his face. "I should have. I'd been drinking the night we met in the ballroom. So, when I saw you, I believed my eyes deceived me."

Her brows came together. "Why?"

He could have told her of her uncanny resemblance to the Oracle, of how he later had convinced himself it had all been the trick of a brandy-soaked mind. But then she would question his sanity, and he didn't want that right now. It was hard to seduce someone who thought you were mad.

"Because you are so beautiful."

Fiona was no fool. Her gaze went to the wine glass he'd emptied right before her arrival. She crossed her arms protectively against her chest, gathering her shawl around her as she did so. "You should stop drinking."

Her tart comment startled a laugh out of him. She truly was unique. He pushed away from the door, coming toward her.

She shook her head. "I think I must go," she whispered more to herself than him. She snatched up his coin purse from the table and would have hurried past him except that Nick caught her arm. He swung her around and without preamble, kissed her.

Fiona's lips parted in surprise. Tension shot through her. She raised her hands to push him away.

Nick wasn't about to let her go. He took her by both arms, turning his head, forcing the kiss, willing her to bend to him. She resisted, she held—and then she opened.

He didn't waste time. He knew what he was doing. And yet, at the first full taste of her mouth, at the first hint of her submission, it was he who was trapped.

Kissing her was different from kissing other women. The spark of lust that had driven him now exploded into something more powerful than he'd experienced before.

And when she melded her lips to his, when she kissed him back—tentative at first, but with growing desire—he had only one wish and that was to scoop her up in his arms and carry her to the bed.

Nick pulled her close, wrapping his arm around her waist, ready to do exactly that when a knock sounded on the door.

It was an untimely interruption. It broke the spell for her. She pulled back, struggling to be free.

At first, he held tight, wanting to keep her, to continue to explore this almost supernatural connection between them. After one kiss, he craved her, *needed* her. Denby and his supper dishes could go to the devil.

Her body arched, the heels of her hands pressing against his shoulders.

Through the haze of lust, he realized she was panicking.

He didn't want that. He wanted to keep her, protect her.

He broke the kiss, and she started to collapse at his feet as if her legs could not bear her weight. He eased her back into the chair by the table.

Fiona struggled for breath, feeling as if she'd run a long, hard distance.

Dear Lord, she was shaking . . . and she didn't dare look at the duke—or else she might rise from this chair and move right into his arms again.

What had come over her?

If it hadn't been for the knock on the door, she feared where that kiss would have taken them.

She'd tried to resist. She'd just met the man. She was no whore. No Hester Bowen. Why, she and her former friend Grace McEachin had parted ways for that very reason. Grace had turned to the stage and to men who would protect her. She'd not understood Fiona's pride. She'd not understood Fiona would think being a seamstress better than being a dancer and ogled by men.

The door opened. She didn't know if the duke had opened it or not. Footsteps crossed to the table where she sat. Covered dishes were set on the table. Fiona kept her head lowered.

There followed the door closing. A wine bottle was uncorked. "Drink this," the duke ordered. He filled the glass close to her place. He poured himself a glass before setting the bottle down.

When she didn't drink he threw himself down impatiently in the chair beside her. He lifted his glass. "To your health, Fiona."

He drained his glass, then put it aside to take hers and place it in her hand. "Drink it. You need the color to return to your face."

She shot him a glance of surprise, her fingers automatically wrapping around the stem of her glass. "Why should you care about the color of my face?"

"We rakes don't like seducing pasty white things," he said in self-mockery. He began heaping food from the dishes onto her plate, his actions more that of a diligent nursemaid than a rakehell.

Fiona took a sip of her wine, the smells of roasted chicken, new peas, and hot bread threatened to make her swoon. Hester Bowen was probably wondering what was going on inside this room. For the briefest second Fiona felt guilty that the woman waited for her, but one bite of the tender chicken erased Hester from her mind.

She tried to eat daintily but within minutes she caught herself holding a piece of bread in one hand and a forkful of chicken in the other. It had been a long time since she'd had a meal such as this.

The duke watched her intently. His eyes were blue, midnight blue. His shoulders were broad and his body long and loose limbed. He moved the chair around to sit by her and stretched his legs out toward the fire, the very picture of a young lord at ease.

"Aren't you going to eat?" Fiona asked, swallowing.

"No, I prefer to drink," he answered, pouring himself another glass of wine. He gave her a lazy, good-humored smile. "You know, you could have given me a false name."

Too late Fiona realized he was right. "How do you know I didn't?" she responded. She'd finished the last of her supper and laid her napkin beside her plate. She should leave now . . . but she found herself in no hurry to go back out into the cold, damp night. Hester would be angry that Lord Belkins had thwarted her plan for revenge and probably rant and rave all the way back to London.

Whereas here, she had a full stomach, a glass of wine, a warm fire, and the duke's coin purse. The purse had been heavy. There was probably not as much as twenty pounds in it, but close. Watching the flames in the hearth, Fiona ticked off all the things she would do with the money: pay her landlord, buy a new pair of shoes, leave London completely . . . she would take Tad into the country where they would be happier—

His lips brushed against her neck. He nuzzled her ear.

Fiona thought her insides would melt.

She gripped the edge of the table knowing she should pull herself up and leave, except it was already too late. He kissed the line of her jaw—and she knew that she wasn't against this. She had to be careful and not let it go too far, but a part of her was fascinated by him. He was the devil, tempting her . . . and what was wrong with just a moment or two more in his company?

He smelled of the night air, of leather and shaving soap. His whiskers tickled her skin. She started to laugh and he kissed her. Just leaned up and took full advantage of her relaxed, open mouth.

This time, Fiona knew how he liked to kiss. Funny, but after her initial, earlier shock, she didn't mind kissing him. The soldiers, her rapists,

had been rough and cruel. The duke was gentle
and yet intent. It was as if he wanted to enjoy this
kiss as much as she was.

With a soft sigh, Fiona leaned toward him. His
arm slid around her waist. She rested her hand on
his chest, surprised by how hard and muscular it
was. A part of her mind warned her she must return to Hester; the other part had no inclination
to do so.

His kiss tasted of wine. Heady, rich, fragrant
wine. He leaned back and she followed, not ready
to end this kiss so soon.

She felt his tongue tease hers. Startled, she
started to pull back. His hand on her back wouldn't
let her move. "It's all right," he whispered against
her lips. "Everything is all right."

Fiona wanted to believe him. Fortunately, life
had taught her cynicism. "I must go."

He kissed the corner of her mouth and sucked
on her lower lip. "No, you don't."

"Hester is waiting outside—"

The duke cut her protest off with another kiss,
this one more demanding than the others.

For a moment, Fiona gave herself over to the
kiss. She let him explore her mouth. Opened to
him. Accepted him.

A low growl came from his throat. "You are

so lovely. So very, very lovely," he whispered against her mouth before kissing her neck, her chin, her ear.

Fiona fought for sanity. She reminded herself that he'd been drinking. A woman should never believe a man deep in his cups. Still, it was wonderful to hear. He was so handsome, so strong, and so bold. She basked in his praise.

He bit her shoulder, soothing her skin with a kiss, and then another and another. He was moving along her collarbone. Common sense intruded into passion, especially when he brought his hands around to cup her breasts and her bodice gaped open.

He'd unlaced the back of her dress.

As she'd been wallowing in his kisses, his clever fingers had been undressing her.

Fiona pushed him away, doubling one fist ready to give him a punch if necessary.

The duke had been diving forward, ready to bury his face in her breasts. He frowned at being pushed aside and reached to bring her back to him, but Fiona quickly came to her feet. She backed away from him, attempting to retie her laces as she moved.

"That wasn't nice," she whispered furiously at him.

Nice? He shook his head in confusion and then

noticed her redoing her laces. "You are wrong," he assured her. "It was very *nice*."

Fiona made an indignant protest. Her fingers were clumsy but the dress was sufficiently retied to be decent. She straightened. "I believe I must go now," she informed him with all the crisp haughtiness of a duchess. She would have marched right out the door, head high, not even worrying about her shawl—except for his holding up the coin purse.

She froze, staring at the red leather purse. She could curse herself. Why hadn't she placed it in her pocket when she had a chance?

"That's *mine*," Fiona said. "You gave it to me in exchange for information about Hester Bowen's plans."

"But I'm not through asking questions," he said with no show of remorse. A lock of his hair fell over his forehead, giving him a boyishly handsome appearance. He was enjoying himself.

"We *weren't* talking," Fiona snapped.

"We would have . . . later." He shook the purse. "Do you want it?"

At that moment, the attraction Fiona felt for him vanished. How dare he hold *her* purse hostage? She'd earned that money. It was vital to her survival.

And yet what could she do?

She clenched her hands into fists, hiding them in her skirts. She dearly wanted to set him in his place. Her hand hit the weight of the vial in her pocket, and she realized there *was* something she could do.

The Duke of Holburn thought he could do as he wished. She'd show him she was one woman who answered to no man.

Fiona smiled. Her earlier shyness fled in the face of her purpose. She slid her hand in her pocket and palmed the vial as she walked toward him. Still sitting in his chair in front of the table, he watched her approach, his eyes alive with interest. Looking past his shoulder, she could see the lip of his wine glass.

She sat on his lap.

The duke brought his legs up to support her weight. His hands went right for her waist.

Fiona smiled down at him. She pushed that lock of hair back from his forehead and slid her arms around his neck, the vial in her right hand. "What must I do to finish answering your questions?"

"Exactly what you are doing right now . . ." he answered, his lips covering hers as his husky voice trailed off.

For a second, Fiona almost lost her will in the

onslaught of his kiss. What was there about him that could rob her mind of reason? She didn't want to be a kept woman, had resisted the notion when Grace and others had recommended it. She'd avoided being this close to men in general since her rape and had never imagined even the intimacy of a kiss after the horror of that period of her life.

The Duke of Holburn had the power to banish her darkest fears. She *wanted* to kiss him. Almost craved it. It was the strength of her will pitted against the powerful lure of lust.

Her arms around his neck, she twisted the stopper from the vial. Her hand was a foot above his wine glass.

His hands cupped her face as he broke the kiss. He looked up at her, his eyes black with desire. "I like you, Fiona," he whispered. "I like you very much. I've not met one who has attracted me the way you do."

He drew a finger across her bottom lip, his smile so wickedly tender, it made her dizzy. He knew his impact on her. Her reaction pleased him. He turned her, bringing one leg over his so that she straddled his body. She could feel the heat and length of his arousal.

For a second, panic threatened. Her breathing

grew shallow. She couldn't control herself. Memories of the rape competed with a yearning, a desire she'd never known before.

The duke frowned, noticing the change in her. His hold loosened. "What is the matter?"

Half embarrassed and half relieved, she said, "Nothing," as she tilted her hand behind him and poured the contents of the vial into his wine. She let the small bottle drop to the table. The duke never noticed, or so she thought.

He drew back, looking up at her. "You aren't easy about this." It wasn't a question.

"I'm nervous." She couldn't meet his gaze.

"Don't be," he said, rubbing the small of her back in the most comforting way possible. "I'm not a man who hurts women or doesn't give a care to their feelings."

She looked to him. "Do you think I'm afraid?"

"I know you are," he answered. "But at the same time, Fiona, you must feel the connection between us, too. I was *meant* to meet you. We were supposed to be here at this time and place. I'll not lie. I want you." He moved her closer so she was sitting atop the hardness of his body. "But I'll not force myself upon you. I won't have to."

She knew he was right. Just looking at him quickened the beat of her heart.

"Here," he said. "Have a drink of this." He

turned and picked up his wine glass from the table to offer her.

"Mine is the other glass," Fiona hurriedly corrected him.

He didn't make comment but reached for her glass and handed it to her. He picked up his own. Facing her, he clinked the rim of their glasses together.

"To you, Fiona . . . and to what I anticipate being a very enjoyable association between us."

She took a sip, watching with a sense of horror as he drained most of what was in his glass. He set it aside and reached for hers.

"Better?" he asked. He turned his attention to her hair, pulling out two of the pins that kept it from falling down her back. He spread it out over her shoulders, combing it with his fingers.

As he leaned in to give a kiss at the very sensitive point where her jaw met her neck, Fiona stopped him with a palm against his shoulder. Her conscience couldn't let her keep quiet.

"I should tell you something."

Annoyance crossed his face. "Later," he murmured, moving to kiss her again.

Fiona placed her fingers across his mouth.

He opened his eyes.

She drew a breath for courage and then let the words spill out, "I am very sorry but I've given you a potion that Hester Bowen said will make you violently ill. I was supposed to give it to Lord Belkins but then he sent you in his place to meet that mysterious Spaniard and, well, I'm sorry I'm not him but you must understand, I can't do this." She said the last as she rose from his lap.

"Can't do what?" he repeated as if she'd been speaking gibberish. "And what potion?"

"It's something Hester gave to me," she said as she swept up the coveted coin purse from the table. "I earned this," she informed him, more to assuage her own conscience than in stating her rights.

"I poured the vial in your wine," she continued as she moved toward the door, backing away so she could keep her eye on him. She'd lost her shawl. It was on the floor by the bed. She wasn't going to walk back by him to retrieve it. "I didn't want to do it but you are too—" She paused, needing the right word. "—*Overpowering* for me. You just scoop me up and I bend to your will. I can't do that. I can't let anyone ever do that to me."

He'd risen to his feet, his expression one of confusion. "You poisoned me—?"

"No," she quickly said. "Hester said it isn't poison but you will be ill." Fiona wasn't about to tell him Hester's exact words about what it would do to his "guts." "I'm sorry," she whispered. Her body still hummed with the need he'd aroused. She tightened her grip on the leather coin purse. "But in this life, we all must do what we can to survive." It didn't help her conscience to see him place his hand against his abdomen as if feeling some distress.

"Good-bye," she said, hating herself for what she'd done, yet having no other choice but to leave. The duke was not going to be happy when Hester's potion took full effect.

However, before she could reach for the door, it came crashing open, forcing her to jump back in alarm.

A pock-faced man with shaggy hair and dark clothing entered the room, followed by two equally disreputable-looking characters. In the man's hand was a pistol, and he aimed it straight at the Duke of Holburn.

Chapter Three

$\mathcal{F}$iona stepped in front the duke. "Who are you? Did Hester send you—"

The duke grabbed her arm and pulled her to stand behind him. Sweat marred his forehead as he battled the potion's effects, but his voice was strong. "What do you want? Did Ramigio send you?"

The leader of the group closed the door. They were a foul-smelling lot. The scent of them sucked up all the air in the room's close confines. "I don't know a Hester," he said, the sound of Ireland in his voice, "and if Ramigio is a man who wants you removed, then I suppose we are from him. That is, unless you have other enemies, Your

Grace?" He didn't wait for an answer but said, "Now kindly take off your clothes and your boots and climb into that bed."

"What makes you think I'll do anything you say?" the duke countered.

"Because I will put a hole in the lass if you don't," the Irishman answered. "And you will still end up dead. My boys and I are a determined lot."

"What of the lass, Thomas?" the henchman on the left asked the leader. "Do we kill her, too?"

Thomas grinned. He was missing two of his front teeth. "We'll see what we feel like doing once we have taken care of the duke. We want it to look as if she murdered him and not us so I suppose we'd best not leave her behind."

Fiona wasn't about to let the likes of them touch her, let alone have the opportunity to rape her. She reached back and wrapped her hand around the top of the wine bottle sitting on the table. So far, only one of them had a gun. He couldn't shoot at two targets at once. She prayed Hester still waited with the coach out in the inn yard.

"Come along, Your Grace," Thomas said, waving the barrel of his gun toward the bed even as his fellows rolled up their sleeves, preparing to use force. "We can make this easy or hard. Either way, it's going to happen. Someone has paid us a lot of money to see you gone."

"Then he'll be disappointed," Holburn promised, aping Thomas's cheerfulness and in one smooth movement lifted the chair he'd just been sitting in and threw it at the gunman.

After that, everything began to happen fast. The chair hit the gunman against the side of his head. He lost his balance, falling back into his mates.

"Run," Holburn ordered Fiona.

He didn't have to tell her twice. She charged toward the door, one hand still gripping the coin purse, her other hand holding the wine bottle. The duke was right at her heels.

Thomas made a grab to stop her. The duke grabbed the wine bottle from Fiona and threw it at him, while smashing his elbow in the face of the third henchman. The man had been caught off guard by the sudden turn of events and had been blocking their way to the door. He fell back into the other two, sending them sprawling again.

From the corner of her eye, Fiona caught a glimpse of a gun. She yanked open the door, practically falling out into the hallway.

The duke took her arm, pulling her with him as he ran down the narrow corridor for the front door. He was breathing heavily. When he stumbled, she realized he struggled with the effects of Hester's potion and she threw her arm around his waist to help him. Their footsteps echoed on the hard wood floor and in seconds Fiona could hear the sound of the Irishmen following.

The jovial Mr. Denby must have heard the noise. He came out into the hallway from a side room to see what was the matter, stepping right into their path. "I say, what's happening here."

"*Out of the way*," the duke ordered, shoving him aside.

"Who are you men?" Fiona heard Mr. Denby say to the Irishmen. "What are you doing in my place—?"

His voice broke off with the sound of fists hitting flesh.

Fiona started to turn. "Don't look back," Holburn growled in her ear. His hand reached past her, grabbing the handle of the front door and yanking it open. He gave her a hard shove forward just as the pistol was fired.

Wood splintered off the door. Fiona couldn't help but give a cry. The duke's arm came around her waist, propelling them both out into the inn yard. The Irishman had missed. He'd have to reload to fire again and now was their chance to escape.

She heard a string of Gaelic curses and then a shout, "Stop them!"

"This way," Fiona said, grabbing his coat sleeve. Hester's coach was still waiting. Hester had been anxiously pacing beside the hired coach as she waited for Fiona. She now stopped in the circle of light around the coach lamps. "What took you so long?" she started and then seeing the duke said, "Who is he? Where is Belkie?"

"Climb in the coach," Fiona shouted.

The driver had been standing by his horse's head. He summed up the situation and, without hesitation, swung up on the box. Picking up the reins, he said to Hester, "You'd best climb in."

The Irish henchmen were outside. The duke was leaning over, one hand on his side as if in pain. Fiona pushed him toward the open coach door first but he held back, motioning her to go forward.

"Please, Hester, into the coach," Fiona begged.

But Hester didn't move. "What's happening?" she demanded. "Why is he with you? Did you give Belkie the potion?"

"It's a long story," Fiona started, taking Hester's arm and attempting to direct her up the step into the coach. "I'll tell you inside."

Hester stepped back. "*What is going on*?" she demanded enunciating each syllable. She was a woman accustomed to having her way. She stepped toward the duke, blocking his way to the inside of the coach. Her pigheadedness gave one of the Irishmen the chance to grab the duke.

It was that moment the potion went to work.

The duke doubled over and lost his dinner with such force it startled the Irishman enough to fall back.

Hester screamed in horror. She moved away. "That's not Belkie," she said. "It's not him."

The Irish were backing away from the duke's obvious illness. Now was their chance to escape.

Fiona grabbed the duke's arm and steered him up into the coach. "Hester, we can discuss this later." She climbed into the coach after the duke.

Hester didn't budge. She faced them, her hands on her hips, "This coach isn't going anywhere until I have answers."

The duke leaned out of the coach to hold a hand out to Hester. "*Come.*" That one word had cost him considerable strength.

She recoiled with disgust. "I don't think so," she said, backing away from him. He grabbed the front of her coat and attempted to yank her into the coach just as a pistol shot filled the air.

Thomas had come out of the inn and stood ten feet away.

The duke came back into the coach, his hand losing its hold on Hester. But it wasn't him the shot had hit. It was the courtesan. Thomas had missed, again.

Hester's eyes widened. "What is going on?" she repeated and then fell to the ground.

"*Drive*," the duke shouted at the coachman as the Irishman cursed his bad aim. He threw the pistol at the coach and shouted to his mates. "If you want your money, *stop them*."

Fiona tried to go to Hester. The duke blocked her with his arm. "It's too late."

And he was right. She had more important problems like the Irishman who followed their leader's order by trying to climb inside the coach with them.

With a scream, Fiona leaned back as the duke came forward. Another shot rang out but it wasn't from the Irish. The fire had come from Holburn's hand.

Their attacker dropped to the ground with a grunt and started hollering in pain.

The duke shouted at the coachman who appeared frozen in fright, "*Drive, damn you*." His words brought the man to his senses. They took off as the duke slammed the coach door shut.

Thomas and his remaining comrade attempted to chase after them, but tripped over Hester's still body.

Fiona couldn't move. "They killed her," she said, shocked by how quickly everything had happened and not believing any of it.

The duke fell back into the corner of the cab's close confines. His breathing was shallow. Deep lines etched his face and his hair across his brow was damp with sweat. "They wanted us," he reminded her.

"No, they wanted *you*."

The driver drove like a madman in the night fog. He let the horse have his lead and the beast was as frightened as Fiona. The coach swayed crazily all over the road. It was all Fiona could do to keep her balance. The duke was a silent, still figure in the corner of the coach, his arms hugging his sides.

At last the driver gained control of his horse and the ride grew smoother. Resettling herself, Fiona shivered from fear and the weather. "I left my shawl back in the room," she said, the complaint sounding inane considering the circumstances. She was surprised she still held the duke's coin purse. She dropped it on the seat as if blaming it for all that had happened this night.

The duke had closed his eyes. He didn't speak. The corners of his mouth were white with pain.

A knock on the roof signaled the driver wanted to talk to them. Fiona lowered the window. "I think we lost them," he shouted at them as if he needed confirmation that they were all right.

"Thank you," she said.

"Do you know where you want me to take you?" he asked.

Fiona glanced at the duke. He had placed one hand on the seat between them, the fingers curled into a tight fist. "Take us where you picked me up," she instructed and raised the window.

She sat back in her seat, her arms crossed against the cold. Several minutes of silence ticked by, allowing a hundred questions to fill Fiona's brain. The duke had his eyes closed but she sensed he didn't sleep.

At last she could contain her curiosity no longer. "You had a gun. Were you expecting to be attacked this evening?"

He didn't answer. Instead, his arm crossed his belly to hold off a cramping pain. Just when she thought he would ignore her, he said, "I had it for when I met the Spaniard."

"Those men weren't Spanish," she whispered.

"I know that," he said, irritation in his clipped tone.

"Do you know who they were?" she had to ask. She had to make sense of what had happened.

His brows came together, his eyes still closed. "No. Do you?"

It was a fair question but it offended her all the same. "Of course not. I don't consort with murderers."

"How comforting," was his dry reply.

Fiona frowned at his sarcasm. "Perhaps you deserved that bellyache," she muttered.

That comment brought a reaction out in him. He sat up, his eyes opened and his face contorted in fury. "Bellyache? Do you believe that's all this is? You *poisoned* me."

"I didn't poison you exactly," she hurried to say. "Hester said it wasn't poison but an elixir that would make you wish it had been."

"And what is that if not poison?" he bit out.

"A potion that would make you heartily sick," she answered. "And it has. But it is what you deserved," she couldn't help adding under her breath.

He heard her.

"*Deserved?* For what? I'd not harmed you. I'd not threatened you—"

"*You did threaten me*," she fired back, guilt making her angry. "You kissed me—"

"*There's* a dangerous action for you," he flared back. "Heaven forbid a man should kiss a woman." He threw himself back in his corner. "Especially when the woman is of Hester Bowen's ilk and approaches the man in a private room designed for seduction and that is let by the hour."

"Let by the hour?" Fiona frowned. She'd never heard of such a thing and then realization dawned. She hated being so naïve. She *hated* that she'd placed herself in these circumstances. "I should have known better than to kiss you. I shouldn't have trusted you."

"On that, we can *both* agree," the duke informed her. "When I saw you weren't the Spaniard, I should have tossed your skirted rump out the door. But no-o-o," he continued, drawing out the word, "you caught me. You slipped right past my guard." He punctuated the words by doubling his fist and hitting it against the side of the coach in his fury.

Fiona drew back, but she had nothing to fear because his abrupt, forceful action upset his fragile hold on his body. He doubled over. "Stop the coach," he muttered. "Stop the coach."

She came up out of her seat and pounded on the roof. The driver either didn't hear or ignored her. Holburn's shoulders were heaving. He was holding it back but he was about to erupt and, having witnessed his sickness once, Fiona didn't want to be closed in with him. She threw down the window.

"Driver! Driver! Stop! *You must stop.*"

This time, he heard her. He pulled the coach over. Fiona opened the coach door and Holburn all but bowled her over to climb outside.

They were in a section of the city not far from where Fiona lived. This neighborhood was not as shoddy but the buildings were just as crowded.

Fortunately, because of the cold and the hour, there weren't many people on the street.

Holburn had the good grace to move toward an alley. Fiona looked to the driver. "We'll only be a few minutes. Please, wait for us."

"Not without being paid what I'm owed," the driver said, not bothering to come down from his box. "This has been an adventure in hell. I'll take my money now."

"If I give it to you, you'll leave," she said.

"No, I won't, miss."

She knew better. "I will give you your money in a moment. His Grace's purse is in your coach."

The moment the words left her lips, Fiona wished she could call them back.

"Your Grace?" the driver repeated, shocked. "Someone was trying to murder a duke? In my hack?" He swore under his breath at his bad luck. "They shot and killed the woman who hired me, didn't they?"

"Apparently," Fiona admitted, feeling more than a pang of guilt. "But we should be fine now." Or, at least, she prayed they would be. Who knew where the Irishmen were or if they had followed. "So, wait. I'll be right back. I have to check on the duke."

She didn't wait for his response but headed for the alley.

Fiona found the duke leaning against the side of a building, heaving his guts up. She stood a distance away, undecided if she should comfort him while he was sick or remain where she was. Watching his distress, she felt terribly guilty. She *had* overreacted to their kisses. When she'd pushed him away, he hadn't forced himself on her. She'd been aware from the very beginning he wasn't like the soldiers who had attacked her.

In fact, she was relieved she could tell the difference, and that their brutality hadn't destroyed the will to be close to a man. That didn't mean she trusted easily.

The duke stopped his terrible retching. He leaned one shoulder against a building's brick wall as if exhausted. His back was to her.

She approached him, daring to say, "What can I do to help?"

"Nothing," he said in a guttural voice. It probably hurt his throat to speak.

Fiona moved close enough to place her hand on his back, but she didn't. She knew better than to touch him right now. "I'm sorry."

His reaction was so quick, it caught her off guard.

He turned and flattened her against the brick wall with his hand on her chest. His face close to hers, his eyes burning with sickness, he said, "When I recover, you'll pay for what you've done."

Before Fiona could respond, his hand dropped away. His body started heaving again. He turned, collapsing at the waist, attempting to fight off the inevitable.

She watched in indecision. Here was her chance to escape, but she couldn't leave him like this. She had to return him to the coach and then she'd let the driver take care of him. She glanced back at where the hack waited and was shocked to see it was gone.

The driver hadn't waited for them.

Bitterly, she realized she had only herself to blame. She shouldn't have told the driver about the money. It was the sort of mistake no one made twice in London.

The duke had sunk to the ground as if too exhausted to stand. He rubbed his head, his movements weak. Murdering Irishmen aside, the city was no place for the defenseless, and Fiona had seen enough violence this night to last her a good long while.

She pushed her heavy hair back over her shoulders and quickly braided it into a plait to keep it out of her way. There was nothing else she could do but take care of the duke. He'd not thank her for it, but at least her conscience would be clear.

Of course, there was the tricky problem of his blaming her for all of this.

She'd deal with that later.

Right now, she had no choice but to take the duke home with her. Putting up with his foul temper would be her penance.

Kneeling beside him, she said, "Excuse me, Your Grace, can you stand?"

He was too far gone to respond. He was also alarmingly pale, even in the alley's shadows, and his breathing shallow.

Fiona lifted his arm over her shoulders. "I'm going to help you to your feet."

Holburn raised his lids enough to give her an accusing stare.

"I know it's my fault," Fiona said. "You've made that clear. Now, come along. We've no choice but to go forward."

To her relief, he managed to rise, using the wall for support. She took his arm, put it around her shoulders. "Lean on me, Your Grace," she said. "I promise I'll take care of you."

He made no response.

Their movements were awkward as they walked toward the street. Holburn could barely place one foot in front of the other, although he kept going.

Fiona took stock of her surroundings and was relieved to realize they weren't that far from where she lived. "Come along, Your Grace. It won't be far."

They moved like two drunkards. Holburn's steps grew slower and heavier as they went. Fiona whispered words of encouragement. She was thankful he didn't have another bout of sickness. She prayed the worst was past.

Her building was pitch black inside. The people who lived here could not afford to waste money on candles and the landlord, Mr. Simon, would never provide them. However, Fiona had never been so happy to reach anyplace in her life. At least, now, she didn't have to worry about the streets or the Irishmen.

She felt her way across the front hall. Four steps and then her toe hit the bottom tread of the staircase. "Your Grace, we must climb two flights of stairs."

He didn't respond; however, when the time came to go up them, he did so. It was a slow, exhausting journey. Her breathing became as labored as his. They were both drenched with sweat, although his had a sickening sweet odor—another sign that

Hester Bowen had tricked her. No innocent potion could have done this to him.

Worried and afraid, Fiona should have felt relief when they finally reached her floor.

Instead, she pulled up short, confronted by a new problem because all was not dark up here. A line of light seeped out from beneath her door.

Someone was inside . . . waiting.

Chapter Four

*F*iona stood indecisively in the hallway.

Holburn rested his head on her shoulder. He was practically asleep on his feet and would be of no service whatsoever if they were attacked. She would have to work this new dilemma out for herself.

She could go to Annie's rooms, which were right next to hers and the closer of the two doors. Annie was notorious for leaving her door unlocked, but she'd left this morning to run off with her lover and hadn't planned on returning. Certainly the landlord Mr. Simon would have locked the door if she hadn't.

A scratching started at Fiona's door. It was Tad.

The big wolfhound knew she was home. He whimpered and she was caught.

The door opened.

Fiona leaned back into the hall's shadows.

Tad came out with a wagging tail as a slim, feminine figure appeared silhouetted in the doorway. Fiona released a sigh of relief, followed by a flash of anger. "What are you doing here?" she demanded.

Grace McEachin, her former roommate, stepped back into the light. She was a lovely lass with coal-black hair and sharp blue eyes. They'd both come from Scotland together but their lives had taken different paths. Fiona had chosen decent work; Grace had turned to the stage. The argument over Grace's decision had made them part ways.

"That was a pleasant greeting," Grace replied stiffly.

"I'm sorry," Fiona countered, "but I haven't seen hide nor hair of you for two months and now you appear? Giving me the scare of my life?" Tad happily waited with shiny black eyes for the pat she couldn't give him because her arms were full of Holburn.

"How did I scare you?" Grace answered. "I thought you would be happy to see me. I brought candles. I knew you could use them. These are the stubs the theater tosses away."

If Fiona had her choice, she would have left Holburn in the hallway until she'd sent Grace on her way. Naturally, he didn't cooperate. He groaned loudly.

"Fiona, are you all right?" Grace asked. She peered out into the darkness.

Well, there was nothing that could be done for the matter. Fiona had to move the duke to a bed. She hefted him up on her shoulder and whispered, "Come along, Your Grace."

It was a sign of how weak he was that he let her lead him in. His feet barely moved. "A bit more," Fiona urged. He protested with a heavy sigh, not even bothering to open his eyes.

Grace had picked up one of her candle stubs and held it so she could see better in the dark. As Fiona came through the door, Grace almost dropped the candle in surprise.

"What do you have there? Or rather *who*?" She didn't wait for Fiona's answer but launched right into, "Fiona Lachlan, don't tell me you've taken a lover. Especially after all the fine words you threw at me the day I moved out. I don't know whether to be happy or spitting mad."

"Be spitting mad," Fiona muttered.

Her "rooms" were really one long room. By the door, there was a hearth, a table, and three chairs. The fire had died yesterday and Fiona had not had money enough to start another, but apparently, Grace had brought coal along with her candles. The room was toasty warm for the first time in a week and a kettle of water was heating over the flames. The only other furniture was a trunk holding Fiona's meager possessions and a chest by the hearth for cooking utensils.

The other half of the room had the window overlooking a back alley and her bed. Fiona had created two rooms by hanging a curtain she'd sewn out of some damaged muslin she'd received from Madame Sophie. The curtain gave her sleeping quarters a sense of privacy. She now dragged Holburn though the curtain and dumped him face down on her bed. He was so tall, his feet hung off the end and his boots almost touched the floor. He seemed to take up every inch of her narrow cot, but that didn't prevent him from immediately taking up a more comfortable position.

He looked so peaceful, she wished she could collapse on top of him.

Unfortunately, Grace was here. "Is he drunk?" she asked from the curtain doorway. She held a plate with several candles burning on it.

"He's not your worry, Grace." Fiona felt Holburn's brow. It was cool, a good sign. He'd live.

She stood and drew a deep breath, planning her next course of action. She could still feel his hand holding her against the brick wall. His threat echoed in her ears. She was going to have to do something to protect herself when he regained consciousness until she could talk sense into him.

"No, *he's* not," Grace agreed. "It's *you* I'm worried about." She still had on the makeup she wore for the theater, but she looked good, well-fed. Her clothes were of far better quality than those she'd owned before she'd left.

"Being an opera dancer must suit you," Fiona couldn't help but comment. If it sounded as if she was jealous, well, she was. It was hard to be self-righteous when the sinner was eating well.

She picked up the empty slop bucket from the corner of the room and placed it beside the bed in case Holburn needed it. Then she turned her attention to his person.

His jacket and clothes were filthy and he needed a cleaning up. She needed to take off his boots first. Tad had been sniffing them. Fiona shooed him away and set to work, grabbing the heel of the boot nearest her.

"It does," Grace said, her chin up. "I earn a decent wage."

"On your back," Fiona couldn't stop herself from saying as she pulled Holburn's boot off with a grunt. "What did he do? Have these things molded to him?"

Anger clipped Grace's words as she took the boot from Fiona and said, "Possibly. This boot was done by Hoby. The best bootmaker in the world." She tossed the boot aside where Tad hurried over for another smell. "And I'll have you know, I've not been with any men, Fiona. I dance. That's it."

Fiona didn't know if she believed her. When she'd first met Grace, the lass had been going from one man to another. Fiona had thought she'd been a good influence on her friend and had convinced her to live decently and right but that influence hadn't held when life grew hard.

"It doesn't matter what I think," Fiona muttered, right now too preoccupied with her own problems to consider the matter. She pulled the heel of Holburn's other boot. This one came off easier than his other and she couldn't help but admire his socks. They were of heavy cotton and finely woven. Apparently he only used the best sock maker in the world, too. "You've chosen your life," she said to Grace. "One that isn't entirely respectable," she couldn't help but add as she moved to the head of the bed and began untying the knot in the duke's neck cloth.

"Says the woman who is undressing a man as we speak," Grace shot back.

Fiona stood as she folded the neck cloth. "What I am doing is my business."

"What I am doing is *my* business," Grace answered.

"Except this isn't what it looks like," Fiona said. "I must clean his clothes, and undressing him is the only way I can do it." Holburn lay so still, he worried her in spite of his lack of fever. She began removing his jacket.

Grace held up a hand as if to beg for understanding. "I'm sorry. You've passed judgment on me ever since I decided to leave Madame Sophie's—where we were working our fingers sore for a pittance—and take up the stage. I hear Madame Sophie let you go because she had a relative that wanted your position. So much for loyalty."

Fiona's temper snapped. She didn't need Grace right now. "Why are *you* here anyway?"

"I brought you candles—"

"*Besides* the candles." Fiona had half the duke's arm out of the sleeve and wondered how she could finish the job without having to use scissors. She was tired and worried and had a full night taking care of Holburn before her. "I didn't *need* candles, Grace."

"Oh, yes, you are perfectly fine in the dark," her former friend answered tartly.

"I am."

Grace threw her hands in the air. "Your stubborn Scottish pride—"

"Obviously you need more of it."

"Oh, no, not if it makes me as headstrong as you are," Grace assured her, but then her manner changed. "I don't want to argue with you, Fiona. I came here because I was worried. I saw Annie at the theater this morning. She told me you were going to take her place doing an errand for Hester Bowen and *why* you wanted to do it. Fiona, don't you have more sense?" she demanded, her Scot's accent broadening with her frustration. "You could have come to me for money. Look at you. You are down to meat and bones."

"I'm fine," Fiona insisted. But she wasn't. Unshed tears blurred her vision.

And it was all the duke's fault. Why did he have to be so difficult to undress?

The next thing she knew, Grace came forward and lifted his body so that Fiona could slip his jacket off.

"Now for his shirt," Grace said.

Fiona moved without thinking. All she could concentrate on was this one task.

Grace helped her pull his shirt over his head. Fiona lowered him to a pillow she'd made from scraps from the dress shop. "He's a handsome one," Grace said with approval.

Fiona wouldn't argue that. Whereas most men of his class were soft from age and an easy life, the Duke of Holburn was all hard muscle. He slept as if drugged and Fiona wondered if this was another effect of the potion.

"Are you going to tell me who he is?" Grace asked. "Or *why* he is here?" She frowned at the stock-still body. "He is only drunk, isn't he?"

"It's a bit more than that," Fiona said and had planned on saying no more because the events of the night were all jumbled in her head . . . however, one word led to another and before she could stop herself she proceeded to tell Grace everything.

Her friend listened, her eyes widening with every new twist to the tale.

When Fiona was done, Grace set the candles on the bedside table and looked at the man spread out on the bed. "You know Holburn is a notorious rake. No one crosses him, and here you've gone and poisoned him."

"He was very angry with me before he passed out," Fiona confessed. She leaned against the wall. Tad sat beside her. Grace had not called the duke by his title. It made him seem less intimidating than thinking of him as "the duke." She rubbed Tad's head. "Holburn was very angry with me the last time we spoke . . . and I don't blame him."

"Fiona, what are you going to do?" Grace asked in round tones.

"I'm going to do what I must," Fiona said. "I'll watch and be certain he doesn't take a turn for the worse and I'll clean his clothes the best I can."

"But he's so angry with you."

That he was.

"I just have to stay out of his grasp until he listens to reason," Fiona said.

"The man's huge." Grace looked him over. "He could break both our necks."

"Not with his hands tied," Fiona answered, an idea forming in her head. She turned and walked into the other room where she kept a hank of rope in her chest.

Grace followed her. "You *are* serious," she said in disbelief.

"Of course I am." The rope was a soft, supple hemp. "I don't see that I have another choice." She also took out the makings for nettle tea. It might help with his healing. "How else can I protect myself? Once he accepts my apology, I'll let him go. You see? It's simple."

"Oh, yes, *simple*," Grace echoed.

Fiona ignored her sarcasm. She had a man to tie up.

In the bedroom, she lay the rope on the bed, drew a deep breath and began unbuttoning his breeches. The room became very hot.

Grace noticed her discomfort. "Have you ever done that before?" Grace asked.

"No." Fiona had the top three buttons undone. She expected him to wear small clothes. By the fifth button, she realized he wasn't.

Shocked, she looked up at Grace. "He has nothing on underneath his breeches."

"No, I imagine not," Grace said. "The young ones usually don't."

Fiona backed away from the bed as if it had turned into a nest of snakes.

"Oh, for heaven's sake," Grace said. She walked over into the room and picked up the clothes from the floor, shoving them into Fiona's arms. "You can start on these. Did you take out the nettle tea for him?"

Fiona nodded, embarrassed that she wasn't as bold as she'd hoped to be.

"Then go make it," Grace said, "while I remove his breeches."

Fiona turned and hurried out of the room. A few minutes later, while she was steeping tea, Grace came out from the bedroom, Holburn's breeches in her hands. "He's decent. I covered him with a blanket." She dumped the clothes on the table and accepted a cup of tea from Fiona. "Thank you."

"No, thank *you*," Fiona said. For a second, she

couldn't meet Grace's eye. "I've been very harsh toward you over the past few months."

"You were concerned for me," Grace said, equally quiet.

"No," Fiona admitted, "I was angry because nothing has been going as it should. I didn't want to go with my brother and his wife to America because I truly believed I was meant to be in London. I felt called to stay here, of course this"—she indicated with a nod of her head her surroundings—"was not where I thought I would be. Or that life would be so hard—"

Tears burned her eyes. She shut them tight, willing the tears away. "I really did believe that with my background, my breeding, life would be better. I made a terrible choice and I took my frustration out on you."

"No, Fiona," Grace said, placing her hand on Fiona's arm. "You were right to be concerned about me. It would be easy to return to my old habits, but I'm trying not to. I admire you so much. You are strong and unafraid—"

"I'm very afraid right now, Grace."

"Holburn will be reasonable."

Fiona shook her head. "It's not him. Life is so hard." She crossed her arms. This time a tear escaped. "And it's lonely. Very lonely. You were the only person I could trust and I behaved rudely to you. I'm sorry."

Grace set down her tea and wrapped her arms around Fiona. "There is nothing wrong with pride," she said. "You've taught me that."

At last, Fiona let go of her shame enough to hug Grace back. "I'm so, so sorry."

"If you say it again, I shall be very angry with you," Grace countered. "And the truth is, I've missed you, too. At the theater they call me the Scottish lass and they don't mean it as a compliment. I grow tired of snappish women who believe they are better than me because of where they were born. Most of them can't even write their own names. I've longed for someone who listens to me and when she speaks has my best interests at heart."

"Even if I don't approve of a life on the stage?" Fiona asked, pressing her cheeks to dry her tears.

"The best of friends," Grace answered, "are those willing to help guide us to be better than we thought we could be."

"Well, if you have any advice for me, please speak up," Fiona said. "Right now, my world has turned into something more than I can manage." She swallowed hard before admitting, "I let him kiss me, Grace."

Her friend's brows shot up. "Who? Holburn?" Immediately, she turned angry. "Did he force himself on you? If he did, Fiona, I'll flog him—"

"No, he didn't," Fiona said, interrupting her before she continued with the wrong idea. "I *wanted* him to kiss me . . . and I kissed back," she admitted, still surprised herself by her reaction to him.

Grace placed her hand on Fiona's arm and brought them both down to sit on the chairs. She looked Fiona in the eye. "He is the worst person for you to trust. He's broken hearts all over this city. Of course, to his credit, all the women I've heard of are those who can take for themselves, but you are different."

"In what way?" Fiona asked.

"You are vulnerable." Grace's expression softened to pity. "You haven't the first idea of how to handle a man like him."

"He hasn't gotten my skirts up yet," Fiona said in her defense.

"But he could," Grace predicted with a wisdom as old as time.

Fiona sat back, unsettled. She couldn't deny her friend's words. The Duke of Holburn had occupied a place in her imagination from the first moment she'd laid eyes on him. But she knew better now. She'd met the real man and although he was handsome, she knew better than to tempt the devil.

"The worst part," she said to Grace, "is that I didn't receive my twenty pounds from either Hester or him—"

Her voice broke off as an idea so daring, so bold, so dangerous took hold of her. "I will hold him for ransom."

"Hold who?' Grace asked, shaking her head as if she already didn't like the answer.

"The duke. Holburn."

Grace set her tea down. "I believe such a thing would be a hanging offense."

"Not if no one knows about it except the duke and I," Fiona said, the idea gathering momentum. "I will tell him he must ransom himself and I'm going to ask for five hundred pounds."

"*No*," Grace said.

"Oh, *yes*," Fiona countered.

"*It's madness.*"

"It's *freedom*," Fiona answered. She lowered her hand and rubbed Tad's head as she thought the matter out. The dog closed his eyes, enjoying the attention. "I know that if it is reported to the authorities I could be in a criminal situation, but Holburn won't turn me over to them. He will not want anyone to know he was bested by a woman."

"You don't know that is true," Grace argued.

Fiona sat forward. "I do know that by the time he comes after me, we'll be long gone."

Grace held up her hand, palm forward. "Don't include me. I'm not part of this. Besides, what are you going to do with that much money? Join your brother in America?"

"America is a wilderness. I want to live somewhere civilized—like Italy." She liked that idea. "On five hundred pounds we can set ourselves up as wealthy widows."

Grace frowned. "Why widows?"

"Because widows have freedom." She put her hand on her empty tea mug and turned it around as she envisioned a new life for them. "We'll find a lovely villa by a lake out in the country and hire a maid. Who knows what could happen from that point? In Italy, our Scots' accents will be considered exotic."

"I don't speak Italian," Grace said unmoved.

"We'll learn," Fiona assured her.

Grace came to her feet and carried her mug over to the cabinet as she said, "You are talking nonsense."

Fiona came to her feet. "Don't dismiss me, Grace. This is an opportunity to change our lives."

"Like you thought earning twenty pounds would do for you tonight?" Grace countered. "Fiona, don't be foolish."

But the idea had taken hold. "I might not receive five hundred pounds," she admitted, "but he will pay me something if he wants to leave my rooms and I won't settle for much less. After all, I saved his life tonight."

"When you go in front of the magistrate, you can explain that to him," Grace answered, unmoved.

"Holburn won't go to the authorities," Fiona said with certainty. "He has the devil's own pride. He reminds me of my brother in that manner. He'll not like paying the ransom, but he'll do it for no other reason than winning his freedom so he can wring my neck. But the world is a big place. He's been looking for this Spaniard for years and hasn't found him. I'll be prepared to run the moment I receive the money."

"And how are you going to leave so quickly?" Grace wondered.

Fiona spread her hands to indicate the bareness of the room. "Other than Tad and the clothes on my back, is there anything else I need from this place? I could be gone in the morning. Of course, I may need some help. If you don't want to leave with me, will you at least help, even a little?"

Her friend stood silent. Her glance went from Fiona to the curtained doorway. "It's madness."

"The best plans usually are. Besides, I come from a long line of daredevils."

"Yes, and look where your brother is now."

"Happy," Fiona answered. "He left for America without even a backward glance."

Again, Grace looked at the doorway. "Is he tied up now?" she asked.

Fiona walked over and picked up the rope she'd set on the cabinet before she made the tea. "He will be in a few minutes."

At last, Grace capitulated. "I'll help you as much as I can, Fiona, but be warned—Holburn isn't the sort of man a wise woman crosses," she advised soberly.

"I'll remember that," Fiona promised. "Any other advice?"

"Yes, you'd best make certain those knots are good and tight."

Chapter Five

*N*ick didn't want to wake. He didn't want to open his eyes, but a blast of cold air was not going to let him sleep. His valet, Gannon, must have left a window open, which was decidedly odd. Gannon never made mistakes.

Furthermore, his gut hurt. True, there were many mornings he felt this way. Excessive drinking was never good for one's constitution. However, today was worse. His stomach muscles felt as if they had been turned inside out. Or perhaps the pain was more distinctive because it was his *mind* that was sharper—

Nick was startled to realize *he was sober.*

His mind was actually *alert.*

He couldn't remember a time since boyhood when he'd been so aware of his senses. It was as if his body had been purged of all poisons.

Nick lay still. While he'd always meant to change his ways, he was uncertain if he was enjoying this new sensation. He felt like hell. His head might be clear but his body had obviously been trounced on by a herd of goats. Even the muscles in his earlobes ached.

A drink would take those muscle aches away.

Slowly, Nick opened his eyes and swore. *This* was not his bedroom in Holburn House. He closed and opened his eyes again before accepting that what he saw was real. He really was in a tiny room that resembled a prison. The place was tidy but nothing could hide the squalor. The walls really were a drab gray from years of soot. The air smelled of a hundred different meals being cooked and from someplace in the building, above or below him, a baby cried, while from another quarter a man gave in to his morning hacking.

Instead of a feathered mattress, he lay on one filled with straw and lumpy in all the wrong places. His stockinged feet—the only clothing he was wearing—hung off the end of the bed.

Thankfully, the sheets smelled clean, but a wise man would climb out of this bed before bugs found him. Nick started to rise—and couldn't.

"What the bloody—?" Ropes banded his body, which had been covered by a thin quilt.

At that moment, he heard a sound at the open window beside the bed.

A huge dog, the size of a small deer, leapt into the room. He gave Nick no more than a passing glance as he padded through a curtain hung across one side of the room.

Nick amended his earlier theory: he obviously *was* drunk.

A hand pulled the curtain back and a serious-eyed young woman entered the room. The dog followed her in, sitting on his haunches by her side.

She wore a simple plain blue wool dress, the clothing of a shop girl, and yet carried herself with the air of a queen.

His Oracle.

Memory returned with a vengeance. The details were still murky but he remembered *her* . . . and the potion she'd poured into his drink. After that, events were unclear. All he remembered was being violently ill.

She was just as lovely as he remembered, although this morning, her eyes were tired. He almost felt sorry for her until she said in her crisp accent, "You are my prisoner, Your Grace."

"That is one of the most ridiculous statements

I've ever heard anyone make," he replied. "Now come untie me."

"I can't," she answered.

"You can," he said.

"You threatened to harm me—"

"I'm certain with good reason," he cut in. He didn't have patience. He needed a pint, or a little cider to take the edge off the morning. "Now, untie these knots and fetch me something to drink. Then, we can reminisce about last night." Before she could respond, a wild, almost dreamlike thought struck him. "Did we really have Irishmen shooting at us . . . or was I having a bad dream?"

"They weren't shooting at us. They were shooting at *you*. They had other plans for me."

"Did I shoot back?" he wanted to know, the haze starting to lift from his memory.

"Yes, you did."

Now he remembered all. "I merely wounded the man. I'd wanted him dead. They shot Hester Bowen. They were aiming at me and they shot her." He frowned at the young woman. "Your name is Fiona." He caressed the word, giving it three distinct, flowing syllables.

She nodded, watching him warily as if she hid a secret.

He plowed on, trying to make sense of it all. "Hester didn't deserve that. I wish I'd killed the man. Those small pistols aren't always reliable when you are aiming at a man while in a moving coach."

Her head tilted in surprise. "Do you shoot people often?"

"Only when necessary," he answered enjoying the response. He relaxed and took a moment to give her a good look over. Drunk or sober, she was a beauty. And being tied up was rather intriguing . . .

"I thought I was waiting for Andres Ramigio," he said, "but you arrived instead. And you thought you were to meet Belkins."

"Who told you the Spaniard would be there," she answered.

Nick looked up at the ceiling, thinking. "There's a mystery here," he said, speaking more to himself than Fiona. "But why? It doesn't make sense."

She took a step closer to the bed. "Hester wanted to teach Lord Belkins a lesson. He'd jilted her without offering a parting gift. So she sent him a note from Annie Jenkins arranging a private supper at the Swan."

"Who is Annie Jenkins?"

"She is my neighbor," Fiona said. "But she eloped yesterday morning and asked me to go in her place."

"And why would you do that?" Nick wanted to

know, searching for anything that made sense out of last night.

"Hester was going to pay me twenty pounds."

"Ah, yes, *money*." Nick remembered his coin purse. "Isn't that the reason for everything?" He took in her body, noting all the assets that a woman could use to make money, and felt disappointment.

He'd wanted her to be better than that. She wasn't. "Twenty pounds seems a pittance to what a woman like you could earn."

Indignation brought color to her cheeks and a flash of fire to her brown eyes. "I'm not a whore."

"Of course you aren't," Nick agreed briskly. "Neither is Hester Bowen or any of her friends. And *I'm* practically ready for sainthood." He smiled, his lips twisting cynically. "I don't know why I'm irritated with you. You are nothing but a pawn in this game. A beautiful plaything who can be bought for twenty pounds."

Her hands formed fists at her side. "How dare you insult me?"

He laughed, the sound bitter. "You insulted yourself for twenty pounds. Now, untie me and let's be done with this. Someone attempted to murder me last night and I'd like to discover who."

Her jaw tightened. Her eyes had grown large in her face as he spoke, but she didn't move.

Nick frowned. "You aren't going to untie me, are you?"

It took her lips a second to form the word, "No." She was obviously aware he wouldn't like her answer.

She was right.

He kept his voice quiet, controlled, silky—the better to make her realize she'd best do as he said. "Do you know who I am, Fiona? How powerful I am?"

She nodded, and then dispelled his notion that she feared him by saying, "But right now, you are naked and tied to my bed and there isn't anyone who knows where you are save for myself. You are at *my* mercy, Your Grace. And if you want to be free, you'll be paying me *five hundred* pounds for the privilege."

Now it was Nick's turn to be speechless.

"What was it you called me, Your Grace? A plaything? A pawn?" She smiled at him. "I don't believe those words apply any longer. You'll have to choose new names for me."

Oh, he had names for her. They spewed from his mouth. To her credit, she held her ground, his words bouncing off her. She was a proud, stubborn queen who listened to him with a complacent half smile.

Nick took hold of his temper. "I'll not pay you. Not even a shilling."

"Then you may rot in that bed," she said pleasantly.

He had to hand it to her, the Scottish lass had courage. Most men quaked in their boots when Nick lost his temper. She hadn't flinched. "Kidnapping is a hanging offense, Fee," he reminded her.

The threat didn't phase her, but her nose wrinkled at the nickname. He'd use it more often.

"Sometimes we must risk hanging to survive, Your Grace," she announced. "Tad, guard." The dog at her side lowered into a menacing stance, his dark eyes taking on purpose. "He's dangerous, Your Grace. A man-eater—"

"Like his mistress?" Nick shot back.

"Yes," she agreed. "So you'd best beware of *both* of us because you are now dependent upon me to eat, to drink and . . . to do other things."

He laughed, realizing she wasn't as invincible as she wished to pretend. "Other things?" he questioned, letting the innuendo of the words flow through his voice. It helped that, in a hair's second, his mind had conjured all sorts of possibilities and his body had fallen suit.

She noticed the change in him. Hot color came to her cheeks.

Nick grinned, enjoying her discomfort while also admiring it. Life hadn't hardened her yet. It would be a pity when it did.

"Is your courage wavering, Fee?" he chided. "Or was it that you were thinking of 'other' things and grew distracted?"

Her brows snapped together. "You are a *beast*." With those words, she turned and marched back through the curtain.

Nick glowered at where she'd disappeared for a moment, but then he couldn't help but smile.

How was she going to keep him tied up? Or do "other" things? She blushed every time she looked at him. All he had to do was look at her suggestively or say something sexual to make her run from the room.

She'd also saved his life last night. He remembered all now. Without her, he would have been an easy mark for the Irishmen.

Still, that didn't mean he would let her ransom him. "You won't find me an easy captive, love," he called out. "You'll have to work for that five hundred pounds."

"Tad, growl," she answered back.

The big dog lowered his head and made a low

menacing sound, but Nick wasn't afraid. In fact, his head didn't hurt so much and he was beginning to feel entertained.

"Nice puppy," he said. "You may have one of my leg bones after I've rotted in this bed."

Tad gave him a wolfish grin as if he'd enjoy the chewing.

"That did not go well," Grace mouthed to Fiona on the other side of the curtain. Her eyes were as big as saucers. Holburn's clothes hung off a line that was strung across the room. They'd spent the night cleaning his clothes the best they could.

"It went *fine*," Fiona snapped. "And I'll not take a penny less just because he's *so irritating*."

"I've never seen you so emotional," Grace observed.

Fiona jabbed a finger in the direction of the curtain. "I *saved* that man's life," she said in a furious whisper. "I *carried* him through the streets of London and does he care? No! The only true reason I tied him up was to protect myself from his insane temper when he woke. And I'm glad I did," she said, moving toward the hearth.

From the other room, Holburn bellowed, "I'm hungry."

Fiona scowled at the curtain. "He needs to be

quiet," Grace worried. "What if Mr. Simon or someone else hears him?"

"Fee, it's time for one of those 'other' things," Holburn yelled. "I'm hungry, Fee."

"I thought you didn't like being called Fee?" Grace said.

"I don't," Fiona answered. Only her brother had been allowed to call her "Fee." How like the Duke of Holburn to instinctively know how to annoy her.

"Fee-e-e," he called. "Fee-e-ed me."

Now he was being silly. "He's testing us," Fiona said. "He doesn't believe I am serious." She stomped over to the hearth. She picked up a bowl from her cabinet shelf.

"What are you doing?" Grace asked as Fiona started ladling the remains of the porridge the two of them had made and eaten for their breakfast.

"He's hungry," Fiona said.

"But you can't feed him *that*," Grace said, hurrying over to the hearth. Keeping her voice low, she said, "He's a *duke*."

"He's a *prisoner*," Fiona corrected, aiming the last word toward the curtain.

"Dukes don't eat porridge for breakfast," Grace answered.

"They do if they are hungry," Fiona replied.

"I'm hungry," Holburn complained from the other room. "I want a steak and a glass of ale, Fee."

"Oh, yes, porridge it is," Fiona muttered to herself. She picked up a spoon and headed toward the curtain.

Grace stopped her. "We must do something about his shouting. His voice carries."

"I know exactly what to do," Fiona answered. She set down the porridge bowl long enough to take his neck cloth off the line. It was still a bit damp. She rolled it up, held it by one finger as she picked up the bowl and went through the curtain.

Holburn greeted her with, "It's about bloody time. Tad and I were growing lonely. Next time, you'd best be a bit more quick about it—"

She cut him off by stuffing a spoonful of porridge in his mouth.

His expression turned comical. He tasted the gruel and then all but gagged. "What is this?"

"Your breakfast, Your Grace," she said serenely. She'd set the porridge and rolled neck cloth on the bedside table so that she could close the open window. "Here now, I don't want you to take a chill. Tad uses this window to go back and forth to do his business."

Still frowning over the taste of the porridge, Holburn said, "He can jump a floor's height?"

"There is a shed against the building. He can climb his way up."

The duke considered her a moment. "You don't fear I'll use this information to plan an escape?"

She picked up the porridge bowl, making a great show of stirring the lumpy gruel, as she said, "I spent hours tying you down last night. I don't believe you will be going anywhere." She deliberately kept Grace's involvement a secret. Holburn didn't need to know everything.

"Open up," she coaxed him, holding up a spoonful of porridge.

He clamped his lips shut.

"I thought you were hungry?" she teased him.

His glower said louder than words what he thought, so she was surprised when he dutifully opened his mouth.

He really was a handsome man. His huge body took up all her cot and his hair was charmingly sleep mussed. A growth of whiskers darkened his jaw in a very attractive, masculine way—

Her pleasant thoughts were abruptly ended as he spit a mouthful of porridge at her. It hit the side of her chin and the bodice of her neck.

Fiona came to her feet. "That is disgusting," she said, taking up the closest thing at hand, his neck cloth, and wiping herself clean. This was her best day dress. She didn't want it ruined.

Holburn laughed with triumph. "I don't like porridge," he reiterated.

"Right now, I don't like you," Fiona returned.

"The feeling is mutual," he countered, and would have said more except that she put the neck cloth to good use. She stuffed the whole thing in his mouth as he prepared to crow again over his actions.

His brows came up in surprise. He tried to spit the neck cloth out but she'd stuffed it well into his mouth. He wasn't going to make another noise.

"Your rudeness earned you that," she informed primly. "And you can go without your breakfast, too." She picked up her bowl and spoon and left the room.

Tad wanted to follow. "Sit," she said and the dog reluctantly went back to his duties.

The truth was, Tad wasn't that good of a watch dog. He was more of a lover than a fighter, but the duke didn't need to know that.

Grace anxiously waited in the other room. "What happened?" she whispered.

"The beast spit porridge on me," Fiona said, irked beyond common sense. She found a cloth and began dabbing at the stains on her bodice. Her hands seemed covered in the sticky gruel and she could feel it dry on her face. She moved over to the last of the fresh water in the bucket.

"I can't believe I stayed up all night to clean his clothes," she complained bitterly. "Or saved his life. I should have *tossed* him to the Irishmen. Then perhaps he'd have a little bit more respect."

She turned to see Grace standing with her hand to her forehead. "What is it?" Fiona asked her friend.

Grace dropped her hand, coming over to her to say, "Let him go, Fiona. This is too dangerous. He's too bold for you."

From beyond the curtain came the sounds of Holburn's frustration. The cot bounced on the floor as he tried to free himself.

Fiona walked over to peek through the curtain. Her knots were holding.

Dropping the curtain, she said to Grace, "I might have agreed with you earlier. However, his spitting the porridge has made me angry. Holburn needs to be taught a lesson so he doesn't continue to carry on like a spoiled toddler. *And I'm just the woman to do it,*" Fiona announced, raising her voice on those last words and directing them in the duke's direction.

He made an angry, muffled response.

"Wait," Grace said slowly, the worry lines across her forehead easing. She held up a hand as if begging a moment's tolerance. "You are enjoying this."

"I am not," Fiona answered, ducking under the clothes line to carry the porridge bowl to the cabinet.

"You *are*," Grace insisted, following. She shook her head. "Fiona, you must be careful."

"I am being careful," Fiona answered. "And I *will* have my five hundred pounds."

"I don't know about that," Grace said.

Fiona turned to her. There was a funny note in her friend's voice. "What are you saying?"

Grace shook her head. "Nothing. Then again, matters are complicated between men and women. I might be wrong, but I think you are interested in *more* than just the five hundred pounds."

Heat warmed Fiona's cheeks. "There can be nothing between me and the duke. You are being fanciful."

"Am I?" Grace smiled with a certainty borne of experience. "Well, we shall see. In the meantime, I have a rehearsal. I'm afraid I can't return until after tonight's performance. Will you be all right?"

"Of course I will," Fiona answered, almost anxious to see Grace gone. Her friend was too wise in the ways of the world. She understood more than Fiona had yet comprehended for herself.

"Don't let him frighten you," Grace advised. "Keep him where he is until I return. I'll see if I can coax one of the night porters to come back with me tonight to help us with Holburn."

"I'm hoping this whole matter is played out by then," Fiona replied.

Gathering up her wool cape, Grace said, "I hope it is, too. But just in case, I shall bring strong arms to help us." She gave Fiona a hug. "Send for me if you need help before this evening."

"I will," Fiona promised and Grace left.

Holburn had gone quiet.

The occupants of the room overhead shut a door. Footsteps sounded going down the stairs in the hallway. People were leaving for wherever it is they had to go during the day.

This was the time, when everyone seemed to have somewhere to be, that Fiona felt the loneliest. The last few days since Madame Sophie had let her go had been torturous.

But now, she had something to do.

She had to take care of her hostage—and her first course of action was going to arrange for his ransom.

Crossing to her chest, she took out a small writing box. It held pen, paper, and ink. Picking up a chair from the table, she went to visit the duke.

He lay on the bed, tied down as she'd left him, mouth full of neck cloth, staring at the ceiling.

She set her chair down beside the bed and took out her writing materials. She placed the small bottle of ink on the bedside table. Tad inched closer to her.

"Now, Your Grace," she said, "I'm going to write a note to your banker and you are going to sign it."

He mumbled something that sounded very profane.

"You shouldn't talk like that," she told him. "It's unbecoming in a gentleman."

Holburn's brows shot together in fury. She smiled, enjoying herself.

She used the top of the box for a writing table.

"Now, let's see, what shall we write your banker?" She dipped the pen in ink and began, "Dear Sir, Please advance the sum of five hundred pounds to the bearer of this letter."

Fiona nodded. "That sounds good, doesn't it?"

Holburn glared at her, and shook the bed with his effort to break free.

"You are wasting your time, Your Grace," she said, not unkindly. "I know how to tie a knot, which is good because you are going to have to stay here until I withdraw the funds. I can't set you free before that."

An idea had been forming in her head since

Grace had mentioned the porter. She and Tad would leave London straight from the bank. She'd hire a lad from the street to free the duke. Of course, she'd contact Grace before she left and warn her to stay away.

It was a good plan.

"I know you don't like being bested. It makes you angry. However, look at this another way. If you don't sign, I shall do everything in my power to annoy you. It shouldn't take me long. A diet of porridge and nettle tea should bring you around soon enough. There's also the boredom of lying in that bed for hours."

His gaze narrowed suggestively.

"Alone," she emphasized. "You will be alone. I'll give you a moment to think over the matter." She set her writing box on the floor and left the room. She took her time brewing a cup of tea. When done, she carried it into his room.

Tasting the tea, she smiled. "Mmmmmm, nettle tea. It tastes so *green.* So different from wine. By the way, do you know what happens when a man accustomed to drinking his weight in grape can't have any? It makes him irritable. Crotchety. All I must do is keep talking and before you know it, you won't be able to stand the sound of my voice. You won't want to eat the food I cook for you and you will want your freedom. Five

hundred pounds is a bargain in exchange for a
good beef steak—"

He interrupted her with a huge groaning noise
and then raised the fingers of the hand closest to
her and pretended to write.

Wearing him down hadn't taken any time at
all. "Very good," she said. She'd wrapped the
ropes around his body on her cot, but had tied
each wrist separately, securing it to the bed frame.
"I'll untie one wrist. You sign the document, and
I'll leave to go to the bank. Unfortunately I will
have to retie you, but you understand. When I
have my money, I'll return to set you free."

There, let him believe he was going to see her
again.

Pleased with herself, Fiona bent over in her
chair to undo the knot around his wrist closest
to her.

What she didn't expect was for his other hand
to come across and reach for her.

Or for the ropes tied around his body to fall
away as if they weren't tied at all.

Before she completely comprehended what had
happened, he dragged her onto the bed, flipping
his body over hers. Holding her down with his
weight, Holburn took out the neck cloth gag and
captured her hands by the wrists.

He smiled, his blue eyes elated. "Surprised?"

Stunned was a better word.

Tad anxiously approached the bed. The duke gave his head a pat and said, "Down." Tad immediately dropped to the floor.

"Your dog isn't much of a guard," Holburn informed her. "And you aren't as good at tying knots as you think you are."

"What are you going to do?" she demanded, surprised she didn't feel panicked. She didn't fear him . . . but she was very conscious of him.

He was hard, aroused, but there was no anger to him. No meanness.

"I'm going to put my breeches on, Fee," he said, "but first, we need a reckoning. Now, what sort of penalty should I extract?"

And she knew he was going to kiss her.

That's when she understood exactly what Grace had meant . . . because she wasn't adverse to that kiss. She'd lost five hundred pounds, but it was part of the game they were playing between them. The game that had started the moment they'd first met.

"You would be wiser to just go," she told him.

"I would, Fee," he agreed, his voice was close to her ear. She could feel his breath against her skin. "But what fun would there be in that?"

His head turned, seeking her lips, and God help her, she let him find them.

Five hundred pounds lost and she would sell her soul for his kiss. What madness was this? She turned, the better to deepen the kiss—

The door to the hallway shook with the force of someone pounding on it. Even the walls seemed to shake. Tad jumped to his feet, the hair rising on his neck, his teeth bared.

"Annie Jenkins?" A male Irish voice, Thomas's voice called out, "We know you live here. Let us in." Without waiting for a response, he said to someone with him, "Crash it down. I'll not have her hiding from us."

Chapter Six

*N*ick came up off the bed and crouched, ready to ward off attackers. At any second, he expected the door beyond the curtain to be smashed to pieces.

But the door remained intact. The sound of splintering wood came from the room next door. The thinness of the walls had carried the sound as clearly as if the Irishman stood in front of theirs.

Tad started to growl.

"Quiet," Nick ordered and was pleased when the dog obeyed.

He glanced back at Fiona. She sat up on the bed, her back against the wall, her face drained of all color.

"Don't worry," he whispered to her. "I won't let them harm you."

Those dark solemn eyes of hers looked to him with a child's trust and it was his turn to have doubts. Damn it all. How had this happened? No one trusted him. Everyone knew he cared about nothing but himself.

"Why are they looking for Annie Jenkins here?" he mouthed.

"She lived next door."

There was clumping around and the sound of furniture being thrown on the other side of the wall. "There's no one here," one of the lads called to his leader who swore colorfully.

"Tear the place up," he ordered, "and then we'll hunt her down. She has to be somewhere around here."

Nick didn't want to face the bastards naked. "My clothes?" he asked Fee.

She nodded toward the curtain.

He moved quietly to the other room and found his breeches, shirt, and jacket hanging to dry. Tad followed him, the huge wolfhound more frightened in spite of his size.

Nick dressed quickly. He heard a new voice out in the hallway. A man shouted, "Here now, what have you done? You can't be tearing down my building this way." At the sound of his voice, Tad grew more anxious. Nick placed his hand on the dog, wanting to settle him.

And then there was the sound of the same man hollering in fear. "No, what are you doing—?"

His question was cut off by a scream and a tumbling sound as if something were bouncing down the stairs. It was followed by silence.

One of the Irishmen, the one Nick was beginning to recognize as the leader, said, "I don't understand why people can't mind their own business." He heaved a heavy sigh. "Well now, she might have stepped out. Find her. Holburn didn't come home last night. I'm thinking wherever she is, he is."

"We'd have to search the city," one of his men protested.

"Do you want your money?" the leader countered. "But first, let's cover the building. You two knock on every door. Bring her to this room if you find her."

"What are you going to do?" one of his men asked.

"I'm going to drag that body up here and store it in the tart's rooms. Who'd have thought the old man would break his neck so easily?"

Nick had finished buttoning his breeches. He pulled on his shirt. Fiona came from behind the curtain with his boots. She set them on the floor beside him. A nervous Tad pushed her hand with his head, wanting reassurance.

"Mr. Simon was the man trying to stop them," she whispered. "He was my landlord."

"There is nothing we can do for him now."

She nodded, a worry line between her brows.

He reached for her hand, lacing his fingers with hers. "Courage, Fee. I'll not let harm come to you."

Before she could reply, there was a pounding on their door. "King's men," an Irish voice announced. Tad growled. Fiona bent to restrain him but Nick caught her arm.

"Don't. Let him bark," he ordered, his voice barely a whisper. "Make them believe no one is here."

Unrestrained, Tad bounded toward the door.

Fee moved closer to Nick. "Do you believe they are really the king's men?"

Nick almost laughed. "The king wouldn't hire the Irish to sweep the streets. They think that phrase will convince people to open their doors."

The Irish pounded again. Tad leaped up the door as if he could charge through it.

"Do you hear that dog?" an Irish voice said. "Sounds like he could tear right through the wood, don't he?"

Tad growled, this time the sound more menacing than when he'd threatened Nick.

"I killed a dog like that once," a companion answered. "Damn cur tried to take me leg off."

"Ah go on," his companion countered. "That dog is probably a wee thing. Not more than yea high."

"Keep searching," their leader barked. There followed the sound of footsteps going down the stairs and more knocking on doors.

Nick crossed to the door, the better to hear what was going on. It didn't sound as if anyone was on their floor any longer. He glanced at Fee. Her body was as tense as a bow string. Deep circles beneath her eyes were another sign her nerves were stretched taut. "They haven't caught us yet," he reminded her. He was actually enjoying himself. It had been a long time since he'd felt so alive.

She nodded. She was obviously not enjoying herself so much.

"How do you think they knew who your neighbor was?" he asked, his voice soft.

"Hester hired the room at the Swan in Annie's name. I don't know how they could have discovered where she lived from there." She pressed her lips together and then asked, "But the more pressing question is, why does someone want to kill you?"

"That is a very good question, and one I shall ask Ramigio when I see him. Or Belkins," he added thoughtfully. "He seems to have taken advantage of the assignation with Annie to set up a trap. I was surprised when Belkins came to me about the ring."

"The ring?" she asked.

"A gold signet ring that Ramigio stole from me nine years ago. I've sent men all over the world searching for him and the ring ever since. Belkins came to me yesterday saying he'd met Ramigio by chance. The Spaniard wanted to return the ring and, knowing how angry I was, wanted Belkins to set up a meeting. He wanted it to be someplace private."

"And you were wary," she said, considering the matter. "That's why you jumped out from behind the door and grabbed me."

"I wasn't expecting *you*," he answered. "Or I wouldn't have been so rough."

She shrugged, dismissing his apology, her mind focused on the mystery. "And after all the time that had passed, you weren't suspicious of Lord Belkins's story?"

Nick shook his head. "Of course, I was. Then again, no one outside of the family knows about the ring or that I've been searching for it."

"Except for the men you've hired to do the search," she pointed out.

That was true. Nick was slightly annoyed to

have to admit it. "Of course they knew. But they were tasked to keep their mission confidential."

"Then how could they ask questions to find the ring?" she wanted to know. "They would have to say something to someone."

Her logic irritated him. "Of course they had to ask questions," he muttered crossly. Wanting to put her off, he reached for his boots, sitting in the rickety wooden chair beside the table to pull them on.

But Fee wasn't one to be deterred easily. "So, *all* of London could have known about you hunting this Spaniard for your missing ring?" she surmised, coming up to stand by the table.

"No," he insisted. "The men I hired were ordered to keep quiet."

The corners of her mouth lifted in doubt. "That's rather naïve of you to think they would, isn't it?" she said. "It's been my experience, there are no such things as secrets. Most men I know would babble anything if it made them appear important. Carrying out the confidential business of a duke would be one of those things."

Nick opened his mouth to tell her she was wrong . . . and then realized she was right.

He turned his attention to his boots while he considered the implications of this perspective.

"The question is," Fee continued as if he wasn't ignoring her, "why would the Spaniard attack you now? What has changed?"

That was the crucial question.

Nick set aside his annoyance with her. He stood. "I think I'd best see Belkins and ask him."

She nodded. "He is the key." She glanced at the front door. "I wonder how long we have to wait for Thomas and his men to leave."

"Thomas?" Nick asked.

"Their leader," she said. "His name is Thomas."

"How do you know this?" he asked.

Fee shrugged. "His men call him by name."

Nick had been toying with an idea but now he made his decision. "You are coming with me."

"Coming where?" she said in surprise.

He took her arm by the elbow. "With me, to my home. You have a good mind for details, and I don't remember much from last night. I need you, Fee."

Her head tilted up to him before she glanced down to his hold on her arm. He resisted the urge to rub his thumb against the inside of her elbow. He was wise.

"I'm not like Hester," she said carefully.

Nick grinned. "I've already figured that out."

"How?" she wondered.

"Your stiffness, your unwillingness to take advantage of the situation."

"I wanted to ransom you for five hundred pounds," she reminded him.

"And a ham-handed attempt it was, too. Come on, Fee, did you really think you could untie one hand and I would sign your letter?"

"If you wanted to be free you would have."

He laughed quietly. "Fiona," he said, enjoying the lyrical sound of her name as he let his gaze drop to her lips, "there are ways around you."

To his delight, her face turned a becoming shade of red. He drew her to him. He couldn't help himself. She was absolutely delicious. In fact the idea of tying *her* to a bed had great merit—

Hurried footsteps tramping on the stairs brought his attention back to the danger they were in.

Tad had been watching their banter with a dog's interest. He now came to his feet and stared at the door.

"I have something," an Irish voice yelled in the hallway. More booted feet sounded on the stairs.

"What is it?" Thomas asked.

"I was asking around for Annie Jenkins," his man reported. "I told her Annie's hair was red and she corrected me. Said Annie Jenkins has yellow hair. Thomas, are we searching for the right woman?"

Thomas's response was to swear.

"What do we do now, Thomas?" one of the men asked.

Nick let go of Fee and moved to the door to listen closer. He noticed she followed him. Good girl. He needed the sharp wits she had between her ears.

"I'm going to go see our client," Thomas said. He sounded anxious. "I'll see what he is willing to do. This job's already been more trouble than we bargained for. And I'll tell him we'll need more money for our trouble."

"How much more?" one of his men asked.

"Double the price. Every time I turn around we're having to cover our trail with another body."

There was a murmur of agreement.

"What shall we do in the meantime, Thomas?"

"Watch this building. We know Holburn hasn't gone home. In fact, when the duke didn't return last night, our client assumed we'd done the job until I told him differently."

"You should have kept quiet," one of the men said. "Then we could have collected our money and been gone."

Thomas acknowledged the truth of his words with a heavy sigh. "Except the cold-hearted bastard had another job for me to do. It wasn't much. I took care of it."

"So how do we find the duke?"

"He's going to be with the girl," Thomas said.

"Find the lass and we find our duke. Liam, you stay in her rooms. John, you watch the door downstairs. That way if she returns, one of you can come fetch me. I'll be back in an hour."

With that, they all went off in their different directions.

Fee whispered in Nick's ear. "What do we do? We're trapped."

Nick shook his head, knowing there was a way out. He took her hand and led her to the bedroom. Seeing the direction he was going, she leaned back. He gave her hand a tug. "It's not what you think," he whispered. Then he couldn't help but lean close to her ear to say, "Not that I would mind. But when I take you to bed, I want to enjoy myself."

Her eyes narrowed at the comment. "That won't happen," she assured him.

Nick smiled. He knew it would happen. He'd be certain of it.

He brushed the curtain aside and walked to the window. "This is the way Tad enters and leaves the building?" He looked to her for confirmation.

"Mr. Simon didn't know I had a dog. Well, he knew but we pretended he didn't," she confessed.

"That was kind of him," Nick murmured as he opened the window, more interested in escaping than in the landlord.

"He *was* kind," Fee said. "He didn't deserve what they did to him." There was a catch in her voice.

"Fee, don't think about it," he warned. "Don't give in to fear—"

"*Fear?* I'm angry. Furious. How dare they do that to him?"

Nick smiled. "We'll make them sorry they did."

"Yes," Fiona answered.

"But first, we've got to escape." He turned his attention back to their escape. The shed against the building that Tad used had a flat roof. Someone had placed a crate on that roof right beneath Fee's window to create a step up to the ledge. From this bird's-eye view, the shed appeared to have seen better days, but Nick suspected if it held Tad's weight, it would hold theirs—at least long enough for them to reach the ground.

"Pack your belongings," he ordered. "And be quick about it."

He didn't wait for a response but went into the other room and took the liberty of opening the chest on the floor. A black wool dress that had seen better days and the muslin dress she'd worn last night were folded neatly on top of some household items. He took the two dresses and returned to the bedroom. Tad padded alongside him.

Fee had spread a swath of blue and green plaid on the bed and was placing a hairbrush and some other toiletries on the center of it. She didn't have much to pack, although he noticed the hairbrush was made of solid silver and she handled it as if it was of great personal value.

"You could sell that brush for a pretty penny," he said as he handed her the dresses.

He was not surprised when she said, "It was a gift from my parents. I'll never part with it."

Her words confirmed his suspicions. Fiona was more than some country girl from Scotland. Her speech, her manner, her intelligence spoke to Quality. There were times when she had more bearing than a duchess.

But he knew better than to question her. She didn't trust him. Later, he would learn her story. "I'm sorry to be uprooting you like this."

She shook her head. "You didn't ask these men to chase you. And I've been 'uprooted' before. I will survive." She said the last more to convince herself than to speak to him.

"You needn't worry, Fee. You are under my protection now. I won't let any harm come to you."

"Perhaps you are the one I should fear most," she murmured, tying a knot in her plaid.

She was right.

He'd not deny she attracted him. His fascination for her was more than just because she was a lovely woman. Or that she reminded him of the

Oracle. He actually respected her. She had a good mind and a steady nature. The ransom trick had been silly, but he could see where such a wild gamble might have worked on a man other than himself.

He picked up her plaid bundle. "I won't ask you to do anything you aren't willing to do, Fee. It's the best I can offer, because you and I are going to be lovers. It's that simple."

Fire flashed in her brown eyes. "Nothing is that simple, Your Grace."

He grinned. "It is now." He changed the subject, holding up the plaid bundle. "Are these your clan colors?"

"Yes," she said proudly. Her chin lifted as she added, "It's a rebel plaid, Your Grace. You might not want to be seen carrying it through the streets."

God, she intrigued him. "I'll take my chances." He crossed to the window. "Tad, jump," he ordered.

"That's not the command," she informed him, even as the big dog leapt out the window.

Nick gave her a conciliatory smile.

Her answer was a glare.

"He likes me," Nick offered.

"Don't assume that just because my dog does, I do."

Nick laughed. "When it comes to you, Fee, I don't assume anything."

He threw his leg over the sill, hoping he had as easy a trip down as Tad had. He wrapped one arm around her plaid bundle. "I'm going first, Fee. That way I can help you down safely. That is, if you *wish* to follow." He jumped.

Chapter Seven

Holburn had jumped carrying all her possessions
in the world.

Fiona knew exactly what he was about. He'd arranged matters so she had no choice but to do as
he said. There were murderers at her door and her
dog was outside with him. Her only option was to
obey—especially since his plan made sense.

That didn't mean she had to like it.

In less than twenty-four hours, Holburn had
gone from being the object of her girlish dreams to
the most arrogant, insufferable, always-in-charge
man she'd ever met, and she'd met a good number
of them.

Then again, would she have found him so attractive if he'd been anything less than what he was?

Holburn was more than an overadmired and cosseted nobleman. He was a loner. An outsider.

So was she.

She knew her own failings, understood her distrust of others. But what drove him?

He could be charming when he chose to be, but there was also a darkness about him. He was searching for something more than a mere ring.

And he wanted them to become lovers.

"Fiona," the duke's hushed voice came from a point below the window. "Hurry."

She glanced toward the curtain separating the two rooms. If she could think of a way past the Irishmen guarding the building, she wouldn't go with Holburn.

It was that hard to trust.

The air in the room seemed to close in around her, making breathing difficult—

She went to the window. Holburn waited with outstretched arms. His breath made small frigid puffs in the air. On the ground, Tad looked up excitedly at the window, overjoyed they were following him.

And then, all doubts fell away from her. A quiet voice came into her mind. *Go with him.* No one spoke aloud and yet she "heard" this voice clearly.

For a second, she thought it was her mother. They'd been close . . . but her mother had not come back to her from the dead.

Fiona shook her head to clear it. She was not one given to fanciful thoughts, but she was bone-tired. Life had been very hard, and that was one more reason to go with the duke. Yes, he was intense in his wants and needs. He obeyed no rule other than his own. Then again, he was a duke. He didn't need to.

She sat on the sill and swung her legs around because she had no other choice. Cold air swirled around her ankles and up her dress.

From this vantage point, the drop to the roof appeared more daunting. She didn't have a shawl or coat and she'd sold her bonnet the week before for food. A shiver went through her.

"Come along," he prodded. "It's cold out here."

"I know that," she answered.

"You're afraid," he announced.

"What?" she demanded, even though he was right.

A grin spread across his face. "You haven't jumped because you are frightened. Don't be. I'll catch you and help you down. It's only six feet."

"More like ten," she informed him. "And I am not afraid."

"Then prove it. Jump."

She really didn't like him. At all.

But she jumped. She used her hands to push off the edge.

Holburn caught her before her feet could hit the ground. He didn't even lose his balance on the edge of the shed's roof. "There you are," he said, setting her on her feet.

Fiona was impressed. She wasn't a large woman but she wasn't petite either. Holburn hadn't even blinked.

"Are you going to lower me down the rest of the way?" she asked, picking up her clothing bundle. If he did, she could be off and running from him before his feet could touch the ground.

But the duke was on to her. "I know what is stewing in that crafty mind of yours. We stay together, Fee. You *and* I. They will hurt you to find me or to cover their own tracks. Don't worry. I'll see to your protection."

You and I. When he'd talked about "protection" before, she'd rebelled. She knew Holburn's reputation and was wary.

But she heard another tone in the duke's voice— kindness. It had been a long time since she'd heard kindness.

It went right through the walls she'd erected around her heart. It made her want to trust him, *even though she knew* she should know better.

"I'll see you on the ground," was all he said before taking hold of the roof's ledge and swinging himself down to the ground, not bothering with Tad's ladder of crates and barrels. He made it look easy.

"Do I have to go down that way?" she asked.

He laughed. "I'd like to see you try."

She was tempted to give it a go for no other reason than to prove her mettle, but one glance over the edge dissuaded her. She tossed her bundle to him and then started to drop to the roof to climb down to the ground. She hated thinking what the filth on the roof would do to her dress.

Holburn stopped her. "Don't climb down those crates. Just jump. You did it once, Fee, and I caught you. Trust me again."

This time the distance was farther. Holburn didn't know what he asked. *You and I.* She closed her eyes and jumped.

Strong arms caught her. Her body was pressed against his hard chest as he absorbed the momentum of her jump. She threw her arms around his neck to keep her balance and because jumping had been more scary than she had imagined. For a long moment, he held her close before slowly lowering her to the ground. Her senses were full of him. The man was rock-solid hard. She believed there was *nothing* he couldn't do. It was that simple. He could protect her.

"We make better bedfellows than enemies, don't we, Fee?" he said, his arm around her waist kept her against him. The warmth in his voice flowed through her.

She started to nod her head—and then came to her senses. "I'm not that sort of woman, Your Grace. My honor is all I have left, that and the piece of plaid I've wrapped my clothes in. Stop this nonsense talk about us being lovers. It *won't* happen."

All humor faded from his eyes. "Don't pass judgment on me, Fee. Don't assume my motives. And don't think I don't understand the meaning of honor. I've spent my life defending my honor."

He let her go then, and she almost lost her balance. He steadied her with a hand on her arm, the gesture chivalrous. Other men might have walked off then. He didn't. He picked up her bundle of clothing.

And Fiona felt guilty. She didn't think she'd jumped to conclusions . . . but the man had just helped her escape a dangerous situation, and she had no choice but to rely on him until she was completely safe.

"I just think it best we be honest with each other." She avoided his gaze, preferring instead to brush at dirt on her skirt.

"Honest?" He snorted his opinion and took her arm, forcing her to meet his eye. "*Honest*, Fee, is saying that I'll not ask for more than what you are willing to give. But I'm growing bloody irritated with you pretending you aren't as attracted to me as I am to you. I'm no bloody lecher."

"I never said you were," she defended herself.

"You don't have to. It's there in the stiffness of your back any time I'm close to you and the prim set of your mouth. But the truth is you are more afraid of yourself than you are me."

That was honest. And true.

"You don't understand," she whispered. "It's not what you think." A headache was forming behind her eyes. She was tired, worn thin, but not just from the events of last night. She'd been raped. She'd been beaten. She needed peace. She needed to feel whole again.

And this man who had occupied so much of her imagination, this man for whom she had stayed in London, was larger, stronger, and more vital than she'd ever expected . . . and she had nothing to offer in return.

He released his frustration with a heavy sigh. He leaned toward her, dropping his voice even though they were alone in the narrow alley, Tad waiting patiently at their feet. "I'm not one to explain myself. I don't understand the twists and turns of fate. I don't know you, not in the way I will know you."

His prediction brought her gaze up to his.

"So let it be," he told her. "Stop thinking beyond the moment. We're here. This is now. That's all that is important."

She could have argued with him. A woman had to think ahead if she valued herself. Fiona had learned hard lessons because she'd trusted.

However, when he took her hand, she silently followed.

And that *was* enough.

Holburn paused at the alley's entrance onto the street. The narrow, winding lane was alive with human traffic. He used his height to scan the passing crowd.

"Do you see the Irishmen?" Fiona asked.

He shrugged. "I assume we saw them last night but I don't remember what they look like. I don't see anyone who appears to be searching for us. There is one burly man leaning against the wall sleeping."

Fiona moved so that she could see and immediately recognized the sleeper as one of their pursuers. "He's one of them. Do you think he is really asleep?"

"I have no doubt of it," Holburn answered. "Look at the slump to his shoulders. It must be hard chasing and murdering people. His mate must be upstairs. Come. This way."

He took her arm and led her in the opposite direction, Tad at their heels. They came out on the street where Fiona had met Hester's coach the night before. It was very busy. Horses, wagons, and coaches clogged the streets while women of every class saw to their shopping, servants bustled along on errands and men on business. A gang of sailors strolled along, obviously fresh from their ship and taking stock of their surroundings.

All was as it should be. While she and the duke had been running for their lives, the rest of the world had gone on.

The duke raised his hand to signal at a passing hack. The driver's cab was empty but he drove on by.

Holburn shook his head. "That was odd."

"We don't appear as if we can afford his fare," Fiona explained.

"Do you think?" the duke asked as he glanced down at his person as if just now realizing what he was wearing. His shirt was open and his jacket was still damp from where Fiona had tried to clean it. He ran a self-conscious hand over the growth of beard. "You're right," he conceded.

"I don't appear much better," she consoled him.

"You're beautiful," he said without hesitation.

The compliment startled her. She knew she wasn't, especially right now. It had been a long, rough night. Her eyes felt gritty and the braid in her hair was coming loose.

He saw another hired vehicle and waved to it. This one didn't stop either.

"It's hard, isn't it?" Fiona couldn't help noting.

"What is hard?" he asked.

"Being like everyone else."

He took her teasing as a challenge. "I'm *not* like everyone else, and well you should remember that, Fee."

"I'm not certain I could forget," she murmured.

The flash of his grin was like the sun coming out from behind the clouds and just as stunning. He'd taken her gentle jab as a compliment. Fiona gave her head a little shake. She could arm herself against his good looks, his strength, his power . . . but the smile could be her undoing.

"Let me prove it to you," he said eagerly, taking her arm.

Fiona gave him a suspicious frown. "You are enjoying this adventure a bit too much."

"I am," he admitted readily, his eyes searching for another hack to hire. "It's a challenge. It's been a long time since I've been challenged."

A new concern grabbed Fiona. She came to a halt. He turned in question.

"My friend Grace McEachin," she said. "She's supposed to return to my rooms tonight. I almost forgot. I must warn her."

"Where is she?" he asked.

"Covent Garden."

"She's in the theater?"

Fiona nodded.

"It won't be hard to send word to her," he said. "Relax, Fee. I'll handle everything." His head lifted. "There's a hack over there," he said and guided her across the street to where a horse and driver waited as they often did since that corner was close to a busy mercantile exchange.

They approached the hack from the rear. Holburn opened the door and all but lifted Fiona into the cab before giving the driver an address.

The driver's manner was immediately one of pleasing subservience, until he caught sight of the duke's ragged appearance—and even then, he was uncertain whether to drive them or not.

It was when Holburn said to the dog, "Tad, climb in," that the driver decided to protest.

"Wait there," the driver protested. "You can't think to put that animal in my vehicle."

Holburn left the door and went to the driver's

box. Fiona could hear them murmuring. The duke returned and said, "Come, Tad."

In truth, Fiona didn't see how there would be room for the three of them. The cab was very narrow and not wide at all. It would be crowded for her and Holburn.

But the duke pointed Tad to the floor and the dog obeyed—which was the most amazing thing of all. Tad hadn't been completely obedient to her of late and he never listened to strangers. It was as if the dog was pleased that Holburn had come into his life.

The wolfhound took up all the floor space. Fiona and the duke had to position their feet around him. Holburn knocked on the roof.

The coach started forward and then stopped with a jerk. Apparently someone had stepped into the hack's path. The driver yelled. Fiona's heart leapt to her throat, her first thought being the Irishmen had caught them escaping. She reached for the door, but Holburn placed his hand over hers.

"Courage," he said quietly.

A beat later, the hack started forward again without further mishap.

"Why don't you rest?" he suggested. "Lay your head on my chest and I'll keep watch."

"I couldn't sleep," she assured him. Every muscle

in her back was tight and her nerves were stretched thin. "Once I know Grace is safe—"

"She will be," he said, cutting off any other protests. Fiona couldn't stifle a yawn. "Close your eyes for a moment," he suggested.

He was right. She should relax while she had a chance. It had been a long night.

It had been a long year.

She closed her eyes, leaning back as comfortably as she could against the hard leather seat. Tad rested his head on her foot and there was only so much room for her to maneuver away from the duke's body heat. She folded her hands on top of her precious bundle of clothing in her lap. All she owned, everything that was either necessary or the most precious to her, such as the silver brush her parents had given her the last Christmas the family was together, was in this bundle. As long as it was with her, she was safe.

"I can stay with my friend Grace," she said softly.

"We'll worry about that later," the duke answered.

Fiona hadn't even known she'd spoken aloud. She was that tired.

His arm came around her shoulders, pulling her head toward him. "Sleep, Fee. You don't need to worry. I'm here."

I'm here. You and I.

This man both comforted and terrified her. He could swallow her whole, absorb her being into his, hurt her in ways she only had an inkling were possible . . . and yet she fell into the deepest sleep of her life with her head against his shoulder.

Cold, damp air brought Fiona to her senses. She sat up with a start, completely disoriented and yearning for more sleep.

The duke's laughing voice said, "Come along, Lazy Ann. We're here."

Holburn.

The hack's door was open and she was alone on the seat. Even Tad was gone.

The duke leaned into the coach, offering his hand. "Come along. The driver has been paid his fare and he wants to be done with the two of us."

Fiona climbed down out of the hack. Her legs ached in protest at the movement. "Where's Tad?" she grumbled.

"He's run over to investigate the park across the street," Holburn answered before speaking to a footman dressed in deep blue livery trimmed in silver braid.

Still not completely awake, Fiona stepped up onto the marble curb. The road here was nicely paved with cobbles that fit tightly together. She glanced across the road at a charming little park where Tad sniffed at the wrought-iron fence. Fiona realized it had been a long time since he'd seen a tree or blade of grass.

The hack drove away. As if realizing she couldn't think for herself, which was true, Holburn took her by the shoulders and gently turned her to face the house.

Fiona woke up.

Before her was a row of four-storied houses that were a study in opulence married to exquisite taste. Their windows sparkled like jewels in the winter sun. Their façades were of decorative brick and marble behind elaborate wrought-iron fencing. It was all so clean and new she almost felt as if she wasn't in London anymore.

These were the neighborhoods of wealth and privilege whose ranks her mother had someday hoped she would join. Her father hadn't cared. He'd had his social concerns to keep him occupied but her mother had been practical. She'd envisioned this life for Fiona, had groomed her for it.

Tad came bounding up to her, overjoyed to have found trees and dirt and certainly a few squirrels. He nudged her hand as if encouraging her to come with him, to see what he had discovered.

Holburn laughed and rubbed the dog's head.

"You are easy to please," he told the dog and then turned to her. "Are you ready to go inside?"

"Inside where?" she asked, afraid of the answer. He couldn't possibly mean to take her, in these clothes, these well-worn shoes, and with her hair looking like it had been through a wind storm, inside one of these houses.

"In this one," he said, and Fiona was robbed of speech.

The house he indicated was the most magnificent in the square, a veritable lynchpin to all the others. The façade and columns were snowy white alabaster. The front door was open and a butler waited along with what seemed to be a column of servants all dressed in the same blue and silver braided livery.

"It's incredible," Fiona said when she could find her voice.

"Thank you," Holburn answered. "My father almost wrecked the family fortune building it. Let me show you the inside. Are you hungry? I'm famished. I hope Cook has—"

He broke off as she hung back. "What is the matter?"

"I can't go in there," she confessed.

"Of course, you can," he said, pulling her arm to drag her along. "I do it every day."

"But the way I'm dressed—? Where's my

bundle?" she asked, slightly panicked to have lost track of it.

"I gave it to a footman. Now, come along, Fee, and stop dragging your feet. It's my house. I can take whomever I wish into it." When she didn't comply immediately, he tempted her with, "How about breakfast? Or a hot bath? A warm, snuggly bed? You won't believe the delights we have in store inside."

Oh, she did believe.

Tad didn't share her reservations. He trotted right into the house, ignoring the group of servants who watched him pass.

Disloyal dog.

"Come along," Holburn said, and she had no choice but to follow.

"Good morning, Your Grace," the butler said as he and the footmen bowed. He was a lean man with close-cropped hair, the only male servant not wearing a wig.

"Morning, Docket," Holburn answered. "This is my guest, Miss Fee—" He caught himself. He pulled her back out onto the step. "What is your last name?" he whispered, keeping his back to the butler.

Fiona feared she would be ill with apprehension. She did not belong here, but at the same time, would not deny her family name. "Lachlan."

Holburn turned to the butler. "This is Miss Fiona Lachlan. She is an important guest. Tell Mrs. James to prepare a room on the family floor for her."

"It is already being done, Your Grace."

The duke smiled his pleasure and led Fiona into a huge black and white marble-tiled foyer where trunks and hat boxes were piled high in the middle of the room. He stopped and looked to Docket.

"What's all this?" the duke asked. "Mother isn't preparing for the country already, is she?"

"Yes, Your Grace," the butler answered.

"She can't do this," the duke said. "She's blocking the door with her possessions." He explained to Fiona, "Mother is making preparations for the country and the family's Christmas festivities. Every year the family meets there. My mother is not only terrible at organizing her life, but she has to take everything she owns. This pile will grow over the coming days."

Fiona didn't see how it could. There was so much stacked up here it was hard to imagine a person owning more. However, all the servants nodded agreement with the duke.

"She can't do this," Holburn decided. "I'll talk to her. Has she come down to breakfast yet?"

"No, Your Grace," Docket answered.

"Well it is time for us to seek ours. Come along, Fee," he said with good humor. "Let's see what Cook has for us."

He didn't wait for her response but guided her along in the direction of his wants, Tad walking along with them. Fiona could feel the looks exchanged amongst the servants. She knew what they were thinking. Holburn must also know, except he didn't care.

She shouldn't either. She was Lachlan, and she'd done nothing for which to be ashamed. Although wrapping herself in pride didn't release the knot of apprehension.

Meanwhile, the duke was all a solicitous host should be. He treated her like an honored guest.

"I'm famished," he announced. "Let us eat and then you may go to your room while I have a talk with Lord Belkins. I want to hear his story."

"I'm anxious to hear it, too," she said.

"Yes, but he'll talk more freely if we are alone."

"Or you'll make him talk," she said.

His response was a nod of agreement. He led her down a hall lined with landscape paintings and portraits to a cozy dining room overlooking the back garden. A sideboard was set up with silver covered dishes. Two footmen stood at attention, waiting to see to his every slightest need.

"Cider, Your Grace?" one of them asked. "Cook mulled it to take the chill off the day."

"At last something decent to drink," Holburn said with feeling. "Fee? Cider? Or perhaps you would prefer chocolate. Williams is a genius at making a pot of chocolate."

Fiona's uneasiness vanished. It had been years since she'd had chocolate. "I would appreciate a cup of chocolate."

Williams set right to work while Holburn turned to the other footman, "Larson, see to the dog. His name is Tad and he's my favorite friend right now. Perhaps Cook has a steak for him."

"I shall see, Your Grace."

"Go with him, Tad," the duke said and to Fiona's surprise that's exactly what Tad did.

The duke watched the servant and dog leave the room before saying to her, "It's so handy to have a dog who speaks English. My mother's dog answers only to gibberish."

Williams swallowed a laugh, certainly unacceptable behavior for a footman, but Holburn didn't mind and a bit more of Fiona's uncertainty lifted. Her father had always said you could judge a man by the way he treated his servants.

There was an easiness between the duke and his servants. They knew who he was. She'd witnessed no disrespect. But it was also clear they liked him.

Holburn lifted the covers over the serving plates on a sideboard. Rich, fragrant aromas reached out and drew her to them.

The duke handed her a plate, but leaned close to say in mock, "Oh look, Fee. Cook forgot to serve your favorite—porridge."

She couldn't stop the smile from his gibe, or cast a glance at Williams who was warming milk in a silver pot over a flame. If the footman overheard, he was too well trained to betray personal thoughts.

Holburn started heaping on her plate everything he put on his own. "That's plenty, Your Grace," she demurred as he reached for a second rasher of bacon for her. She took her seat at the round linen-covered table. Williams set her chocolate by her plate.

Outside the window, she noticed Larson leading Tad out into the garden. The wolfhound stood stock-still for a second and then greedily investigated every inch of ground, paying special attention along the garden's brick wall.

Sitting beside her at the table, the duke said, "What do you see?"

"Tad," she said. "That dog used to run for miles when we lived in Scotland. He hasn't had a good run in almost a year."

As if giving truth to her words, Tad began running in a huge circle as if chasing a demon, his dog smile growing wider until his tongue was hanging out and his eyes bright with happiness.

Both Fiona and the duke laughed before turning their attention to their own plates. Fiona was hungry, but her first act was to take a sip of chocolate. She released a sigh of pleasure. "You are very good at chocolate, Williams."

Williams bowed, acknowledging the compliment.

"You appear almost as happy as Tad," Holburn said.

"I am," Fiona replied over the brim of her chocolate and took another sip. "There is a happy atmosphere in this house," she said. It belied all the rumors she'd heard of Holburn.

"Williams, make Miss Lachlan another pot of chocolate. This is the most content I've ever seen her."

Fiona laughed, surprising herself at how carefree the sound was. How long since she'd felt this relaxed? Or had good food in front of her?

Holburn watched her with a bemused expression. "I can't remember the last time I heard someone laugh under this roof. Certainly I've never done it—"

He was interrupted by the sound of a small dog

barking and the click of heels coming down the tiled hallway.

Holburn and the servants tensed. Fiona turned to the door, uncertain of what to expect.

A beat later, a tall, regal, blond woman appeared in the doorway. She was dressed all in black from her laces to the stones in her rings that she wore on almost every finger. She carried a skinny, brown pointed-nosed dachshund who was yipping as if expressing his displeasure with the world.

"Dominic, I am so *glad* you are here," she said waving a black handkerchief in her free hand at him. "Such tragic news! Who would have thought it? He was so young to die! Why I only saw him two weeks ago."

"Saw who, Mother?" the duke said. He stood as she entered. Fiona did also.

But the duchess's attention wandered to the sideboard. "Oh, Williams, fix a plate for Master Rockford. He's starved. Can't you hear him?" She pinched the dog's nose. He snarled and shook his head before yipping again. "I'll take a plate, too."

Fiona's gaze went from mother to son and back again. He was dark and she fair, but they had the same clear, blue eyes.

In her youth, the dowager duchess must have been an acclaimed beauty. Even now, she would turn male heads. But Fiona sensed a calculating mind behind his mother's blue eyes. It was there in her overstated mourning dress and her dry eyes.

Or perhaps it is something that one woman can sense in another, and men never understand.

Whatever it was, Fiona didn't trust the duchess.

"Mother, who died?" Holburn asked again.

"Terrible story," the duchess said, throwing herself into the chair Williams held out for her. Master Rockford sat up in her lap, one paw on the table as if demanding his breakfast. His beady eyes took in everything with the air of a bored debutante. "Louise's note begged me come to her side as quickly as possible. Poor woman. It's so tragic to lose a husband, but a son, too—"

Her attention landed on Fiona. Both duchess and dog gave her the same beady stare. "Who are you?" the duchess asked. "Holburn, who is this riffraff sitting at my table?"

Fiona was stunned by her rudeness.

To his credit, the duke was equally insulted.

"Mind your tongue, Mother," he warned under his breath. "This is Miss Fiona Lachlan. Fee, this is my mother, the Dowager Duchess of Holburn."

The dowager made a little sniffing sound before saying, "Miss Lachlan."

Fiona bobbed a quick curtsy, but she'd caught the secret smile that had crossed the dowager's lips, and it spoke louder than words to Her Grace's character. Here was a woman who dealt in small duplicities. She would try manipulation first to achieve what she wanted.

Meeting her explained a great deal about Holburn's attitude toward the world. It was to his credit he didn't allow her to run roughshod over him.

And Fiona knew the best way to deal with this sort of woman who feigned innocence while delivering insults was to be gracious and generous. It was a trick her mother had taught her.

"Please, Your Grace," she said. "I'm certain it is a surprise for Her Grace to discover you have a guest. Especially when she is mourning the loss of a friend."

The dowager turned her head and gave Fiona a hard, clear-eyed stare. Fiona returned her gaze with a level one of her own, all the time keeping a smile on her face.

After all, that was what "riffraff" did.

"Yes, well, thank you for understanding," his mother said to Fiona at last. She didn't apologize for her comment, but broke off a bit of sausage and hand-fed it to Master Rockford. Fiona knew she was considering ways to remove her from the house.

"Mother," Holburn said, his patience at an end, "who died?"

"You are very testy this morning," she complained. "But since you should know, it is Lord Belkins. You did know him, didn't you? They found his body in the park."

Chapter Eight

"*B*elkins is dead?" Holburn repeated.

Fiona felt the food she'd eaten churn in her stomach. She sank into her chair. The duke came behind her and placed his hands on her shoulders, giving them a small squeeze. She knew he was reminding her to be brave. However, the movement was not lost on his mother.

Her eyes turned to shards of blue. "Didn't I just say as much?"

"Mother, this is a shock," he said.

"I'm shocked as well," she told him.

"I saw Belkins yesterday at my club," he continued. "He was hale and hearty. How did he die?"

"I don't know," his mother answered. "It's not

even in the papers yet. His mother Louise and I have been friends for years. I had a note from her two hours ago saying her son had been found dead in the park and begging me to come around. Poor Louise. Belkins was her favorite since he was the heir. She lived under his roof. I don't know what will become of her now. His brother will inherit and she doesn't know *what* that means. I'm so fortunate, Holburn, that you have made provisions for me in case of your demise. I would *hate* for my fate to be left to Brandt and Maven. I don't see how my husband could have such disagreeable brothers." She gave Master Rockford another bite of sausage. "Why, they would turn me out into the street, and then what would poor Rocky and I do?" She kissed the dog as he was licking his snout.

"My uncles wouldn't turn you out, Mother," Holburn answered. "They might make your life miserable, but you wouldn't be on the street."

"Don't be so certain," she said. "They've never liked me. They'd plotted against me for years."

"Well, you no longer need to worry," he said as if they'd had this conversation before. "You'll have a very healthy independence upon my death. They can't touch that money."

Her Grace held out her hand to him across the table, the gesture coming off disingenuous to

Fiona. It must have struck him the same because he didn't make a move toward her. The dowager pulled her hand back, her lips pursing into a pout. "Such a good son," she cooed. "His only weakness is women."

The air crackled with Holburn's temper. "I'm not weak around women."

"No, they are weak around you," his mother said agreeably. "Aren't they, Miss Lachlan?"

Fiona did not want to be dragged into this. The woman was impossible.

The duke looked at Williams. "Leave us, and take that damn dog."

"He stays with me," the dowager said but the footman had his orders. He slipped Master Rockford out of her arms and carried him out.

Holburn stood, leaning on one hand across the table to confront his mother. "Miss Lachlan is a guest," he said, his voice in tight control. "For the period that she is under my roof, she will be my ward—"

"Ward?" his mother queried. She fussed with the black lace around her neckline. "Wait until Brandt and Maven hear this. They will roar their disapproval."

"They can howl at the full moon for all I care," Holburn returned evenly. "What I won't tolerate is any disrespect shown to Miss Lachlan."

There was an edge to his voice that brooked no disrespect.

His mother eyed him mutinously and then said, "Oh, very well. Do as you wish. You always do anyway. I'm still miffed at you for advancing my allowance."

The duke's expression grew stony. "We've been over this."

"I'm still not happy."

"You rarely are," his son said.

"Am I to have no say about my life?" she said, coming to her feet. "Look at her. Her dress is atrocious and that hair would suit a witch—"

"*Enough,*" he said. Fiona wished she could hide under the table.

The dowager raised a hand. "You are right. I am too blunt in my opinions, although it is a trait we both share, my son."

Every time she said, "my son," a chill went up Fiona's spine. She wondered if the duke felt the same way.

"If you want your ward, you may have her." She picked up her black handkerchief. "I must be going. Louise is waiting. We were so close at one time, Louise and I. All I need is Master Rockford and I'll go. You and Miss Lachlan may be alone—"

At that moment, there was a din of dog barking coming from the butler's pantry. The dowager reached the door first and threw it open. Master Rockford streaked into the room, a brown blur of running feet. She swept him up into the safety of her arms.

The footmen followed. They held Tad by a rope line. "I'm sorry, Your Grace," Larson said. "Master Rockford wanted the wolfhound's steak."

"And that huge dog attacked him?" the dowager said shrilly.

"No, Your Grace," Larson said, "Master Rockford attacked old Tad here. Went right after him as if he thought they were the same size." Larson sounded dutifully respectful, but Williams was having a hard time keeping his humor in check.

"Of course he would. Rocky is not a coward," the dowager replied, soothing her shaking dog.

Larson looked to the duke. "Tad really did try and keep his temper," he said. "But when Master Rockford sank his teeth into his steak, the wolfhound had enough. He put one paw on Master Rockford and continued eating. That was what the barking was about. Master Rockford was upset."

"As well he should be," the dowager declared. "Dominic, I want that monstrous dog gone by the time I return today." She didn't wait for an answer but went charging out of the room.

Fiona was mortified. Nor was she going to let Tad leave without her. They would go together.

"I know what you are thinking, Fee," Holburn said, "and don't worry. Tad isn't leaving. My mother makes pronouncements like this all the time. The house is large enough for both dogs to live peacefully, and they probably will if she stays out of it."

His words were exactly what she wanted to hear. Over breakfast, she had adjusted to the idea of staying here, even if it was only for a day or two. "I'm sorry Tad upset Master Rockford."

"I'm not," the duke said. "Rocky has needed a comeuppance for a while, hasn't he, lads?"

The footmen nodded. They were openly grinning now. Williams scratched Tad's neck.

The duke held out his arm. "Come, Fee, let me show you to your room. Are you coming, Tad?" The wolfhound joined them.

Once they were out in the hallway, he murmured, "What were you saying about a happy atmosphere?"

"I stand corrected," she confessed. "Is she always like that?"

His expression grew troubled. He didn't answer right away but waited until they'd reached the top of the stairs. It was clear they were alone here. The servants were off doing other things.

"Yes, she is always like that," he said in answer to her earlier questions.

"I'm sorry," she said and meant the words.

He shrugged. "It's just her silliness. Mother doesn't feel she fits in. She always has believed the *ton* frowned on her, and she's right. They have. She was a lovely opera dancer who captured the heart of a duke. My father wasn't a practical man like his brothers."

"Is that the Brandt and Maven she referred to?"

Holburn nodded. "Lord Brandt and Lord Maven, my illustrious uncles. She's right to dislike them."

"They have been cruel to her?"

"Not cruel—disapproving. They disapprove of everyone who doesn't fit their rigid set of expectations. They earned their own titles through service and money in the right places but they have little consideration for mother, who earned her title using the oldest method of all—love."

"So she and your father were a love match?" Fiona asked, anxious to find something good about the dowager.

"On his part," the duke said. "Mother is so mercurial, she feels one thing today and another tomorrow."

"It must be hard to have a woman like that in your life."

Holburn gave a quick shrug. "I understand her. She always attends to her own welfare. I see her when she wants something or, like downstairs, when we happen to meet. Otherwise, we stay out of each other's way. You won't need to worry about her. Come," he said, changing the subject. "Let me take you to your room."

Fiona had other questions she could have asked, but she knew when the subject was done.

Nick led Fee down the hall to the room he'd directed for her use. Tad followed.

"I'm going to Belkins's house to pay my respects and see if I can learn something about his whereabouts last evening," he told her. He stepped back and let her enter the bedroom first.

She took two steps in and then stopped dead in her tracks. Her breath came out in a soft sound of appreciation. "This is lovely."

Nick thought *she* was lovely. He no longer saw the crumpled clothes or the mussed hair. Instead, her spirit seemed to glow around her. He had to pull his gaze away to look around the room and see it as she did.

Soft yellow walls, India carpets, cream-colored furniture with blue bed clothes. It looked the same as the other rooms in his home, except now he was seeing it through her eyes—and felt a twinge of pride as she walked around, her eyes admiring everything. Tad went straight to the fire in the grate and flopped down.

Nick was especially pleased that the servants had placed a bouquet of flowers on the bedside table.

Fee saw those immediately. "Roses?" She turned to him. "How can you have roses in winter?"

"There's a hothouse in the back. The gardener prides himself on his flowers." Nick had never paid particular attention to the flowers before. It had been another of his father's lavish fancies.

But right now, watching Fee touch the velvety petals in wonder, seeing her lean down to smell them, he thought it the best thing his father had ever done.

She smiled at him. "I'm amazed. They're beautiful . . . or is it that they are all the more special, because I wasn't expecting to see them?"

Just as he hadn't expected to see her smile.

For a second, Nick stood transfixed by that smile. Fiona Lachlan was a lovely woman by anyone's standards. Since setting eyes on her, he'd wanted her. He liked her. He'd be happy to bed her.

However, that smile . . . it didn't just change her face, but created in him feelings he'd never experienced before. He wanted to touch her, yearned to put his arms around her. Breathing became hard, as if his heart beat twice as fast.

An image floated in his mind, an image of her

smiling not over roses but over him. Over her pleasure at *being* with him, *trusting* him . . . *loving* him.

Nick took a step back, startled by the directions of his thoughts.

He didn't believe in love. No one he knew was in "love," at least, not with their spouses and relationships with mistresses never lasted.

Nick *had* witnessed one-sided love, but he considered that lust. His father had been a prime example of that. He had lusted for Nick's mother and "won" a dubious prize.

"Is something the matter?" Fee asked, coming toward him in concern. "You've gone pale."

"I'm fine." He held up a hand to ward her off and searched his scrambled mind for a safe topic. "Tell me the name of your friend again. I'll stop by the theater and warn her not to go back to your rooms."

"Grace McEachin."

"Covent Gardens, right?"

"Yes." She peered up at his face, obviously not convinced he was fine. "Let me feel your head. Perhaps you are still feeling the effects of that potion."

Nick knew he couldn't let her touch him, not with a bed close at hand. He backed away. "You need to sleep. You have huge circles under your eyes."

"I am tired," she admitted and yawned.

Dear Lord, even her yawns were attractive. "If you need anything, pull the cord by the door and ring for a servant."

He didn't wait for her answer but left, closing the door behind him.

At last, he could breathe again.

Nick leaned back against her door, still dizzy from being close to her inside her room. He'd never gone buffle-headed over a woman before. He'd wanted them, liked them, had them.

Beware innocence.

The mystery behind the Oracle's prophecy haunted him. Fee wasn't an innocent. A woman didn't survive on her own without learning hard lessons. She'd paid a price. He saw it in her eyes . . . but that didn't make her "safe."

The Irishmen, Belkins's death . . . the vision of Fee's face as the Oracle. Forces were at work that he didn't understand. Or that a sane man would refute.

He glanced up and down the hall. This was his home, and yet he felt a stranger. It was an eerie feeling.

Nick walked to his room and was relieved to open the door and see his valet Gannon waiting with fresh clothing. The world fell back into place again.

"Is something the matter, Your Grace?" Gannon

asked. He was a short man with frizzled gray hair and impeccable taste.

"Why do you ask?" The words came out sharper than he had intended.

"You seem preoccupied, Your Grace. That is all."

Nick forced himself to relax. He reached for an excuse. "Lord Belkins died either last night or early this morning. I'll be paying a call on Lady Belkins as soon as I'm dressed."

"Yes, Your Grace," Gannon said as he turned to the bureau of drawers and pulled out a black armband.

"Oh, and another matter, Gannon," Nick said as he prepared to turn himself over to his valet's skillful administrations, "I have brought home a guest. She's my ward." Like the other servants in the house, the valet was too well trained to even so much as raise an eyebrow. "She needs clothing and all the toiletry articles a woman likes. See to it while I'm out. I know you'll do well."

"Yes, Your Grace. Should I also assign one of the maids to her?"

"Of course," Nick said. "Just don't let it be one of my mother's favorites. I'll have no carrying of tales."

"Understood, Your Grace."

With that, Nick sat in the chair in his changing room and let Gannon do his magic. Less than an hour later, he was out his door where a groom walked his favorite mount, a dark bay gelding by the name of Jack.

As Nick started to mount, he caught a movement amongst the trees in the park across the road. A pasty white face had pulled back just as he'd looked in that direction. It had to be one of the Irishmen. He wondered if it was Liam or John or even their leader, Thomas.

He leaned over to the groom. "Peter, there is a man lurking in the park. Don't look. You'll see him eventually. He isn't that bright. I want you to keep your eye on him. I believe he is going to follow me. You stay close to him wherever he goes. I'll want a report at your first opportunity."

"Yes, Your Grace," Peter said, pulling on his cap.

Pleased, Nick reined Jack around and set off down the road to learn what he could about Belkins's death.

But first, he was going to stop by Covent Gardens and speak to Miss Grace McEachin. Yes, he'd pass on the warning but his true mission was to satisfy his curiosity about Fee. He'd not delay such a visit a moment longer no matter how many Irish murderers were on his trail.

Three hundred thousand pounds had recently been spent to rebuild the Royal Opera House at

Covent Garden after it had burned down in a fire the year before. Nick had attended the opening celebration in September and kept a box here although he didn't go to the theater often. His time was better spent at the gaming tables that kept the family fortunes alive. Instead, his uncles and other family members used the box.

However, his mother also rarely went to the theater. That seemed curious for a woman who grew up on the stage, although she took great pains to distance herself from her common background—and hence, her reaction this morning to Fee.

Nick frowned. He and his mother were not close. It was hard to have any sort of relationship with such a difficult woman, although he did care for her. She was his mother.

In truth, she spent as much time at the gaming tables as he did and always had. More than once he'd had to settle her debts, but lately they had risen to a ridiculous amount. Six weeks ago, he'd warned her it would have to stop. She couldn't continue to be so careless. He would cut her off, and she knew he meant it.

At the stage door, he gave the porter Grace McEachin's name and pressed a guinea in the man's hand.

"Should I tell Mrs. McEachin who is calling for her, my lord?" He used the term "Mrs." because in the theater many women pretended a dead husband. It was a protection of sorts, and sometimes there truly was a dead husband—or a live one whom she had escaped to seek her fortune.

"Tell her Fiona Lachlan wishes to speak to her," Nick answered.

The porter didn't even bat an eye at the name Nick used but pocketed his money and went in search of the dancer.

The back stage was a decidedly inelegant space in contrast to the lavish theater on the other side of the curtain. Here, pulleys, ropes, curtains, and props took up a good portion of the space, leaving narrow paths for the humans who created the magic on stage.

A few minutes later, the porter returned with a lovely woman with curling black hair, porcelain skin, and vivid blue eyes dark with concern.

She recognized Nick. Her step slowed. She stopped. He knew she debated whether to run or not.

"I'd like to speak to you a moment in private," Nick said without introduction. He moved toward a fake wall assuming she'd follow. She hesitated a moment, crossed her arms in indecision, and then joined him.

"What has happened to Fiona?" she demanded, her low angry voice carrying the lilt of Scotland.

"I swear, Your Grace, if you have hurt her I shall carve your heart out myself."

"You Scots are a blood-thirsty lot," Nick commented. "And I assure you, Fee is fine. She's under my protection right now."

This information did not mollify Miss McEachin. She flew at him with her fists. *"What have you done to her?"*

She was a petite woman and he had no problem deflecting her blows. He caught her wrists. "Nothing. I've done nothing to her. She is safe and she is well."

"You haven't touched her, have you?" she demanded, her concern that of a loving sister. "She's not like me."

Nick gave a small laugh. "Miss McEachin, when would I have had time? Since I've met Fee we've been too busy trying to stay alive to think to seduction."

Miss McEachin glared at him as if divining the truth of his statement. She pulled on her wrists. He let her go. She moved a step away from him, distrust still etched in every line of her face. "But you'd like to," she said at last. "Wouldn't you?"

"I'm here because she asked me to see you," he said, uncertain whether he was offended by her charge . . . or guilty of it. "The Irishmen who attacked us last night broke down Annie Jenkins's door this morning. Fiona," he said, making a point of using her full name, "was afraid you might attempt to visit her and she didn't want you caught up in this."

Her brows came together in concern. "I thought they wanted you."

"They do, but that hasn't stopped them from killing others. Hester Bowen died last night when a shot aimed at me hit her instead. I also suspect they have murdered an acquaintance of mine. To be safe, I have Fee with me."

"And you don't know what all of this is about?"

Nick couldn't help a cynical smile. "Other than someone wants me dead, no. But I will find out."

Some of the tension left Miss McEachin's body. "Then she's safest with you."

"I believe so."

She shifted her weight from one foot to the other. He could leave now. The message had been delivered . . . but he wanted more.

He was rewarded when she said in a quiet, thoughtful voice, "You must be careful with her. She's not as hard as she pretends."

"I know."

She shook her head. "No, you don't. You are like everyone else. So judgmental. But she's Quality, Your Grace. She was bred and groomed to marry a man such as yourself. Her father was one of the most respected magistrates in Scotland. A true and honest man."

Here is what he'd really come to Covent Garden for—information about Fee.

"What happened to him?" he asked.

"He was murdered," she said with a bitter smile. "He stood up to the landowners who wanted to clear their property of the crofters and clansmen who had been loyal to them for centuries. In the Highlands, he is revered as a hero. His son, Fiona's brother, became a rebel against the Crown and had to run to America. Fiona was left alone. Life is not good for a woman alone. Bad things happen."

"Such as?"

She shook her head. "It's not for me to say. Fiona will tell you, if she has mind to."

"Why didn't her brother take his sister with him?" Nick would have. He wouldn't have left her behind.

"He offered. Fiona refused to go. She's a stubborn one, or have you not discovered that already?"

"Will you gloat if I admit I've learned that fact—repeatedly?"

Her manner changed to one of friendly commiseration. "I know she can be a trial, but in truth,

Your Grace, she is one of the kindest, most loyal women I know. The man who wins her heart will be blessed."

Nick smiled. "Is your opinion of me changing, Miss McEachin?"

"No, Your Grace," she said without hesitation. "I know your reputation with women. You don't deserve Fiona. However, I also know your reputation for pistols and swords. You'll protect her for no other reason than the challenge of it."

Her words hit him wrong. "Just for the challenge?" he repeated, letting her know she had offended him. "No more, no less?"

But Grace McEachin was not intimidated. "Does it matter—?" she started, and then stopped as if struck by a new realization. "Wait. You are angry at what I said."

"What man of honor wouldn't be—"

"It's more than that," she said, cutting him off. "You *like* her. You may actually be fond of her."

Fond? Such a light word for what he actually felt. He took a step toward the door.

Miss McEachin followed. "Could the heart of the Duke of Holburn, a rake who has lived in the bowels of hell, actually be falling in love with my friend Fiona Lachlan?"

There was that word again. Love.

"Don't be foolish, Miss McEachin. I don't have a heart."

"And I'm thinking you might be wrong, Your Grace," she said.

No, Nick wanted to say, a strong, forceful word, but the denial stuck in his throat.

She smiled with knowledge borne of experience. "You can't escape Fate, Your Grace. You may already be trapped."

He turned and left the theater, feeling as if the hounds of hell were chasing him in her statement.

Chapter Nine

*N*othing attracted company like tragedy.

The Belkins's townhouse was mobbed, the street outside it jammed with coaches and horses. People waited to enter the house while others gathered in front discussing the sudden loss of one of their number. It wasn't officially a wake, but rather the initial gathering of family, friends, and the curious.

More than a few lifted their eyebrows in surprise at Nick's arrival. He wasn't known for obeying the niceties. As he gave the butler his hat and his name, several mothers waiting in the entrance hall herded their daughters away from him.

Of course, those same daughters craned their necks for a better look.

Lady Belkins was a short, horse-faced woman with prematurely graying hair and crying didn't become her. She held court in her sitting room, a tragic, red-eyed figure whose life had changed overnight. She'd been one of the top heiresses of her Season years ago. Nick was fairly certain Belkins had blown through her fortune and he wondered what she would do now. He wasn't the only one in town who'd held Belkins's markers, although at least he wouldn't call them in. Belkins had already paid a terrible price, one his wife shouldn't have to pay.

Nick took a moment to murmur his condolences to the distraught widow and then moved into a side room, where he found a place to stand, giving him a view of the hallway and the receiving rooms. He took a punch cup off the tray of a passing servant and listened to the conversations around him, marveling at the two distinct sides to Belkins's life. Here was the one of respectability. And then there was the other, the life that included Hester Bowen, gambling, and possibly Andres Ramigio.

Then again, Nick couldn't criticize. His life was the same. A pretense of duty and honor and a reality of doing as he damned pleased.

He heard his mother's voice and was surprised she was still here. He caught sight of her in the hallway, which was absolutely a crush of people. She was standing close to the wall, speaking earnestly to a woman who could have been the same age. The black pheasant feathers on his mother's hat bowed and jerked with her animated head movements.

Nick wondered what had his father seen in this woman? She was silly, vain, and manipulative. His father had given her everything, including naming her his duchess and yet, Nick always had the sense that it hadn't been enough.

Over to his right, two of Belkins's relatives were lamenting his death at such a young age . . . and Nick was taken back to the time of his own father's funeral. They had said such things about his father, too.

Nick had been ten and away at school when his father had died. Docket had come for him, and Docket had been the one to explain that his father had been found dead on the library floor. No one knew what had happened. He'd returned from a ride, gone to his desk to see to some papers and apparently had fallen where he stood.

The memories made Nick uncomfortable. He wasn't a man given to introspection. He saw no purpose for it. But for the first time, thinking back to those days with the rational mind of a man and not a boy, Nick wondered if perhaps his father had been disappointed in his own marriage. Like everyone else, he'd assumed the unequal class distinction had meant his parents had been wildly in love. Had love turned sour? His parents had not had more children.

A male voice close by said, "I heard he was found face down in the road. Hit his head on a rock. His horse was found running loose in the park."

Nick glanced over and saw the speaker was Sir Lionel Hemly, who was holding court with two other gentlemen he didn't know.

"Which park?" one of the gentlemen asked.

"I'm not certain," Sir Lionel answered. "Of course the mystery is what was Belkins doing out that early in the morning. It was not a fashionable hour for a ride."

"He could have been coming in," one of his companions said and the men laughed, knowing what he meant.

"Still, it's deuced bad business," Sir Lionel concluded. He reached for the punch tray a servant carried, set down his empty glass and took a fresh one. "'Tis a somber note for the Christmas season, eh? He's left his family with nothing. His wife may have to move back in with her family."

It was what Nick had suspected. Belkins had

been a done up. He'd offered to arrange the meeting with Andres Ramigio in exchange for his markers because he had no money. At the time, Nick had been so excited at the mention of Ramigio he hadn't considered an important question— how had Belkins known the man? Or that Nick had wanted him? It wasn't a matter Nick mentioned outside his immediate family. Other than his uncles and his cousin Richard, he doubted if anyone else knew.

Belkins's death could have been an accident, but Nick didn't believe so. The numbers of dead from last night were piling high.

He wasn't about to be next. The time had come to be bold.

Mourners were still entering Belkins's front door. Few were leaving, since this impromptu wake gave everyone the opportunity to visit.

Nick wandered down the hall, giving his punch glass to a passing servant. Most London townhouses were laid out in the same manner. There was a front set of stairs for guests, and a back set for family and servants. Nick found the back stairs and quietly climbed them, thinking he'd pretend to be searching for the water closet if a family member or a servant came across him.

If there was one person who might have knowledge of where Belkins had been last night, it would be his valet.

Nick wasn't certain which room was the master's suite. He opened two of the doors in the hallway before he found himself in a larger bedroom than the others. He stepped inside and gave a start when he saw a body, fully dressed in riding clothes and lying on the bed as if asleep.

He started to back out of the room until he realized the man was Belkins himself. His body had been laid out here to be dressed.

Later, per custom, the family would probably retire the body to the receiving room or the dining room for the viewing.

However, right now, the room was quiet. It was just Nick and Belkins.

Shutting the door behind him, Nick moved to the bedside for closer inspection. Belkins was apparently wearing the same clothes he'd had on at the time of his death. The boots were scuffed but the jacket and shirt were clean. The muscles of his face were rigid and there was still a very faint hint of color to his complexion. Coins had been placed over his eyes and a bandage wrapped around his head where there were still the marks of an ugly bruise.

Nick wanted to know what was under the bandage. He knew he must move fast lest he be caught poking and prodding the body. *That* would do nothing to enhance his reputation.

The bandage had probably been tightly bound when it was first applied, but because the body was dead, the swelling had gone down. Nick could ease the bandage enough to see that the center of Belkins's forehead was caved in, the bruising a sign of blood around the injury. Perhaps the man could have fallen off his horse and hit his head hard on the ground—but then his clothes would be dirty.

Or more likely, some one had bashed in the head good and hard. Nick wondered if the back of His Lordship's jacket and breeches were as clean as the front? He doubted it.

Belkins had been murdered. The family could believe what they wished, but Nick would not ignore the fact Belkins had been too good of a horseman to have fallen head first off his mount—

"I beg your pardon, sir?" a clipped voice asked from the other side of the room.

He'd been caught.

Thinking fast, Nick slumped his shoulders as if in grief. He turned to meet the valet who walked into the bedroom from a changing room. Nick hadn't even heard the man moving.

The valet was roughly Nick's age, and half his height. His eyes were red-rimmed from grief and he held a black scarf in his hand.

"I'm the Duke of Holburn," Nick said in what he hoped was a stricken voice. "I had to see him. We were friends. We were supposed to have dined together last night. I can't believe he is dead."

"It is tragic, Your Grace," the valet said.

"Yes," Nick said, lingering over the word before saying, "Belkins never showed for dinner. Didn't even send word." Being wise in the way of servants, even the most loyal ones, he reached into his coat pocket and removed some folded pound notes. "His plans must have changed. I don't suppose you knew what they were?"

The valet's shrewd eyes narrowed on the money. Since his employer had died, the man knew he'd soon be without a position. One had to be practical, even in the face of death.

"He stayed in last night," the valet said, taking the money.

Nick peeled off several of the notes and laid them on the bed beside Belkins's body. "Did he stay in all night? Or receive a message that would have called him away? After all, he wasn't found here."

"There was a message," the valet said.

Nick placed another note on top of the others. "When did it arrive?"

"Earlier in the day yesterday, before my lord woke." That spoiled the theory Nick had been developing that someone had called Belkins out of bed.

"Was he expecting it?" Nick asked.

The valet nodded. "Although it upset him."

Nick's interest quickened. "Did you by chance read it?"

The valet stiffened. "I don't do that sort of thing, Your Grace," he announced. "Lord Belkins burned the letter."

Damn, Nick thought.

But then the valet unbent enough to confide, "However, I did manage to catch a glimpse of what it said."

Nick placed the money left in his hand on the bed. The valet picked up the bills and pocketed them before saying, "The writer said he'd received His Lordship's message about the Swan."

"Who signed the letter?" Nick questioned, his heart pounding with excitement.

"I didn't have enough time to make sense of it, but the name was Spanish."

"Andres Ramigio or the Barón de Vasconia?"

The valet nodded. "I saw the word Andres."

Nick received this news with mixed emotions. He'd really not wanted to believe Ramigio a killer . . . although he didn't know him well. After all, they'd spent one night carousing and enjoying each other's company. That wasn't a character recommendation—and yet, the two of them had bonded immediately. Nick had thought himself a fairly good judge of character. That was the reason the theft of his ring made him so angry. "And Belkins burned the note?"

"Yes, I watched him do it."

Damn the bad luck. Nick would have liked to have seen the message for himself. "Did you see who delivered it?"

"I didn't. But a footman said it was handed over by one of the street lads."

Nick could have chased down a description but he knew it would be impossible to find the lad who had delivered the note. London's streets were filled with boys who would run an errand for a half penny.

He looked at the body on the bed. The poor bastard had paid the ultimate price for betraying a friend. "But why would he have done that? What motivated him to send me to that inn?"

"Money," the valet answered before Nick realized he'd spoken aloud. "His lordship was to be paid handsomely to arrange a meeting with you. There was a line in the note telling him he would be paid if all went well at the Swan. I couldn't read if the letter said where and when His

Lordship would receive his money. However I suspect he left early to collect it."

"Why do you believe that?"

"I overheard him mention to Lady Belkins that he would give her pin money this morning. She wasn't happy. She wanted it last night and he said he couldn't pay it until the morning."

God bless the servants. "Any idea when he left this morning?"

"Around four. That's when the groom said he came for his horse. He walked into the stables, gave Billy a shake, and ordered him to saddle his Nell up."

And after that? Nick released a sound of exasperation. The trail had gone cold.

At that moment, the door opened. A maid entered. "My lady would like—" she started and then stopped seeing Nick in the room. "Oh, I beg pardon."

Nick patted Belkins's arm. It was stiff. Nick turned and walked out of the room, his mind full with this new information. He took the back stairs again and found the crowd of callers in the hallway had thinned considerably.

His mother was still there. He caught sight of her in the dining room. He was moving toward her to mention he was leaving when he realized she was talking to his uncles, Lord Brandt and Lord Maven.

It was too late to avoid them. They'd seen him.

His mother appeared relieved at his presence. "I told you Holburn was here," she informed the uncles in a carrying voice so Nick knew his presence was expected. She welcomed him with a big, motherly smile.

His uncles were twins and alike in almost every way. They dressed in somber, austere clothing. They were of the same height, almost as tall as Nick, and their expressions were ones of cheerless gloom. Life was a serious matter to them and they did not understand Nick or his frivolous mother.

"Gentlemen," Nick greeted them as he approached. Ignoring their bows of acknowledgment, he asked, "Mother, are you ready to leave?"

"Oh, yes," she said waving her black handkerchief in front of her face. "Past ready. This all reminds me so much of the sadness surrounding your father's passing. So tragic to lose a husband so young in life." If she had said this to garner sympathy from her in-laws, she could have saved her breath. Nick's uncles didn't so much as flicker an eyelash over the mention of their brother's death.

Nick supposed they would feel the same about his death as well.

Or perhaps they'd be more enthusiastic, since his uncle Brandt would inherit the title—and *there* was a motive for murder. Both Brandt and Maven had earned their own titles, but that didn't mean they didn't covet his.

It's a disquieting thing to consider the idea that one's relatives might consider murdering him. It had been a random thought but it started to take shape in his mind.

What had Fee said? The person who had hired the Irishmen would be the one who would gain the most from his death. Neither uncle thought Nick worthy to be duke. They'd said as much often enough.

But would they stoop to murder?

He forced himself to smile at his uncles while inside every fiber of his being recoiled from them. "Will we see you Christmas at Huntleigh?" Nick asked, already knowing the answer. His uncles never missed an opportunity to inspect the estate.

"Of course," Brandt said. He took out his snuff box and flicked it open with his thumbnail. "I trust, Daisy," he said to the dowager, "that all is as it should be, or will you be dependent upon our wives' help again?"

"I can manage," his mother said quickly. She was sensitive to the use of her given name. His uncles rarely afforded her any respect in private or public.

"Yes," Nick said. "She has it organized already. Everything is packed and waiting for the moment she leaves." He changed the subject. "Mother, didn't you have a coat?" He caught the eye of a servant. "The duchess is leaving. Please see her to the door and fetch her coat. I'll join you in a moment, Mother."

His mother seized the opportunity to escape, made cursory farewells and went running off.

Nick faced his relatives whose faces seemingly held no guile. He knew differently. His uncles could be ruthless men.

For a moment, he debated confronting them. They would deny hiring the Irishmen or any involvement in Belkins's death. He decided the best course would be to have them followed. Until then, he would be all that is pleasant. "It was good seeing you, Uncles, even under these circumstances."

"We don't see you enough, Holburn," Brandt said. "Perhaps we should have supper together before we leave for the country? Richard has returned from India with some interesting stories to tell."

And give them another chance at him in the city, where there were hundreds of escape routes for their assassins?

No, if they took another shot at Nick again, he wanted it to be done where the killers would be out in the open and on his own land where he was law. His cousin Richard's stories of India would have to wait.

Inspiration struck. "I'm afraid I will be unable to dine with you before Christmas. I leave for Huntleigh on the morrow." He'd be better able to protect himself and Fiona there.

"But Christmas is another two weeks away," Maven said.

"I have some business to attend to on the estate," Nick answered.

"What of Belkins's funeral?" Brandt agreed.

"That's why I'm here today," Nick answered, giving them his best smile.

"Or the settlement?" Brandt said. "I was under the impression Belkins owed you a great deal of money."

"He owed everyone," Nick said, his suspicions being reinforced by such a callous statement. "But considering the circumstances, I will not collect upon the debt. It would not be the action of a gentleman."

"He owed us," Brandt said. Seeing Nick's surprise, he said, "We had shares in a sailing venture we wished to sell. This was before we realized how deeply into the duns he was. After all, his wife had come to him with a great fortune."

Therefore Belkins would be in a position to do as they bid.

"And will you forgive the debt?" Nick challenged them.

His uncles exchanged glances. "We shall see," Maven answered, speaking for both.

It took all Nick's willpower to stand his ground and not back away from these men who had disapproved of him all his life. "Well then, we shall enjoy a cup of Christmas cheer before the fire at Huntleigh when you arrive. Now, if you will excuse me. I need to see to my mother." He turned and left his uncles without acknowledging their bows.

To his surprise, his mother wasn't waiting for him by the door. He glanced outside. Her coach still stood by the curb, the door open, the step down.

He turned back into the house, finding it curious his mother wasn't there. He searched for her in the receiving room.

Lady Belkins was sobbing in the arms of one of her friends as others surrounded her offering condolences. One woman offered smelling salts; another held out a cup of tea.

Nick wandered through the room and caught a glimpse of his mother in the far corner. She was talking to a square-jawed man of average height. His steel-gray hair was close cropped to his head and he had the presence of a military man.

His mother saw him. Her face was flushed and her eyes bright. She seemed agitated. Meetings with the uncles always upset her.

She waved him over to join them. "Holburn," she said, "this is a particular friend of mine. Colonel Harry Swanson. He was cavalry," she added, and Nick realized she wasn't even thinking about his uncles. Her infatuation for him was clear for all to see. "Colonel, this is my son, the Duke of Holburn."

"Your Grace," Swanson said, he clicked his heels like a Prussian as he made his bow.

"Colonel," Nick acknowledged. He didn't mind his mother having a suitor. In fact, he was rather surprised she hadn't had *more* men in her life. She was still very attractive and rather young. But ever since his father's death, she hadn't taken a lover or mentioned remarriage.

Now, Nick sensed it was different. Without being told he knew the colonel was his mother's paramour. The signs were there in the way she leaned toward him and how solicitous he was to her.

"I was thinking, Dominic," his mother said, reverting to the informality of his given name, "that Colonel Swanson could join us at Huntleigh for the holidays."

"That's a capital idea," Nick said. The colonel would keep his mother occupied under what, if Nick's suspicions about his uncles were correct, could be a trying family visit. Besides, he needed a chance to make the officer's acquaintance. After all, it would be up to Nick to approve or disapprove the match if his mother decided to remarry.

His mother's smile was as giddy and excited as a young girl's. "See? I told you my son wouldn't mind your presence."

"Well, then, I accept the invitation," Colonel Swanson answered.

"Good," Nick said. He turned to his mother. "Are you ready to leave?"

It was obvious she wasn't anxious to depart now that Colonel Swanson had arrived but she had no choice. They had already stayed far too long.

As he was leading his mother down the front steps of the house, Nick asked, "Why hasn't he ever come to the house?"

"He has," she told him.

That was news. "I've not met him."

She paused on the coach step. "Dominic, are you really that interested?"

Her jaded response surprised him. "Of course I am."

His mother shook her head. "I think not. You are far too busy with your own life to consider mine."

"That's not true," he countered, having heard this complaint before. "I take great interest in your welfare."

"When you aren't enjoying your *own* pursuits," she charged.

"Well, it appears you have 'pursuits' too, Mother," he responded.

"He's very special," she said, referring to Colonel Swanson.

"I'm certain," Nick said, closing the coach door. "I will see you at home?"

"I have some errands to perform so I might not be there until much later. In fact, I am to see friends at dinner this evening."

So that meant he and Fee would dine alone.

Nick liked the idea.

He also noticed that Colonel Swanson now stood on the front step. His mother pretended to just see him and waved. "Dominic, you don't mind if I ask Colonel Swanson to accompany me?"

For a second, Nick debated saying no, and then realized he was being overprotective. "No, mother, I don't mind. By the way, I'm leaving for Huntleigh tomorrow. I have some business to attend to."

The brightness left her eyes. "Are you going to take your 'ward' with you?"

"Yes," he said without hesitation. "After all, Gillian is there." Gillian was a distant cousin who was one of many who depended upon him for her support, but she was one he liked. She lived year round at Huntleigh.

His mother pressed her lips together, but in the end could only nod. "Have it your way." She sat back in her coach and dropped the flap over the window. The driver flicked the reins.

Nick watched his mother's coach leave. It stopped at the end of the street and picked up Colonel Swanson.

He turned his horse homeward, anxious to share his suspicions and his new information with Fee.

Once home, he went directly to her room. Tad was sleeping in front of her doorway, which surprised him since when he'd left the dog had been inside the room.

Tad looked up as he approached and wagged his tail. Nick took a moment to give him a pat. "It's a good thing you are a big lad," he told Tad, "because I don't believe you are much of a watch-dog."

Tad licked his hand in response.

Nick gave a light knock on the door.

There was no answer.

He'd assumed Fee was inside, because Tad was here. He glanced up and down the hall. There was no servant to ask. The thought crossed his mind that perhaps Fee *couldn't* answer the door. Immediately a hundred scenarios leapt to his imagination from her running away to some scoundrel Irishmen being on the other side of the door with a knife at her throat.

Nick opened the door, Tad right on his heels. He slipped inside and was relieved to see Fee in deep sleep on the bed. She lay on her side, her lashes half moons on her cheeks, her body as limber as a cat's.

Tad slipped past him and went to lay on the floor beside her. Lucky dog, Nick thought, and then, because he could no more stay away from her than a knife blade can resist the pull of a magnet, he, too, moved toward the bed.

A part of him wanted to wake her. He had much news to tell her.

Then again, she appeared so at peace, it gave him pleasure. She was under his care now. He'd not let harm come to her.

The intensity of this wave of protectiveness caught him off guard. He'd not felt this before.

No, he amended, he'd not *let* himself feel this before.

The servants had been in the room. There were toiletries on the dressing table. He assumed they had found dresses for her and had hung them in the wardrobe. He wondered what she'd think when she saw them. He hoped she'd be pleased but Fee was an independent spirit. She might not thank him.

So, Fiona was a magistrate's daughter, which explained why she was intelligent and well-spoken. Nick was discovering that when it came to his Fee, he wanted every one of her secrets.

No, he wanted something more. He wanted her to trust. He wanted to be her hero.

He almost laughed out loud at the whimsy of his thoughts. Who was he fooling? He was a far cry from the sort of man a woman like her could love.

But for the first time, he discovered he wanted to be.

He backed away from the bed, his gaze never leaving the sleeping woman.

The Oracle had warned him—*Beware innocence.* He'd avoided it for years.

But now, his Fee had found him . . . and as he

closed the door to let her sleep, he realized they had been fated to meet from the moment they were born.

The question now was, had she come to help him? Or destroy him?

The answer was, it no longer mattered. The tides of fate were in motion.

PART II
Courage

Sisyphus of Corinth was as cunning as he was clever and delighted in fooling the gods. He challenged the Oracle at Delphi, "Can a man escape his Fate?"

"If he is unwilling to meet it," the Oracle answered.

"Then," Sisyphus exclaimed with triumph, "that means man determines his own destiny. If he has a choice to act or not act, he alone and not the gods decides his Fate."

The Oracle's response was a smile.

Chapter Ten

*F*iona woke to the sensation of Tad's cold black nose nudging her hand.

Slowly she opened her eyes and was momentarily confused by her surroundings in the early morning light. She realized she'd been dreaming. It has been over a year since she could recall dreaming.

She lay with her head resting on the soft counterpane, able to feel her heart beating as memories came rolling back to her.

Her mother had been in her dream. They'd sat in this very bedroom with its yellow walls and plush blue upholstery and bed curtains. They'd talked the way they always had. Her mother had been her closest friend. Her confidante. Her advisor.

She'd sat by the dressing table wearing the green high-necked gown that had been her favorite. Fiona had been on the bed where she lay now. They'd talked . . . laughed, and yet, Fiona could not recall one word that had been said no matter how hard she strained her memory.

All that remained of the dream was the fleeting sense of her mother's presence and that she was not unhappy where she was—and that was something precious.

In fact, the love in her mother's smile had been genuine. Her skin had been radiant with health.

Fiona's last memories of her mother in life had been far different. She'd wasted away, lost in the pain of humiliation and disappointment. She'd been unable to go on without her husband or the prestige that had once been theirs.

This hadn't been just a dream, it had been a blessing . . . and Fiona wondered why it had come at this moment in time? In the days and months after her mother's death, she'd prayed for such a dream without solace.

Again, Tad pushed her hand again with his nose, wanting her to rise. That's when Fiona remembered where she was. She gave the dog a scratch behind the ears.

"Have you gone out?" she asked him. "Or run over to that park?"

The dog panted his answer and nudged her for more pets.

"Give me a moment to wake," Fiona said, stretching her arms. She yawned, feeling completely lazy and relishing it. The room was toasty warm. A servant had come in and laid a fire in the hearth that lacked the soot and smoke of the one in Fiona's old rooms.

Perhaps *this* was the dream, she wondered, and she'd wake to all her old worries. Her stomach would be empty, her feet cold, and she'd be anxious over whether or not she'd have money to make it through the week.

At that moment, the door to the room opened and a maid with a mob cap carrying a newly pressed dress of periwinkle wool over her arm quietly entered the room. She walked over to a changing screen and hung the dress.

Fiona feigned sleep. *Was the dress for her?* She'd been so tired she'd slept in her blue one, which was now hopelessly wrinkled.

Tad wagged his tail. Apparently the maid wasn't a stranger to him. She wore the ducal blue uniform with a huge apron tied around her waist and a mobcap over her frizzy brown and gray curls. Her cheeks were as rosy as cherries and her mouth appeared always ready to smile.

She gave one of those smiles to Tad and it was in looking in his direction that she realized Fiona was awake.

"I beg pardon, miss. You surprised me. It is time for you to wake but you've been sleeping so soundly, I'd not had the heart to disturb you."

"What time is it?" Fiona asked.

"Why, half past seven. You slept right through the afternoon yesterday and into the night. It's early but His Grace is hoping to be on the road for Huntleigh after breakfast. My name is Sarah. I've been with the family a long time and His Grace asked that I look after you."

Fiona frowned at the news that Holburn expected her to travel with him. What was he up to now? She pushed the tangled mess of her hair back over her shoulder. Her makeshift braid had come undone and now her hair was a sign of how hard she had slept. She sat up.

"Where is Huntleigh?" she said and then paused as she realized her silver brush was in the bed with her.

She picked it up. She didn't remember using it the night before. However, in her dream, her mother had held it in her hand. Her mother had always handled the brush when she'd come into Fiona's room. She'd said she liked the weight of it. That's the reason she had purchased it as a gift for Fiona.

"The family home is in Lynsted in Kent. The title is an old one and has gone through several changes," the maid talked as she bustled around the room opening the drapes and setting things right. "They were once the Earls of Lynsted, but when they were made dukes, the king decided to change the surname. Who knows why? Kings do as they please."

Fiona managed a quiet, "Yes," to Sarah's tale of family history. The brush brought out a superstitious chill in her.

"I'll have hot water sent up for a bath, miss," Sarah said. "However, until then, this water in the basin is warm. I've set out tooth powder and a cake of the finest soap you will find anywhere." She walked over to the dressing screen. "I also took the liberty of pressing a dress for you to wear today. If it isn't to your liking, I can always bring another."

"That dress is for me?" Fiona repeated, wondering if her still sleep-addled brains were letting her hear correctly. She threw her legs over the side of the bed and went over to the dressing screen to investigate. Tad came along with her as if he'd had a hand in the surprise.

The dress was marine blue and made of the softest wool Fiona had ever touched. Pleats had been sewn across a bodice trimmed in snowy white lace. "It's lovely," Fiona said.

"Well, if you don't like it," Sarah answered, "you may take a look at the ones in the wardrobe and choose something different."

"The wardrobe?" Fiona repeated. She hurried over to it, flinging open the doors to find at least a half dozen dresses hanging there. There were several as warm and serviceable as the marine wool, but there were also dresses of finer materials. Dresses that could be worn to dinner or church or anywhere there was good company. There were also three pairs of slippers on the wardrobe floor and several shawls hanging from a peg.

"Where did these come from?" Fiona asked, turning to Sarah. She knew first-hand how long it would take to make dresses of this quality.

"His Grace had his man Gannon see to the matter," Sarah answered, smiling as if she was pleased by Fiona's reaction. "Between he and Docket, there isn't anything that can't be done if His Grace wants it. There's all the frillies us women so like in the dresser drawers as well. I'll be back to lay them out once I've given the word to send the hot water up for your bath." She left the room.

Fiona looked at Tad, who regarded her with bright, shiny eyes. "Yes, I know," Fiona said. "We have landed in a field of clover." She knelt beside the dog, putting her arm around him. "But what will he expect in return?" Still, she couldn't resist a happy sigh. "Did you notice that one of the dresses is a riding habit?"

Tad cocked his head, and Fiona laughed. It had been a long time since she'd ridden. Another lifetime ago.

She rose to her feet, catching her image in the mirror. She shouldn't accept the dresses . . . "But then, what would I have to wear?" she asked the image, and the image smiled, knowing she was going to adore wearing such fine materials.

Fiona walked to the basin and began washing her face.

Once again, Sarah had been right.

The soap *was* the finest she'd ever seen.

By the time she was bathed, coiffed, and dressed, Fiona felt like a new woman. She went down the stairs to the dining room. Tad followed at her heels.

Sarah had proved a godsend. She had a supply

of creams and lotions that made Fiona's skin feel smooth again. She was also talented with a brush and had styled Fiona's hair up high on her head. Between Sarah's ministrations and the marine-blue dress, Fiona felt like a lady again.

Docket met her at the stairs with the information that the duke was enjoying his breakfast in the dining room. Fiona took a moment to quell a new nervousness.

Holburn's generosity had opened her heart. Yes, he was an attractive man, and a duke! But in her experience, not many men would demonstrate such consideration. Or be so generous.

His kindness raised the stakes. It made that attraction between them more than simple lust.

He could not have been so thoughtful if he didn't care about her.

And she was beginning to care about him. Deeply.

Common sense warned her to be careful, but this morning, she didn't want such warnings. This morning she wanted to bask in the glow of her happiness. She wanted to believe anything could happen, including falling in love.

She walked into the dining room.

Holburn sat at the end of the table with the morning papers in front of him and his customary mug of cider. The light of a winter dawn came through the window overlooking the small back garden and framed his broad shoulders and dark hair. He appeared confident, roguely handsome, and every inch the duke in his riding clothes.

He looked up at the sound of her entrance and his surprised reaction to the "new" her was everything she could have wished. A slow, approving grin spread across his face.

He rose from the table and came around to her. "Fee," he said, the heat in the one word of her nickname saying volumes. And then he laughed at his own awkwardness and she could only smile happily.

"Thank you," she said, her throat threatening to close with the pent-up emotion behind the words. "The dresses are lovely. Everything is lovely."

"It's my honor." There was so much warmth in his gaze as he spoke, heat rushed to her cheeks.

If she had her way, they would stand here forever, the two of them in perfect accord.

"Come, sit down," he said. "You must meet my Aunt Agatha." He stepped back and Fiona saw a petite woman in turban and shawls sitting at the table. Fiona's attention had been so focused on Holburn she'd completely overlooked the tiny woman's presence.

The duke led Fiona over to the table. Aunt Agatha was crumbling toast. She didn't look up but concentrated on her task.

"Aunt Agatha," the duke said in a loud voice. "This is Miss Fiona Lachlan. Miss Lachlan," he said with formality, "this is my great aunt, Lady Kensett."

Fiona was beginning to think the woman senile, when Aunt Agatha turned remarkably sharp eyes up to her. Fiona curtseyed. Lady Kensett smiled her approval. "Pretty manners. Pretty girl. I can see why you like her, Holburn."

The duke laughed. "Aunt Agatha seems sweet," he said to Fiona, raising his voice loud enough for his aunt to hear, "but she's as sharp as a tartar. Keeps me in line."

Lady Kensett snorted her thoughts and began chewing her toast. Tad moved over to her chair and laid down at her feet, waiting for crumbs. Fiona would have called him off but the duke waved her objection aside.

Instead, he leaned close. "Your night's sleep agreed with you."

"I haven't slept so well in years," she confessed. "And thank you, thank you, *thank you* for this dress. I know I shouldn't accept it—"

"Don't be ridiculous. I'm a duke, you know." He drawled his words like a pink of the *ton*. "My household has a certain image it must maintain. At least, that's what all my relatives tell me."

"I'm not a relative—"

He cut her off. "No more objections, Fee. A few dresses are a small payment for your saving my life. And for right now, you are my ward. Aunt Agatha will be our chaperone on the trip so rest easy. By the way, our Irish friends seem to have disappeared."

"What do you mean?" she asked, her attention diverted from his use of the words, "for right now."

The duke drew her over to the sideboard and handed her a plate. In a low voice he said, "One of them was watching us yesterday. He was hiding in the park. I had a groomsman keep an eye on him and follow him if he left."

"And?" Fiona prompted.

Holburn speared a slice of beef and put it on her plate before saying, "And nothing. According to Peter, the Irishman followed me to Belkins's house. Peter kept an eye on him but there was a crush of callers yesterday. The man slipped away and has not returned. He's vanished. I sent other men to watch your building, but no Irishmen there either."

"Did you see Grace?"

"Yes, I warned her."

"What did you learn from Lady Belkins?" Fiona asked, wanting to know everything.

Holburn brought his head closer to hers. "I know Belkins didn't die from a simple fall off his horse. Everyone can say what they wish but I saw his head. Someone bashed it in."

Fiona's appetite fled. "What are we going to do?"

"We are leaving today for the country."

"That's what the maid said." She shook her head. "I don't understand. How will that help?"

"Because they can't hide from us out there the way they can here. We're going to draw them out, Fee. Don't worry. You will be safe. I'll have good men riding with us in the coach. Of course, once we are in Kent, we'll be on my land and I'll control the battle." He carried her plate over to the breakfast table and set it down beside where he was seated. "But I've been thinking about the question you asked—who has the most to gain?"

He glanced over at Aunt Agatha. She was still eating toast and sipping tea. Fiona noted there were no servants in the room.

Holburn swung his gaze to meet hers. "I suspect my uncles," he said.

"Family members?" she repeated, stunned by the thought.

"They are the only ones who gain since they are next in line for the title."

"But members of your own family . . ." She let her voice drift off, troubled by the implications. "What of this Spaniard?"

"You've made me reconsider this matter. It is too simple to blame Ramigio. His name was on the letter Belkins received the afternoon before he died, but the truth is, Andres hasn't been heard from for years. I've sent men in search of him and they have returned without any information. For all I know, Ramigio could be dead. Certainly there were a number of men who have probably wanted to kill him."

"Good heavens, why?" she asked, startled by the pronouncement.

"He was a charming scoundrel. A good drinking companion but not someone who could be trusted. He proved that to me . . . back in the days when I was much the same way. Those are the sorts of men who usually find themselves in the worst trouble. To be honest, there have been many times I could have throttled him over the ring."

"Then whoever has plotted this knows you wanted the Spaniard," she surmised.

"Exactly. And the only people who knew how much I cared about the lost ring were family."

"Are you close to your uncles?"

"No. After my father died, they had my guardianship until I turned one and twenty. I had to wrest control of my estates from them and then learned they'd made poor business choices on my behalf."

"But why attack you now?" she asked.

Holburn frowned. "I don't know."

"Is there anyone else who knows about the Spaniard who could gain something by your death?"

"Possibly Mother."

Fiona sat back in her chair. Aunt Agatha was concentrating on her fruit compote. "Would you really suspect her?" Fiona asked, keeping her voice low.

Holburn shrugged. "You asked who stood to gain. She receives an inheritance upon my death."

"But to attempt to murder one's own child?" Fiona shook her head. "No woman is that depraved."

"I like to think not," he agreed. "Then again, Mother enjoys the privileges of being a duchess, even a dowager one. She needs me for that. My uncles would ship her to Australia if they could."

"So, she isn't a good suspect."

"A not likely one," he conceded.

That was a relief. "Although it was kind of you to see to her welfare. Most men don't seem to concern themselves with the care of their family members upon their death."

Holburn gave her a sharp glance and she knew he'd heard the deeper meaning in her words.

"My father," she said, feeling as if she should explain or defend him in some way. "His death left mother and me ruined."

She said no more. She couldn't.

Holburn set his knife and fork down and leaned toward her. "I want you to trust me."

Fiona didn't look at him as she folded her own napkin. "I do."

"No, you don't," he answered without heat. "But someday you will."

She turned to him, conscious of Aunt Agatha's presence. "Why should you care?" There it was . . . she was opening herself up to her doubts, her fears. "You know nothing about me," she explained. "I could be some—" Her voice broke off. Some things were best left unsaid.

"Rebel?" he suggested.

"You and Grace had a conversation." She was not pleased. She wasn't angry. Uncomfortable was the better description.

"She didn't betray any confidences."

Fiona didn't know that. She crossed her arms.

Holburn turned so that his back was to his aunt. "Don't be unhappy with your friend. While you slept I asked my man of business to make discreet inquiries as to your father. That was my doing, not Grace McEachin's."

"And what did you discover?" Fiona asked, a knot tightening in her chest. This was her fault. She shouldn't have mentioned her father or criticized him. Her brother Gordon had warned her.

To his credit, Holburn didn't evade the question. "I learned that your brother Gordon Lachlan has a price on his head. That your father, a Scottish magistrate, died in disgrace speaking out against the king's law."

"He *didn't* die in disgrace," Fiona answered. "He died because he spoke for those who couldn't speak for themselves. He made the gentry feel guilty, and that's really why he died. One doesn't turn on one's own class."

"He's considered a hero to many," Holburn informed her.

That was something. "How did you find out?"

"I used the power of a duke."

She nodded. It was unfortunate her family hadn't had that power years ago. "I don't know why you asked those questions."

"Because I want you to feel safe. And that brings us back to the question of trust," he said, placing a hand on her arm. "Fee, I don't want you to hide from me. I want you to trust me."

She laughed, a bitter, angry sound. "I don't know how to trust."

"Then let me teach you."

His gaze held hers. She was aware of the sounds of the servants in the butler's pantry and the hallway, of the ticking of a clock, of Tad's nails on the wooden floor where he lay.

And she was aware of every nuance, every muscle, every lash, every pore of Holburn.

"You can't teach me that," she whispered, her throat tight. "It's something I'd have to give to you . . . and I don't know if I can. Not just to you, but to anyone."

To her surprise, her admission didn't warn him away. So, she added, "I'm not ashamed of my family. I won't ever be. I'm proud of them."

"As you should be," he answered. "But you shouldn't hide either."

Good Lord, she was crying. One tear had escaped and she swiped at it angrily. Aunt Agatha had realized something was wrong. Fiona caught her curious glance before the woman lowered her head and pretended to fall asleep.

It didn't matter. She was tired of running from the past. Of pretending.

"I wasn't hiding," she informed Holburn. "It's just that the people my parents trusted didn't want anything to do with me after my father's death. They turned me over to the soldiers, Your Grace. Those men wanted my brother Gordon and they would do anything to bring him out."

She'd not go into details. She couldn't.

"I also assumed that I would do better for myself in London—" For a moment, she hesitated, wondering how far she dared go, and then decided she had nothing to lose.

"Gordon wanted me to leave with him. He'd come to fetch the woman he loved. Her name was Constance Cameron and she had gone to a ball to meet you."

"I barely remember her," he said. "We weren't promised to each other."

"No," she said and then confessed, "I saw you at that ball and in that moment, I knew I needed to stay in London. I felt . . ." She let her voice trail off, at a loss of the right word.

He supplied it. "A connection?"

She nodded, dazed that he understood. She had expected him to laugh or make some comment on her naiveté.

Instead he leaned closer to her until it was as if there were only the two of them in the room. "I remember catching a glimpse of you at that ball. But I thought my mind had played a trick on me."

She had her arms crossed and tight against her

stomach. He pulled one hand away, running the pad of his thumb along her index finger before saying, "Fee, I don't know how to explain this without sounding as if I'm ready for Bedlam, but I had a vision of *you* almost ten years ago. I was at the ruins of Delphi. Ramigio had stolen my ring and I was furious. There was an old woman there who appeared to be twice the age it seemed of Aunt Agatha. She changed before my eyes. She grew younger, beautiful . . . vibrant. Fee, she changed into you."

Chapter Eleven

There, Nick had confessed all. He'd played all his cards and now waited for Fee's reaction. He'd not told one soul that story. Not ever.

Her brows came together in concern. He was certain she really did question his sanity. Either that, or she was waiting for him to laugh and confess it was all a joke.

But it wasn't. The vision in Delphi was as real to him as her sitting here.

"Wasn't the priestess at Delphi the one who would have visions about the future?" she asked.

He nodded.

"Did I tell you anything?"

Nick drew back. It was one thing to have heard what the Oracle had said, another to share it.

He swept an imaginary crumb off the table linen. Fee covered his hand with hers, holding him in place.

"Trust me," she told him.

Nick had to smile at being persuaded with his own words. Still, he felt a bit ridiculous in saying, "She said, beware innocence."

Fee wrinkled her nose. "Beware innocence? What an odd prophecy."

"I know it sounds outrageous," Nick said, "but, Fee, my life changed after that meeting." He glanced over at Aunt Agatha. Her eyes were closed, her chin on her chest. Tad was also asleep, his large body taking up a good section of floor.

Nick drew Fee closer. "Before I went to Delphi, I had atrocious luck at the gaming tables. I rarely won. My father was also known for being a poor, albeit devoted gambler. After that vision, I rarely lose at cards."

"You win *all* the time?"

"No not all, but after an evening's work, I'm always ahead."

She tilted her head, her disbelief clear in her eyes. "And you attribute this to the vision."

"I know how it sounds. I feel silly, but it is the

only explanation I have for why my luck had changed."

"Perhaps because you changed," she suggested. "You were upset over losing the ring. Perhaps it led to some sort of new maturity. Or it could be just a simple change of luck."

"Fee, I've *tried* to lose. It's unnatural how it works. It's almost as if I've been cursed. I'm fortunate in games of chance but on other investments, I fail. I've bought into two ships, both lost at sea. I have invested in numerous schemes that have all lost every shilling."

She brought her head close to his. "Your Grace, those schemes probably carry risks. Many men have lost fortunes investing as you have. As to winning at cards, it must be a pleasant curse."

"But what if it all ends, Fee? What if this is the end? Whatever the Oracle predicted that day seems to be happening. I can't describe it but I sense something started back then is nearing its finish."

"Because I look like the Vision?"

He almost hated to admit, "Yes . . . and because of the mention of Andres and mad Irishmen attempting to murder me. I asked the Oracle that day for my ring. I don't believe it was destroyed and I think I will see it soon."

"Beware innocence," Fee said thoughtfully. "*Whose* innocence?"

"What does 'beware' mean?" he countered. "Trust me, I have racked my brain for years trying to understand."

Fee sat back in her chair, her expression somber. "My father was a scholar of the Greek myths. I remember him talking about how the Oracle's message was always very obscure so it could mean anything. For example, once a king asked the Oracle if he should go to war. She said, 'If you go to war, a great civilization will be destroyed.' He thought that meant he would win so he went to battle. Instead he lost and the civilization he destroyed was his own."

She shook her head. "Your Grace, your message is the same. It could mean anything. Or nothing."

What was it about women that they could see the logic with blunt clarity? Nick didn't know if he should be pleased or disappointed.

"You don't think I'm a fool?" he asked.

Her face softened into a smile. "I'm the one who has harbored affections for a man I laid eyes on only once."

Nick raised her hand to his lips and kissed the back of her fingers. "I won't believe in happenstance, not when it has the power to bring you to me."

Fee thought she would melt from the heat in his gaze. All the hardships she had suffered had been worth this one look—

The sound of Master Rockford's barking could be heard out in the hall. It was followed with the swish of skirts and the click of heels on the tile floor.

Nick stood, knowing his mother was about to arrive.

She came to the doorway looking as if she hadn't slept all night. Heavy circles were under her eyes and her skin was pale. In contrast, her hair had been styled and her clothes were as immaculate as usual.

He'd seen her like this before. Recently. It meant that she'd played for heavy stakes and lost.

Nick didn't want the conversation he knew would be forthcoming.

Keeping his voice pleasant, he said, "Mother, what are you doing up this early?"

She raised a distracted hand to rub her temple. "I had trouble sleeping. I knew you were leaving and thought to say good-bye." She frowned. "Is that your Aunt Agatha?"

"She heard from Brandt that I was leaving for Huntleigh today and sent a note asking if she could ride with me."

His mother's turned cynical. "What? Is she going to be your chaperone while you are with your 'ward?'"

"As a matter of fact, yes."

His mother smirked. "She's half deaf and almost blind. Good choice, Dominic. She'd not provide any difficulties there for you."

"Mother," he said, warning her to mind her manners.

Master Rockford had noticed Tad and began yipping and squirming to have a go at him. For his part, Tad wisely went around to the other side of Aunt Agatha's chair and sat with his back to the dachshund.

His mother walked toward the sideboard, her anxious dog in her arms. "Where are the footmen?"

"Preparing for the trip," Nick answered. "I'm taking them with me. As a matter of fact, it is time for us to leave," he said as congenially as he could. He stood and offered a hand to Aunt Agatha, thinking he would escape without a confrontation when his mother's voice stopped him.

"Dominic, I need to speak to you."

"My plans are to leave now. Perhaps we can talk at Huntleigh—"

"Please," she interrupted him. Tears filled her eyes. "We must talk."

Nick hated it when she cried. She knew it, too. He did not want this confrontation.

She noted his hesitation. "You are unwilling to give your mother a moment of your time?" she demanded, her voice rising.

Damn it all, she *was* going to make a scene. It was as he suspected. Nick felt trapped. To his left, Fee frowned, but considering her concern as she watched his mother, he didn't think it was directed at him. Aunt Agatha's hearing had improved in the last few seconds. She was awake and alert, and he envisioned fodder for months of family gossip.

Knowing he had no choice but to indulge his mother, Nick rose and offered Fee his hand. "Would you take Aunt Agatha to the drawing room?"

"Of course," Fee said.

His aunt wasn't as accommodating. "I don't know why I should leave. Can't she say what she has to say in front of me? We're family."

"And have you dine for a week on what is said between my son and me?" his mother said. "Absolutely not."

"I'll find out anyway," Aunt Agatha said serenely.

Over her head, Fee shot Nick a sympathetic gaze. Even Tad was happy to abandon him. He quickly followed his mistress.

After the door was shut, his mother set Master Rockford on the floor. The small dog strutted around the table, proud that he had run the big dog out of the room.

Nick returned to his chair. His mother didn't move from the side board. She ran a finger along the edge as if tracing the wood grain before saying what he already knew, "I overplayed last night. I lost."

"That's unfortunate," Nick answered.

"I need you to cover the debt," she informed him.

"How much?" he asked.

She closed her eyes, breathed deeply. "Four thousand pounds."

He almost fell out of his chair. He'd played deep before but then he had been certain he would win. "What were you doing playing so deep? Especially after our last conversation?"

"I don't believe it kind of you to question me," his mother replied, still meeting his eye.

"What sort of response is that? Three weeks ago I helped you out with a loss that was a quarter of that amount," he said, struggling to keep his voice calm. "Then last week, you lost another two thousand. I told you then, that I would not come to your rescue a third time."

She turned to him then. "You *must.*"

"I can't, Mother. I have estates to run. There are bills that come before gaming debts."

"Oh, yes, like the money you'll throw at your 'ward.'"

"I have not thrown over six thousand pounds at her," he countered.

The blue in her eyes flashed with defiance, and he knew he wasn't going to escape the inevitable. "I need the money, Dominic. *It's a matter of honor.*"

"You used that argument for the last two losses. I warned you, Mother, and now I'm honor-bound to stand by my word. Sell your jewelry if it is so important to you, but don't look to me when you've gone aground for these amounts."

Her lips curled into a sneer. "*When did you turn into such a paragon?* Your father would be shamed to hear you now. *He* would have covered me."

From forgotten pieces of his childhood memories, Nick recalled fights between his parents, times when his mother reacted just such the way as she was preparing to do now. "I stand by what I said," he said, and braced himself for the worst. He was wise to do so.

With a squeal of frustration, his mother swept the dishes off the sideboard. Plates, sausages, kippers and everything else went flying to crash against the wall. Master Rockford's little legs started pedaling after a sausage rolling across the floor. He snatched it up and went running to hide under a chair to chew on his bounty.

Nick sat calmly, refusing to give into her tantrum this time.

"*I want the money,*" she demanded. "I'll be refused play if I don't pay."

"Then perhaps that will be best."

She stared at him as if not believing her ears, and then pushed away from the sideboard. Her shoulders slumped. "You can't mean that, Dominic. I'm a duchess. I can't be refused. How will it look?"

"Sell your jewelry," he repeated.

She screamed her rage and threw a chair on the ground with such force it splintered the wood.

"You are ruining me," she said, her face a mask of misery.

"You are ruining yourself, Mother—"

"*Don't you call me that.* A son takes care of his mother." She shook her head. "You are turning into your father, always telling me no."

"Actually I haven't said it enough, Mother."

"I am not happy, Dominic. Not happy at all. I've been so good to you, running your household and all. Now that I am enjoying a bit of pleasure, you want to ruin me." She didn't wait for his response but marched to the door. She flung it open before Aunt Agatha, who had obviously been eavesdropping, could move out of the way. Fee stood on the other side of the hall with Tad sitting on his haunches next to her. They both appeared embarrassed.

His mother glared at the two of them and then stormed down the hall. Master Rockford chose to remain where he was, under the chair gnawing on a sausage.

"Well," his aunt said, drawing out the word and raising her eyebrows to her hairline.

Nick nailed her with a look. "You will not say anything about this to anyone."

Aunt Agatha sniffed. "You are too protective of her," she said. "I told your father blood would out. I warned him not to marry her. She used to carry on this way all the time. Of course, she was younger and still had her looks. A man will put up with anything when a woman has those." His aunt's words confirmed those childhood memories of his parents battling behind closed doors.

"She just recently started these tantrums," Nick said.

"I'd heard she stopped after your father died," Aunt Agatha said. "But before that, she made his life miserable."

He was conscious of Fee's presence. "Aunt, we should leave this conversation."

Aunt Agatha dismissed his concerns with a lift of one shoulder. "Talk to Brandt and Maven. They've witnessed a number of her scenes. But she didn't dare carry on that way with them."

"We've discussed this enough," Nick answered.

His aunt didn't agree. She opened her mouth to argue but Fee took her arm. "Do you have everything packed, Lady Kensett? I believe the duke wishes to leave within the hour."

"I do," Nick said, thankful for her interruption.

"I am ready to travel," Aunt Agatha said.

"Unfortunately, I'm not," Fee answered. "If you will excuse me?"

"I also have a few things I need to see to before we leave. Aunt, do you wish to wait for us in the drawing room since the breakfast room is indisposed?"

His aunt took a glance inside the room and frowned. Master Rockford had moved on to sniff at more delicacies on the floor. Still sitting by Fiona's side, Tad watched him with more than a little jealousy on his face.

"I'll wait in the drawing room," his aunt said. A maid had come from the direction of the back stairs and she waved her toward the small dining room. "Girl, see to that, will you? And help me down the hall, Holburn." Aunt Agatha took his arm.

As the maid looked into the dining room and discovered the damage, Nick led his aunt and Fiona toward the other side of the house. He was pleased that Fee waited for him to settle his aunt comfortably before the fire.

As they walked up the stairs, Tad trailing behind, she said, "I couldn't pull your aunt away from the door, but she is strong for an old woman."

"And proud of it," Nick agreed. "I have to admit, I hadn't realized what a bold old buzzard she was. She showed no remorse for listening at the door."

"Well, one didn't have to put her ear up to the door," Fee said with her usual tactfulness.

As they reached the top of the stairs, he said, "Go ahead, ask. I can hear your mind work. You are buzzing with questions about Mother."

"Does she always lose her temper with such violence?"

Nick leaned a shoulder against the stair post. The servants were all busy and they were alone. "Not as often as she has lately."

He hesitated a moment and then continued because he *did* need to talk to someone about this. "I seem to remember her having fits when my father was alive. But after his death, she rarely carried on in that manner. Of course, I was away at school." He studied the weave of the hallway runner before confiding, "She was always one to horde things. She'd build piles of possessions, much like her growing mountain of luggage downstairs in the hall. I suspect her need to gather her belongings has something to do with her past. She went from a commoner—an *actress*, no less—to duchess almost overnight. The two of them had eloped and no matter how hard my grandfather tried, he couldn't break the legality of the marriage, especially after I was born."

"You must have felt an outsider, too, since they were so critical of your mother."

For the first time in his life, Nick felt someone understood. "It's hard when you sense something is wrong with your family, but don't understand." Needing to justify emotions he'd struggled with most of his life, he said, "Mother *doesn't* fit in with the *ton*. She has friends, most as nervous as herself. They are the sort who live on the fringe of society and they always lead her in the wrong direction. After Father's death, my uncles were named my guardian and had control of all my affairs, including those affecting Mother. They are overbearing, arrogant men. They wear their disapproval like coats and can make a person feel like the worst failure."

"Are you speaking for your mother or for yourself?" she wondered.

"Both. When I had to tell them that Ramigio had stolen the ring, they acted as if I'd committed an act of treason."

"And that is why you are so determined to find it?" she asked.

"I'm determined because the ring is a symbol of my birthright and stealing it was a betrayal of a friendship. I *trusted* Andres. I *liked* him. Mother wasn't the only one who felt alone after Father's death."

"What is your relationship to your uncles now?"

He smiled grimly. "I do as I please, and they disapprove of it. Of course, Mother isn't as strong. They can crush her with one word of disapproval. That's part of the reason she is so anxious to have her gambling losses covered. My uncles always find out what we are doing."

"The truth is I would be upset about such gambling losses," Fee said. "You are right to stand your ground."

"Even when she is throwing sausages around?"

"Especially then."

Nick frowned his concern. "She's always played for high stakes but this past month her losses have been ridiculous."

"What has changed?"

He smiled. "The Fiona Lachlan question—what has changed?" He considered the matter. "Colonel Swanson." At Fee's puzzled look, he told her about meeting the officer the day before. "However, I don't know how long she has known him. The only other change is one that has no effect on

Mother now. I established a trust for her in my will."

"Why did you do that?"

"She feared being left under my uncle Brandt's protection if I died and he inherited the title. I don't blame her," he said with feeling. "Since I plan on outliving her, the trust seemed a simple way to ease her concerns."

"But if you die . . ." Fee let her voice trail off.

Nick immediately rejected what she was suggesting. "I don't see Mother hiring Irishmen or paying for my murder. She's a distracted parent but not an unfeeling one."

"She was very angry downstairs."

"You heard my aunt. She's had these tantrums for years without killing anyone."

Fee raised a conciliatory hand. "You are right. It was a flight of fancy on my part. I'm starting to imagine murderers behind every door."

"That's why we are going to Huntleigh." He took her arm and walked her to her bedroom door. "However, I am worried about my mother's tantrums. She invited Colonel Swanson to join the family gathering over Christmas. His visit will give me the opportunity to know the man, and perhaps sound him out about this gambling. She often goes out with friends, but she must be meeting him."

"He may even be the one encouraging her to gamble so recklessly," Fee suggested.

"I'd like to find that out, too." He opened her door for her. "Will you be ready within the hour?"

"Of course, Your Grace. I can be ready sooner, if necessary."

"Then let us leave in the half hour. I'll call the coach around."

As she started to enter her room, she asked, "How long will it take to travel the distance to Huntleigh?"

"About seven hours if we stop for lunch, which we will. Aunt Agatha enjoys her meals."

Fee laughed.

"You and my aunt will be in the coach. I prefer to ride."

A pleading look came to her eyes. "Could I ride? There is a riding habit in the wardrobe."

"Of course you may," Nick said, pleased. Riding was one of his passions. "I'll have a horse saddled for you."

The smile she gave him in return for this small gesture made him feel as if he'd just handed her the moon.

Maybe he *was* falling in love.

But instead of being frightening, it was rather nice.

"I'll let you change," he murmured—and almost tripped over Tad who had laid down behind him.

After that embarrassment, both he and Tad escaped as quickly as they could.

The footmen Williams and Larson rode as outriders and two armed men rode with the coachman. Sarah, Fiona's maid, traveled inside the coach with Lady Kensett and Gannon, Holburn's valet.

The day was overcast but there was no danger of rain and Fiona's spirits were high. The riding habit was a lovely emerald-green velvet trimmed in black braid *à le militaire*. On her head she wore a black beaver riding hat accented with one green pheasant feather. She'd even been outfitted with black riding gloves that fit perfectly and a pair of half boots that were a touch too large but she didn't care.

She loved to ride. Holburn had given her a handsome, well-behaved gelding named Monty. His horse was a dark bay with four black legs and a massive chest. Tad ran along with them.

Within an hour, they'd left the city behind and Fiona felt she could breathe freely again.

Holburn nudged his horse beside hers. "You are a good rider."

"I used to hunt," she admitted proudly. "I could take a hedgerow as well as any man."

"Could you now?" he said as if not quite believing her.

"Do you wish to test me?" she challenged.

A competitive light came to his eye. He glanced at the footmen. "We're going for a bit of fun, Williams. Keep an eye on us, but don't stay too close." To the coachman, he said, "See you at the Golden Stag."

With those words, he turned his horse and jumped the fence alongside the road. He looked across it to Fiona. "Well? Are you coming?"

To the laughing encouragement of the others, Fiona cleared the fence and kept going, riding right past Holburn. The duke had no trouble catching up with her and for the next two hours they had a merry chase across the cold, bare fields and through the trees of the countryside with Tad trying to keep up.

Fiona couldn't remember a time when she'd felt more alive and excited about life. At one point, her hat had flown off her head and the duke had gallantly retrieved it. She'd noticed Williams and Larson then, dutifully riding at a distance. Tad had grown tired and fallen back to travel with them.

"Should we wait for them?" Holburn asked.

"No," Fiona said and kicked her horse. They were off again.

The Golden Stag was a welcoming inn along the road. The coach was waiting for them by the time they arrived. They had an enjoyable meal and then it was back to the road. This time, she and Holburn walked their horses.

The duke liked her.

There wasn't a woman worth her salt on the face of this earth who could mistake the expression in his eyes every time he looked at her. And his affections were more than just physical lust. *He* liked *her.*

And she couldn't help but fall in love with him.

The conversation between them was easy. They discussed everything from religion to social opinions to teasing remarks about their riding. The more she grew to know the duke, the more she admired him.

He wasn't the hardened rake as everyone had portrayed him. She found him intelligent and thoughtful. He was unafraid to be his own man, a quality she admired, and one that would give him the reputation of being a loner.

Too soon they arrived at Huntleigh.

She and Holburn had left the coach to take a shortcut across the fields. They rode around a bend and over a hill into a stable yard. The barn was of pale brick. It was larger than most houses and the yard was paved with cobblestones.

Grooms came running out to greet them. Holburn tossed his reins to one of them, slid off his horse, and moved to help her dismount. He put his hands on her waist and swung her out of the sidesaddle and to the ground as if she weighed nothing.

"You *can* ride," he said with approval.

Tad had followed them and now came panting up to join them. Fiona gave his ears a scratch. "You enjoyed that, didn't you?"

The dog yawned an answer.

"Come," Holburn said, linking his arm in hers. "We'll walk up to the house."

"My legs need the stretch," she admitted, knowing that tomorrow she would pay for the day's exercise. She gracefully caught the long skirt of her riding habit by the wrist band sewn in at the hem and let him lead her through the barn which was cleaner inside than most houses she had visited.

On the other side were paddocks and a small pond with geese. "There are swans and wild ducks in the summer," he told her, proud of his home.

Tad started to chase geese. Fiona would have stopped him, but Holburn let him go. Of course, the dog was no match for a fat, angry goose. The goose's hissing scared Tad back to hide behind

Fiona's skirts and there he stayed as they started up a gravel path built into the side of the hill.

Even in winter, one could see that great care had been taken with the landscaping. Fiona was paying so much attention to her immediate surroundings that it wasn't until they came out at the top of the hill that she realized the house was right there—and it robbed her of breath.

She walked past Holburn, stunned by the size of the house built in the same pale brick as the stables. The windows sparkled in the late afternoon sun and the front of the house had a marble portico that was amazing in its size and the whiteness of its stone. The London house was a cottage in comparison.

"This isn't a house," Fiona said, "it's a palace."

"It was intended to be," Holburn answered. He led her along a stone path from the hill to the front door. "My ancestors always had high hopes for advancement."

"And where does one go from duke?" she acknowledged.

He smiled.

Someone from the stable must have warned the serving staff that the duke had arrived. The front door opened and out poured a host of servants in the same blue livery worn by the London staff.

Their enthusiastic greeting was genuine.

Holburn nodded and accepted their warm welcomes as he gently guided Fiona through the door with a hand placed on the small of her back. "The coach is following," he told the butler whom he introduced as another Docket. "They are brothers," he explained, although this Docket had more hair than the other.

The inside of the house was more magnificent than the outside. The floors were a dark wood, polished to a high shine, and covered with patterned carpets. The high ceilings were painted with scenes from mythology and the cream-colored walls decorated with family portraits and landscapes.

A tall woman with laughing eyes and hair the color of honey came forward to greet them. "Holburn, I am so glad you came early. It's rare that we have time to spend without the rest of the family."

"Only because you refuse to come to London, dear cousin," he said, leaning for her kiss on his cheek. He straightened and looked around the house. "I see you have been busy decorating for Christmas." Garlands of holly were everywhere, over the doorways and down the staircase. Red velvet bows and holly nosegays were arranged on the tabletops.

He introduced Fiona. "Gillian, this is my—" He paused, smiled at Fiona and said "My ward. She saved my life, Gill. Fee, this is my second cousin Gillian Ranson, Lady Wright, and every year she spends days upon days decorating the house for Christmas."

"It's only a little holly," his cousin answered.

"It's like this all over the house," Holburn assured Fiona. "Even in the water closet. Gillian must have the servants cutting holly for days."

"No, Holburn, I'm not that carried away," Lady Wright said, laughing.

"You are," he assured her and Fiona found herself smiling with them. They had the easy banter of true respect for each other, the sort of thing found in the best of families.

"It's a pleasure to meet you, my lady," Fiona said.

"She's Scot," Gillian said with surprise. "What a lovely accent. And, please, don't be so formal. I'm Gillian here. I can't stand my title because I never could stand my husband."

Her bluntness caught Fiona off guard.

Gillian frowned. "Have I startled you? I'm sorry," she replied without any true apology. "We who live in the country have a tendency to speak bluntly."

"You have not offended, my lady," Fiona said.

"Blunt speaking is a way with us Scots. I was surprised to hear it from an Englishwoman."

"I can't be any way other than outspoken," Gillian admitted.

"I have the same flaw," Fiona answered. "Although I refuse to think of it as a flaw."

Gillian laughed and took her hand. "Then we shall be friends. I can't tolerate anyone who doesn't speak her mind. For that reason, Holburn is the only one in the family I trust. Come, let me show you to your room. You must be exhausted if you rode alongside Holburn. He has a bruising hand with the horses."

"I'm a fine horseman," he countered.

"Bruising," Gillian insisted and Fiona laughed. It had been a long time since she'd felt enveloped in the warmth of family. After her experiences with Holburn's mother, she had not anticipated Gillian to be so welcoming.

Gillian led them to the back stairs. This house lacked the formality of Holburn's London residence. The carpets were as thick and the floors as polished, but the furniture was more comfortable. The chairs and sitting arrangements were testimony to countless evenings spent over a chess board or listening to conversation or music. And, of course, everywhere, on mantels and tables, were arrangements of holly. Fiona wondered if there was a holly tree left with branches within a mile of the house.

"Are you musical?" Gillian asked as they passed the door to a large music room with the chairs arranged around a pianoforte.

"Not very," Fiona admitted.

"Good, neither am I. But everyone else in the family sings, including Holburn who has a passably fine voice."

He winced. "Gillian, must you tell all my secrets?"

"Every one of them," she answered with unconcern, leading them up the stairs to their bedrooms.

Fiona's room was done in a fresh mixture of greens. The spread on the bed was white but the rest was as relaxing as an oasis. "I feel as if I'm walking into a garden," she announced, pleased with her accommodations.

Holburn nodded, looking around the room as if he'd wanted to confirm for himself all was as it should be. "I'll let you have a moment to yourself," he said. "The coach should arrive momentarily and I'll help Aunt Agatha. If you need anything, Fee, ask Gillian." He ducked out of the room before she could give a saucy reply.

Gillian looked at Fiona, her expression thoughtful. "I haven't seen him so happy and relaxed in years. And he usually doesn't make an appearance here until Christmas Day."

"We had a good ride," Fiona answered.

"No, it's you," Gillian said. "He likes you."

Fiona felt a tug of happiness in her heart, but she had to be practical. "He is a kind man."

"No one has *ever* said that about Holburn," Gillian retorted. "I've heard him described as ruthless and more often than not, arrogant." She shook her head considering the matter. "But never 'kind.' May I call you Fiona?"

"Of course."

Gillian smiled and moved toward the door. "I fear, Fiona, that you are either blind to Holburn's faults or in need of a rest." At the door, she paused and looked back at Fiona. "Dinner is early. Your maid will know the details." She opened the door. "I'm glad you are here. I think you are good for my cousin."

"We've only just met," Fiona confessed.

"Sometimes that's best," Gillian answered. "Sometimes people just know when they should be together."

"Did you 'know' with your husband?"

Gillian's smile tightened around the edges. "You *are* blunt."

"I'm sorry. I didn't mean offense—"

"I'm not offended. Shocked, perhaps. Few are

as plain-spoken as myself. It's rather refreshing, and a bit disconcerting. The one thing I know—you are perfect for Holburn."

Fiona shook her head, yearning for Gillian's words to be true and yet too pragmatic to believe them. "He's above my touch," she said.

"Let him be the judge of that," Gillian answered softly and left the room.

Chapter Twelve

*H*olburn did have a good singing voice. It was a strong baritone that resonated in Fiona's soul.

After dinner that evening, he and Gillian sang a sad, poignant duet of "Barbara Allen" and then followed it up with a joyous rendition of "The Saucy Sailor." Holburn threw in so much enthusiasm and eyebrow waggles that everyone in the room was laughing to the point of tears.

Fiona and the duke hadn't been the first to arrive for the family Christmas celebration. Besides Aunt Agatha, two other sets of relatives were already in their rooms and accepted Fiona amongst their numbers without question.

By the end of the first evening, she was relaxed and enjoying herself.

Holburn was a generous host and obviously well-liked. "Much more so than his uncles," Gillian confided.

"Why is that?" Fiona asked.

"Lords Maven and Brandt put on airs as much as Daisy the Duchess does but in a different manner," Gillian answered and then clapped a hand over her mouth. "I shouldn't have called her that," she confessed, the laughter in her eyes removing any apology from her words. She leaned closer to Fiona. "It isn't a secret that Holburn's mother is a bit high strung. We all avoid her, and that little dog of hers. Master Rockford barks at everything, especially my cat."

Gillian's white long-haired cat was peacefully curled on a pillow in front of the fire. Tad lay beside him, his nose almost touching the pillow, his eyes boring holes into Kitty as if waiting for a moment to pounce—but he had enough good sense to stay where he was. Everyone marveled at Kitty's nerves. The cat seemed truly unaffected by Tad's attention, although Fiona had been told by several people the cat detested Master Rockford and had chased him with her claws on more than one occasion.

"The uncles are reserved," Gillian said, picking

up her original thought. "They fancy themselves more ducal than Holburn. If something happens to him, Brandt is next in line for the title. We all pray Holburn remains alive and happy. Brandt would ship me off to my husband without any regret."

"Would it be so terrible to return to him?" Fiona dared to ask.

"Yes," Gillian said, her good humor vanishing. She tactfully changed the subject. "Oh, look, the children are going to sing. I'm thrilled you have no musical talent," she offered as an aside.

"My mother wasn't," Fiona answered and Gillian laughed, at ease again.

After a delightful evening, Holburn made a point of leaving the room with Fiona and escorting her upstairs. Fiona could feel the speculation amongst the relatives as she left the room.

On the way upstairs, she said, "They believe we are involved. They don't think I'm a 'ward.'"

"They have suspicious minds." His response betrayed no emotion, and her pride wouldn't let her question him.

Perhaps she was nothing more than a temporary ward, someone he was protecting from coming to harm because of her association with him.

But she wanted there to be something more.

At her bedroom door, she braced herself, hoping

for some sign of his intentions. It seemed like forever since they'd been in that room in the Swan and shared hungry, greedy kisses. She could almost believe she'd imagined them.

To her disappointment, Holburn behaved the perfect gentleman. He left her at the door with a kind "good night."

Fiona watched him walk to his set of rooms located down the hall from hers, wondering about his return of her affections. Or had he lost interest?

At his door, he paused, turned to her.

The look he sent her was so heated, it was better than a kiss.

She opened her door and escaped inside, almost overcome with her good fortune. He treated her as if they were courting—

Fiona broke off her thoughts. She couldn't let herself think in this direction.

In spite of having been the daughter of a once-respected magistrate, she wasn't worthy to be any man's wife, let alone a duke's. No matter how attracted she was to Holburn, she had to remember her place and help him keep in mind of it, too.

Fiona had come to respect him. To admire him. To enjoy his company. They were compatible. They shared the same values—and that's why she knew he deserved someone better than herself.

He needed a woman who was whole and pure and could give him children untainted by disgrace. He needed a woman with social connections and money.

Fiona was no longer any of these things . . .

If she loved him, and she did—then she mustn't let a relationship between them go further. In this respect, she agreed with his mother. It was for his own protection.

However, the next morning when her maid Sarah woke her with the message that the duke wished to know if she would join him for a morning ride, Fiona did not say no.

And that evening, she let Holburn walk her to her bedroom door.

He didn't so much as take her hand but he lingered, leaning his shoulder against the wall. Laughter and music drifted up from the stairs where the late night set still enjoyed themselves. They stood in the hallway teasing and flirting with each other. He treated her with the respect expected of one borne to her station in life—and she loved him all the more for it.

They rode again the next morning. She was beginning to know the grooms by name and they all greeted her cheerfully. They did not question Holburn's precaution of having an armed groom accompany them. He also informed her privately that he had men patrol the estate but no one had seen hide nor hair of the Irishmen or any other strangers.

Fiona prayed they were long gone . . . although she was in no hurry to return to her former life. Huntleigh was a heaven on earth. She enjoyed being surrounded by family and everyone she met from the scullery maid to the butler was happy.

She complimented Gillian about it that evening, assuming much of the attitude in the house was her doing.

"Oh, no," she said, looking up from her embroidery. "Everyone is always this way when Holburn's in residence. The servants adore him and they should. They were the ones who raised him." She'd leaned closer to confide, "They like you, too. My maid Molly told me so. They think you are good for him."

"They can't think that?" Fiona blurted out, not modulating her voice in her surprise.

Several heads were raised from the games they were playing or conversations being held. The family, a number growing by new arrivals every day, gathered in different seating arrangements around the oversized sitting room every evening. A rush of heat burned Fiona's cheeks.

She glanced at Holburn to see if he'd overheard. He sat in an upholstered chair by the fire with two of his youngest cousins, a three-year-old boy and five-year-old girl, in his lap. They were playing that he was going to bite off their noses and they laughingly alternated between pretending to hide and daring him to do so.

Sensing she was looking at him, he raised his gaze to meet hers over the head of the youngsters and smiled in that way that made her happily dizzy.

"Because of that," Gillian whispered in her ear. "We've all noticed how he looks at you, and how you return that look. But there is more. His manner has changed. Before he'd make an appearance at Huntleigh for Christmas but was always in a rush, always preoccupied as if he needed to be someplace else. Usually around those cursed gaming tables. This year, he doesn't seem to have a desire to be anywhere else but here. And he's at peace. I hadn't realized how unhappy he must have been until I saw him in this light."

"It can't be me," Fiona said in complete honesty.

Gillian touched her arm as if she'd been teasing. "You can't be so naïve, Fiona."

"I'm trying to be cautious—"

"Don't be," Gillian ordered. "Throw caution aside. Holburn *likes* you, and that is a gift. My husband is the sort of man every mother wants for her daughter, except he never liked me very much. I'm not certain he even knows I am a person with feelings and intelligence. In truth, I'm jealous that the two of you enjoy each other's company."

Her attention was claimed by one of the children, who wanted help with a sampler she was making. Fiona sat beside them, pretending to be interested in a fashion magazine. Anyone seeing her would have thought her serenely calm, except that wasn't true.

For the first time since her parents' deaths, happiness bubbled inside her.

Her mother would have been proud. They'd shared so many hopeful conversations for Fiona's future, dreams that had been abandoned after the soldiers' attack.

But now, Fiona wondered if her mother wasn't her guardian angel? Could she guide Holburn to her?

What if she confessed her humiliation at the hands of the soldiers to Holburn? What if she allowed the duke to decide if she was suitable instead of making the decision for him? Gillian's words gave her courage.

She toyed with the idea of speaking to him this very night when he walked her to her room. She prayed she didn't lose her courage.

In the end, Fate made the decision. When it came time to excuse themselves, a great uncle, Lord Morris, and his very young wife went upstairs with them leaving no opportunity for a confidence of any sort.

So it was that the next morning, Fiona was especially looking forward to their ride. The groom would be following but Fiona thought she might manage a moment of privacy.

Fiona took extra care with her appearance, ignoring both morning chocolate and the knot of anxiety in her stomach. In the back of her mind was the fear he could reject her once he knew the full truth. She tried not to think on it.

She and Holburn usually met by the back door to walk down to the stables together. However he wasn't there this morning.

A footman approached. "His Grace is in the front hall," he informed her. "He asks you to join him. His uncles have arrived."

The infamous uncles . . . Fiona didn't know if she was prepared to make their acquaintance and yet the footman waited to escort her to them. She gathered the hem of her riding habit over one arm and followed.

The front hall was a flurry of activity. Servants carried trunks and bandboxes up the steps. The uncles, both dressed in somber black, were easy to identify. However, Fiona hadn't anticipated they were also twins. No one had told her. Identical gray eyes turned to frown as she approached.

A less bold woman would be shaking in her riding boots. Fiona was made of sterner stuff. She also had Holburn, who held out a welcoming hand, inviting her to join him.

He drew her close, perhaps even too close. "Fee, this is Lord Maven and Lord Brandt, my father's brothers. Uncles, this is Miss Fiona Lachlan of whom you may have heard."

Fiona bobbed a curtsey, conscious of the way the uncles' eyebrows had shot up at Holburn's use of his pet name for her. He'd been using it around the house from the first day and no one had appeared to care.

But if the duke had noticed their reaction, he gave no indication. Instead he easily continued, "Miss Lachlan's father was the well-known Scottish magistrate, Sir John Lachlan. Her mother was related to Marlborough. I believe they are second cousins. Isn't that right, Fee?"

Her mother and the Duke of Marlborough were actually third cousins but Fiona was too surprised that Holburn had this information to correct him. She nodded dumbly.

"How interesting," Lord Maven murmured.

His lack of enthusiasm didn't dampen Holburn's

spirits at all. If anything, he seemed happier. "And this," he said, taking Fiona over to a tall brunette dressed in the same somber hues as their lordships, "is my aunt, Lady Brandt. Auntie," Holburn said with enough cheekiness to make her frown deepen, "this is Miss Fiona Lachlan of Scotland and you heard all the rest. She is my special guest."

If he had announced he was marrying her within a hour, their reactions could not have been more surprised. It was the warmth in his voice that did it. Even Fiona was stunned at his blatant show of favor.

At that moment, another traveler entered through the front door. He was close to Holburn in age although he was much taller, almost a giant. He had dark, deep-set eyes and strong features that went with his height.

"And this," the duke said, "is my cousin Mr. Richard Lynsted. Richard, this is Miss Fiona Lachlan."

Of the group in the hallway, Richard appeared the most untroubled by being introduced to Fiona. He made a bow before handing his hat to a footman. "Your servant." He let a footman help him with his great coat.

"Richard is Lord Brandt's son," Holburn said

off-handedly. "We went to school together. We don't rub along well."

His cousin made a face as if he'd heard this all before. "That isn't entirely true, Holburn."

"Close enough?" the duke suggested. He didn't wait for an answer. "Welcome to another Christmas at Huntleigh. I'll allow you all to settle yourselves. Gillian and the housekeeper have seen to rooms. Fee and I are off for a ride."

He took Fiona's hand and started for the back hall leading to the path toward the stables when Lord Brandt informed him, "Your mother will be along later this afternoon."

"Good," Holburn said. "I look forward to seeing her."

"She is bringing a guest," his wife chimed in. "Some soldier. Did you know?"

Fiona frowned at the condescension in the woman's tone.

"I did know," Holburn said easily. "Colonel Swanson, I believe. I invited him."

"I'm concerned, Your Grace," Lady Brandt said, approaching him. "I've made inquiries. I fear your mother and this colonel might be paramours."

"And?" Holburn asked. "Is this our business?"

"Everything involving the family is *your* business, Your Grace," Lord Brandt said.

"Then the matter is being handled," Holburn said easily. "You needn't worry."

"But I must," Lord Brandt insisted. "For example, I have concerns about Miss Lachlan. You see, I, too, have made inquiries. I'm hoping she is your paramour because what I've learned makes her unsuited for anything else."

His cold pronouncement sucked the air out of the hallway. Fiona couldn't breathe, couldn't even think in the face of the man's charge.

Holburn had no such problem. Whereas before he had been genial and good willed in the presence of his uncles, he now, in a blink, turned as aloof as themselves, with one notable exception—he actually was the duke. If anyone had any question, they had only to witness the change in his demeanor.

His presence seemed to fill the hall. His voice was pleasant, and all the more threatening because of it as he said, "I know you didn't mean that the way it sounded, Uncle."

Lady Brandt stepped forward, placing her hand on her husband's elbow as if prompting him to respond. His cousin Richard had gone stock-still. Fiona sensed he wished he was anywhere but in this hallway at this moment.

Surprisingly, he was the one of the family who found his voice first. "I'm certain my father didn't mean to suggest—"

"*I did,*" Lord Brandt cut in. He met Holburn's eye. "I know what I said. Is it wrong to wish to prevent a mistake before it happens?"

Holburn walked back to him. "You have insulted my guest," he said, his voice so low, Fiona had to strain to hear it. The servants that had been in the hall had all been wise enough to fade into the background.

"My question to you," the duke continued, "is would you stake your life upon the charges against her good name that you are making?"

Fiona feared her knees would buckle beneath her. She didn't want them to duel over her . . . especially when Lord Brandt was right about her reputation. This was what came of keeping her silence.

She opened her mouth to speak but at that moment, Lord Brandt said, "I forgot myself." He made a deep bow in Fiona's direction. "I beg you to forgive my lapse in manners, Miss Lachlan."

Holburn didn't wait for her to respond but advised, "I would not make that error again." He took Fiona's arm and they left the hall.

She waited until they were outside and on the path to the stables before saying, "How did you find out about my mother?"

"I had some people ask questions," he said as if it was not important.

Fiona pulled up short, anger and guilt rising in her all at once. "What else did you find out?"

A look of annoyance passed across his eyes. "That your family connections are impeccable," he said. "And my dear uncles had best treat you with respect."

She was going to have to tell him. "Is that all?"

"Is there more?"

Here it was, her chance to confess—but she discovered she wasn't ready. The words wouldn't form on her lips. And this was too public a place. Anyone could come upon them. "Let's go for our ride," she said, her conscience twisting miserably.

Their horses were saddled and waiting in the stable yard. Marvin, the head groom, had chosen a handsome dark bay gelding for her mount. Holburn rode a spirited chestnut filly.

The air was brisk and the day a good one for riding. Fiona put her frustration in her riding, waiting until the horses were suitably warmed up to give a kick and jump the nearest hedgerow.

Holburn immediately jumped after her. Usually she waited until he joined her, but today was different. She had the desire to outrun all her worries and she did so.

The bay was ready for a race and Holburn's filly was more than up to the challenge. Fiona lost track of where the groom was. At this moment, he didn't matter.

Instead, she gave her horse his head and let him run. Holburn's filly easily matched hers stride for stride.

They raced across the pasture, jumped three fences and then turned off onto a road beside a rushing stream. The horses' hooves clattered over a small wooden bridge.

Fiona turned hers up a path leading to a knoll overlooking the estate. However, before she could go very far, Holburn's hand reached for her horse's bridle. She reined in, surprised, turned to him—and his lips met hers.

For a second, Fiona couldn't think . . . and then she kissed him back.

Their horses slowed to a stop. Fiona let go of the reins and slipped her arms around Holburn's neck. This was what she wanted, what she needed.

She was going to have to tell him the truth, but first, she had to be certain she meant something to him—because the truth be known, he meant everything to her.

He lifted her off her side saddle and brought her over to sit in front of him. The kiss deepened. Her legs rested on his thigh, his arms surrounded her. He was hard, aroused. The length of him pressed against her thigh.

This wasn't what she'd planned to do. She had something to say to him, something very important—but she could no longer remember what it was.

Holburn broke the kiss first. He jumped down from his horse. She realized they'd not gone far from the stream but were in a small clearing near the road. Bare-limbed trees and holly berry bushes provided a shelter. He placed his hands on her waist and swung her into his arms. "I told the groom to stay back," he said.

"Good," she answered before his lips came down on hers again.

When at last they had to break for air, he said, "I've wanted to do that for a long time."

"I have, too," she managed to answer and they would have kissed again except that a cold steel tube came in between them. She pulled back in surprise and realized it was the barrel of a gun.

Holburn recognized the same. He quickly placed himself between her and the man holding the gun. They had been so preoccupied with kissing each other, they had not seen or heard him approach.

At first, Fiona feared it was one of the Irishmen.

He wasn't. This man had a swordsman's slimness with broad shoulders. His straight, blue-black hair was tied back into a neat queue beneath a wide-brimmed hat. He was dressed for riding in a black coat and neck cloth over a white shirt and gray leather breeches. A growth of whiskers gave him a roguish air and his eyes were the most extraordinary silver-gray.

"*Hola*, Your Grace," he said softly in accented English. "I understand you have been searching for me."

Immediately, Fiona knew this was the Spaniard. The man Holburn suspected wanted him dead.

Chapter Thirteen

*N*ick faced his enemy. The years had not been
kind to Andres. His former friend showed
signs of weariness. It was there in the harsh
lines around his eyes and mouth. Unfortunately,
the hand holding the pistol was remarkably
steady. But instead of fear, the gun made Nick
angry.

"So, it *was* you," he said to Ramigio.

"It was *me* for what?" the Spaniard answered.

"Attempting to kill me?" Nick reminded him,
irritated that Andres would play ignorant. "So what
has happened now? Have you tired of paying
Irish thugs and decided to do it yourself?"

"Thugs?" Ramigio frowned as if he either didn't

understand the word or didn't know what Nick was talking about. He raised the gun. "Are you asking about this? What else would you have me do? I must protect myself."

"Protect yourself from what?"

"*You*," Ramigio declared, pointing the gun at Nick, who pushed it away.

"What did I ever do to you?"

"*Este hombre me esta frustrando*," he muttered. "Are you saying you have not sent *hombres* to kill me? But I have fooled you! I came here to tell you to leave me alone. *Suficiente.* We are done. You have hounded me like a dog."

"I have sent no one to kill you. But I want my ring back. Give me the ring and I *will* leave you alone," Nick assured him.

"You are so ridiculous," Andres answered, punctuating his words with his pistol in the air. He never could talk without using his hands. "I don't have your ring. You chase me all these years for what I do not have. I never worried because your men are *incompetente*. I give them a little money, they say they can't find me, and you are allowed to pay them again to look. Your men and I have become *amigos*. However, now, you shoot at me and make me angry. You leave me alone. You do not touch anything I have."

"If you do not have the ring, where is it?" Nick

demanded, but Fee had heard something he should have noticed.

She stepped out from behind him. "Someone is shooting at you?"

"*Si*," Andres answered. "That is what I said. And I don't like it."

"Who is after you?" Nick asked, realizing the importance of Fee's question. "The men I sent were not to harm you but to fetch the ring back. They are two burly characters, both English."

Ramigio released his breath with a weary sigh. "Those men, they are buffoons but not killers. They did not shoot at me. The man who shot at me had very good aim." He poked one finger at the place on the sleeve of his jacket close to his heart where the bullet had hit him. "You see, I was lucky."

"I think we may need to talk," Nick said.

"I don't want to talk," Andres answered. "I want you to leave me alone. I am tired of being chased and I don't want to be murdered."

"Understood," Nick said. "I would feel the same, but first, I have some questions for you. And then I'll leave you alone," he added, thinking he was being completely reasonable.

"Forever?" Ramigio asked.

"Forever."

The Spaniard raised his hands in acceptance.

There was a fallen tree close to where Nick and Fee had been kissing. Andres made himself at home by sitting on the log. "Go ahead. What questions do you have?" he said, gesturing with his pistol.

No longer fearing being shot, Nick crossed over to the fallen tree. Fee followed. Their horses were grazing not far away and perfectly happy to do so. "Let us start with the easy question," Nick replied. "Where is my ring?"

Andres made a face. "Always with the ring. You would think a better friend would ask about someone trying to kill me."

"All right then," Fee said, expressing the same exasperation Nick felt. "Who is trying to kill you?"

"I don't know," Ramigio answered. "That's why I came here. I thought it was Holburn."

"Listen, *tío*," Nick said derisively, using a word that had once indicated their friendship, "answer her question politely."

"*Tío*," Ramigio repeated. "We were friends. Good ones."

"Until you stole from me," Nick countered.

Andres raised his hand, holding the gun to his heart. "Sometimes a man does not realize in doing what he must, there is a cost. I have not fared well since that day. I wish I had not done it."

Nick wished he had not done it, too, and had a great deal to say about the subject but Fee stepped between the two men.

"Why don't you tell us your story from the beginning?" she suggested.

"Yes, start with stealing my ring," Nick agreed and earned a hip bump from Fee for his insubordination.

Ramigio looked from one of them to the other, and then let his eyes fully take in Fee as if he had not completely noticed her earlier. His grin turned wolfishly charming. "Not bad, Holburn. You were always a lucky man with women, but this one—you have outdone yourself. While I have lived like a peasant, you have wooed a *princesa*—"

"The ring," Nick cut in, annoyed. The Spaniard had too handsome a face and too much charm with the ladies.

"Or I'll take that pistol from you and make you eat it. You are on my land now and here, I have all the power."

Andres shrugged, unimpressed. "My story is simple. I came to England because you sent me the letter. You should have done this long ago, *tío*. I thought you sent for me . . . in a nice way. Not any of this nonsense about men trying to do me harm like you have for years—"

"When did you receive this letter?" Fee asked, cutting through his complaint.

"Two weeks ago. I received it in Amsterdam. I was a member of the court there."

"Yes, probably as a hanger-on," Nick couldn't resist drawling.

"A man does what he must," Andres agreed without taking offense and Nick was reminded of why he had liked the Spaniard so much years ago. He'd been a good companion who held no pretenses and had been like fresh air in Nick's life.

Nick's anger vanished. "I didn't send a letter to you, Andres."

"But it was delivered by one of the men you had following me."

This *was* startling news. "My last report said they had lost track of you."

Andres frowned. "They lied to you?"

"They'd *been* lying to me," Nick countered. "It was *you* they tried to trick this time," he pointed out and had the satisfaction of hearing Ramigio swear in Spanish.

Fee took charge again. "Do you have the letter?"

Ramigio set aside his pistol and pulled the letter from his coat. Nick took it from him, unfolded it, and read it quickly. "This is a request, supposedly from me, asking Ramigio to meet me in London by the Tower the same night we were attacked.

It says that I want to make peace. I don't recognize the handwriting but it isn't mine." He looked to Andres. "Did you really go to the Tower?"

"I did," said the Spaniard.

"You came all the way from Amsterdam?" Nick questioned. "Why?"

"I am tired of the chase," Andres said, and then added, "What I did, taking your ring, was not good. My conscience, it bothers me. Besides, I would like to visit England. I think there are opportunities for my talents here."

"You almost made me soften to you with your talk about a conscience," Nick said. "But then you included your true motive for coming to England— to make money. To find more fools like me."

"I do not think you are a fool. What I did was not right."

"But you did it," Nick accused, reminding himself more than Andres.

Again, Fee brought them back to the important subject. "Who could have sent this letter, Your Grace," she asked, "using your men?"

Nick shook his head. "I hired them. I met with them privately. No one knew of them other than myself . . . and apparently Andres."

"Maybe all of London," the Spaniard said, the gibe striking home that Nick's secret plans weren't that secret.

"When you reached the Tower, what happened?" he asked Ramigio.

"Someone fired a shot from a distance. I think the plot was I would be shot, fall into the Thames, and they'd be done with me. But he missed. He fired again. He really wanted to kill me. I pretended to be hit and fell in the river on my own. I don't want to do that again. I ruined my best coat."

"And then what happened?" Fee asked.

"I came looking for Holburn," Andres said. "You have been hard to approach, *tío*. You've ridden with armed guards most days."

"Except for today," Nick said.

"Yes." Andres's silvery eyes lit with laughter. "And I am able to appreciate why you wish to be alone." He said this with a nod in Fee's direction. "In fact, I apologize I had to interrupt."

Fee's cheeks bloomed with color and Nick was torn between an urge to kiss her shyness away or to rip out Ramigio's eyes. He focused on the matter at hand.

"We don't know who sent this letter," he said, "but it had to be someone close to me. Someone who knew of my connection to you. Who could that be, Ramigio?" he demanded, at last coming to the most important question of all.

Andres stood. He had always enjoyed the drama of the moment. "I would think it might be the men who hired me to steal your ring. You see, Holburn, I don't have your ring. I was paid to take it and paid well."

"Who paid you?" Nick demanded.

This time, Andres didn't prevaricate. "Lord Livermore. I delivered the ring to him."

Lord Livermore had been his sponsor on the Grand Tour. Nick knew immediately that Livermore wouldn't want the ring. No, he had been acting for someone else . . . for the men who had arranged the Grand Tour.

For a long moment, Nick felt as if the world was shaking beneath his feet. All that he had known, all that he had trusted was being shown to be a sham. He'd been searching for years . . . when the ring had always been close at hand.

Fee placed a worried hand on his arm. "Who is Lord Livermore?"

Anger rose in him like bile. "The bloody bastards . . ." Nick's voice trailed off as he moved to action. "Andres, where is your horse?"

"I tied him on the other side of that knoll."

"Take Fee's horse to collect it. Come, Fee, you double up with me. We are returning to the house."

He grabbed his horse's reins, leapt up in the saddle, and then held a hand down for her. She looked up at him in confusion. "My uncles stole the ring, Fee. My uncles have had it all this time."

She shook her head, as if her mind couldn't understand all the implications. "But why?"

"That's what *I* want to know."

Fee took the hand he offered and he lifted her up to sit in front of him on the saddle. They collected Andres's horse and then the three of them rode to the house's front door.

Holburn dismounted, tossing the reins to a footman who was surprised to see him. Taking a moment to help Fee down from her horse, Nick marched into the house. Both Fee and Ramigio followed. Tad came running up to greet them. He'd been out on the hunt when Nick and Fee had left for their ride. The dog was quickly taking over the estate. However, Nick was in no mood to give him attention now.

"Where are my uncles?" Nick asked Docket.

"In your library, Your Grace."

"Follow me," Nick ordered Fee and Ramigio and started down the hall, anxious for the confrontation.

"Perhaps I should wait here," Fee suggested.

Nick stopped. "No. I need you." He didn't wait for her answer but continued to the library.

He found both Brandt and Maven making themselves comfortable amongst his books. Richard was also with them and the thought struck him that his cousin could also have been a part of the theft. It was inconceivable that they had deceived him for so long. His mind hadn't even begun to consider that they may have hired men to murder him, but he was quickly overcoming his aversion to the accusation.

Never, in spite of knowing how little his uncles considered him worthy of the title, had he suspected they would betray him. The Oracle's warning so many years ago took on a new and more ominous meaning.

Beware innocence, she had said. He now understood it was his *own* naiveté she had warned him against. His own innocent trust.

"Uncles, I have a visitor I believe you should meet," he said, entering the room without preamble.

His three relatives came to their feet in deference to his rank. They always did what was expected albeit without enthusiasm. Nick stepped aside to allow Ramigio to enter the room. He watched their faces for signs of recognition.

Only Richard knew who the Spaniard was, although by the puzzlement in his expression he couldn't quite place where they'd met. Or was it a ruse?

Nick didn't know who to trust any longer.

His uncles looked to him for introductions.

"You don't know him?" Nick demanded. Fee had come in to stand by the door.

"Should we?" Maven asked.

"I know him," Richard said with dawning awareness. "We met in Greece, didn't we? During our Grand Tour? He was the Spaniard you befriended. Am I correct?"

Nick would have jumped to the conclusion that Richard had been guilty of stealing the ring. However, the sudden wariness in Brandt and Maven's expressions gave up the game. Richard did not share any of their alarm.

"You hired Ramigio to steal my signet ring," Nick quietly accused his uncles.

The twins exchanged glances as if silently asking each other what to say.

"*Steal* your signet ring?" Richard repeated. "I thought you lost it?" That was the story Nick had put about. He'd been too embarrassed by Ramigio's deceit.

"Your father and his brother know differently," Nick said. "Richard, excuse us."

His cousin frowned, obviously unwilling to leave until his father motioned to go to the door.

Nick waited until he had closed the door behind him. "Let's hear it all," he said to his uncles.

They could have played dumb. They could have protested they weren't aware of who Ramigio was or denied having anything to do with the missing ring.

Instead, Maven announced, "You didn't deserve the ring. Your behavior was disgraceful in those days. Actually, it was little worse than it is now."

"So you wanted to make me see the error of my ways by stealing from me?" Nick lashed back.

"We hoped to *preserve* the ring," Brandt answered. He moved to stand beside his brother. "The way you were behaving, you were going to lose it. Or gamble it away without a care or concern and tossed aside centuries of your heritage."

"I would *not* have," Nick countered.

Maven snorted his disagreement. "You already were. We *saved* that ring."

"No, you *stole* it," Nick corrected him. "You paid a man to befriend me and then when I was not aware of it, take my property and deliver it to you."

"Those are the sorts of friends you have," Brandt said. "He didn't do anything more than a dozen or more scoundrels were attempting to do every night."

Nick could not believe their arrogance. Who were *they* to speak to him this way? And to maintain they were in the right in the face of his anger? Did they not know who he was?

Or was it they didn't care?

He let his voice go deceptively calm. "Where is the ring now?"

"In my possession," Brandt answered.

"Of course," Nick said, choking back his cold fury. "You are the next in line. You probably felt you deserved the ring."

"I've seen that it was treated properly," Brandt answered, completely unruffled.

"You will return the ring to me," Nick said. "*Now*. I don't care if you must send horsemen to London, I want that ring. It is mine."

At last he received a reaction he could understand from his uncle. A dark spot of indignant color appeared on each of Brandt's cheeks as if he wished he could defy Nick—but knew he couldn't. "As you wish," he said at last.

"I also 'wish,'" Nick continued with equal formality, "to know what your reasoning is behind attempting to have me murdered?"

Both men's jaws dropped at the accusation. Brandt was the first to recover. "We haven't attempted to have you murdered."

Nick moved into the room. "Miss Lachlan can testify in a court of law to that fact. You are the prime suspects, uncles, because you stole the ring. And because by your own admission, you do not wish me good will."

"But murder?" Maven shook his head. "We would not go that far, Holburn. The idea is preposterous!"

"You tried to murder me, too," Ramigio chimed in.

The twins looked at each other dumbstruck. "This is ridiculous," Maven insisted.

"Miss Lachlan, is the charge serious?" Nick said, asking for her corroboration of his accusation.

"It's very serious," she responded. "His Grace barely escaped with his life on the first attempt. There has been more than one. Your men tried to hunt him down."

"If it wasn't for her, gentlemen," Nick said, "I would be dead, and one of you the duke. Greed is always a reason to cause harm. And then there is my friend the Barón de Vasconia. Tell them your story, Andres."

"Someone lured me here, claiming to be His Grace and then shot at me. He wanted to throw my body into the Thames."

"Apparently they weren't successful," Maven said as he reached for his snuff box in his pocket.

"Do you insult me?" Ramigio said.

"I merely point out how convenient your story is." Maven looked to Nick. "Whatever our opinions of you, we've always respected your title. We would not taint it with murder. Whereas this man, an admitted thief—after all, that is why Livermore hired him for us—has everything to gain by lying."

"First give me the ring," Nick answered. "Then we shall discuss the other matter."

He anticipated them to say they would need time.

Instead, the twins exchanged glances, coming to a consensus between themselves. Brandt untied his neck cloth. He pulled a chain out from beneath his shirt and held it up so the ring dangled in the air.

"You've been wearing it?" Nick said.

"From the day Livermore delivered it to me. I have not taken it off once."

Brandt made it sound as if he'd performed some heroic sacrifice in duping his nephew. Nick struggled with a desire to smash the smug look off his uncle's face. Instead, he held out his hand. His uncle slipped the chain over his head and placed the ring in Nick's palm.

The signet felt lighter than Nick remembered. It seemed more fragile. He broke the chain and placed the ring where it belonged—on his left ring finger.

For a long moment, he looked at the engraved lines of his family's crest. The depth of his uncles' betrayal roiled inside him. He remembered his father wearing this ring.

He raised his head to face his uncles. "I trusted you. When I lost this ring, it was like losing my father again. I felt I had failed him. *And*, I had the difficult task of presenting myself to the two of you and confessing what had happened. Do you remember what you said?"

Neither man answered.

Nick spoke for them. "You said you weren't surprised." He gave a bitter laugh. "All the time you had me twisting with guilt, you possessed the ring." He shook his head. "Leave my house."

At first, the two men acted as if they hadn't heard him correctly.   .

Nick looked them straight in the eye, for the first time in his life he felt completely the duke in front of them. *"Leave."*

"But we just arrived," Maven protested.

"You will pack up your wives and your servants. You will be gone by dinner. When I return to London, I will speak to the magistrate and ask for an inquiry into the attempts on both mine and the Barón de Vasconia's lives. You will also be tried for the murder of Hester Jenkins. You may have heard of her, uncles. She was a well-known courtesan and favored by many highly placed gentlemen. I'm certain the story of that night will make your names gossip fodder for years."

"We had *nothing* to do with the attempts on your life," Brandt insisted. "We never hired men to do anything against you."

Nick closed his fist, feeling the weight of the

signet on his finger, and held it up for them to see. "You hired someone to steal this. Why should I believe you now? Instead, you may protest your innocence to the magistrate. Of course, we will also tell our stories."

"This is *unreasonable*," Maven replied.

"Be gone within the hour," Nick answered and turned to leave the room. He offered his arm to Fee, who quickly took it as if she wished to escape the tensions of the library.

Ramigio fell into step behind them, but they had not gone far when Nick said to him. "You need to leave, too, Andres."

The Spaniard frowned. "But we have no quarrel between us. I thought we were *amigos*."

"We were never friends," Nick answered. "You came here out of self-interest. What? Did you expect me to be grateful that you finally did what a friend should have done in the beginning? It's too late, Andres. There is an inn in the village you can stay for the night. I will send a footman to let them know to have a room prepared, but on the morrow, you will be gone. I want you nowhere close to me."

There was a beat of silence. Nick waited, studying a place on the wainscoting.

At last, his voice quiet, Ramigio said, "As you

wish, Your Grace. You needn't worry about the footman or showing me out. I shall take the back way so that I don't inconvenience you."

He didn't wait for a response, but left.

The barón was wrong for stealing the signet ring but Fiona's heart went out to the Spaniard as he turned from Holburn and walked down the hall. She liked the man. She understood now how Holburn could have so quickly made him a friend and then felt deeply betrayed by him.

She couldn't fault the duke for cutting the Spaniard out of his life, especially in light of his uncles' duplicity. It was all too much to absorb. Perhaps later, the duke might relent in his stance toward Andres, but not now.

"Are *you* all right?" she asked the duke.

His brows came together. He didn't look at her as he said, "I will be. I must be."

"Trust is a fragile and valuable commodity in this world," she whispered. "You had no choice but to make the decisions you did."

He frowned "There are always choices, Fee. What is unsettling is that all my life, the ones closest to me have meant the most harm. Is the title so important?"

"Some think so."

His lips twisted cynically. "They are the ones who don't have it, and the responsibilities."

There was a great commotion coming from the front hall. Fiona had thought it would be the uncles leaving—and then she heard the annoyed yipping. The dowager had arrived. Her heart sank.

"Mother," Holburn said under his breath. He didn't sound overjoyed at her arrival either.

Docket had his hands full directing traffic in the hall. Servants and luggage were coming and going.

"Dominic," his mother said happily in greeting, standing right in the middle of it all. She held a squirming Master Rockford in her arms and was dressed in the height of fashion with a bit of a Christmas cheer. Her green velvet pelisse and red hat made her appear like one of Gillian's holly berry arrangements. Her smile momentarily vanished at the sight of Fee by his side but she quickly recovered.

"How good of you to greet me," she said to her son. "Please, give your mother a kiss, right here."

Holburn hesitated and then dutifully did as instructed, his words of greeting perfunctory. His mother didn't notice. Her attention had been claimed by the way a servant was handling several hatboxes. "Here now, don't be clumsy."

Gillian and many other relatives had come to welcome this new member but Fiona noticed there was little warmth in their manners. One of the children asked to hold Master Rockford.

"He's not a pet," the dowager haughtily informed the child and passed the dog to her maid. "Please see to his needs," she ordered.

At that moment, a well-dressed gentleman of military bearing entered the house. His clothes were well tailored and obviously new. As the servants worked to move the bandboxes and trunks upstairs, the duchess announced to all, "This is a particular friend of mine, Colonel Harry Swanson. His Grace has invited him for the holidays." She smiled at the colonel, a secret, proud smile. "Gillian, what room have you prepared for him?"

"The blue one has been aired for him," Gillian answered.

"The blue one? *That* will never do. I want him in the chamber next to mine."

Gillian's eyes widened at her instructions. She glanced at Holburn, who maintained a stony silence. Fiona knew his mind was on other things than his mother's bald announcement, but Gillian didn't.

Gillian glanced at the housekeeper before saying in a conciliatory manner, "I'm sorry, Your

Grace, but we've already placed Lord Maven in that room."

Before the duchess could speak, Holburn announced, "Maven will be leaving. As will Brandt and his family."

At that moment, both uncles came into the hall from the receiving room. They overheard what the duke had said. Their jaws tight, they made no comment but went upstairs.

The relatives looked from one to the other but no one asked any of the questions brewing in their minds, save the dowager. A smile spread across her face. "Well, we may have a good holiday after all." To Gillian, she chirped, "You shall see Colonel Swanson is placed in the better room."

"Gillian is not the housekeeper, Mother," the duke said. "If you want something done, you may address Mrs. Sims. Now, if you will excuse me, I have another matter to attend to."

Holburn went outside where a footman still walked the horses they had ridden earlier. Someplace between the kisses and the Spaniard's gun, he had lost the hat he'd been wearing. He didn't bother with it now but mounted his chestnut and took off for a ride. Tad happily charged after him, running with all of his strength to not be left behind this time.

"Isn't that like him?" his mother observed to

the world at large. "I arrive and he goes riding off. Come along, Colonel. *I* shall show you to your room." The dowager swept up the stairs, the berry plumes of her hat gracefully moving as she proudly began giving the colonel a tour of Hunt-leigh starting with the importance of all the ancestors whose paintings lined the stairway wall.

Fiona moved to the front door. She sensed that Gillian and the others had questions, but she wasn't going to answer them. The grooms were bringing coaches around for Lord Maven and Lord Brandt.

Holburn wasn't anywhere to be seen.

For the first time since Fiona had arrived at Hunt-leigh, dinner was a dull affair. The duchess had taken over.

Duchess Daisy, as Gillian had irreverently dubbed her, dominated the conversation at dinner. Everyone knew she was smitten with Colonel Swanson. She giggled like a schoolgirl, made a production of keeping his wine glass full, and pouted when the ladies excused themselves from the table after dinner to let the men enjoy their port.

Fiona had no doubt the colonel was enjoying himself. He seemed to have an eye for fine things. Her suspicion was seconded by Gillian, who swore she'd caught him turning over a piece of china on a hall table to check its marking.

"It's as if he's valuing everything right down to the half penny," she whispered to Fiona.

The general family was very confused. A good number of them thought well of Lords Maven and Brandt. They didn't understand their abrupt departure or why the duke had not returned. He had sent a groom to the house with the instructions to not wait dinner for him, but that didn't stop Fiona from worrying. She was glad he had Tad. She prayed the dog would guard him well.

The gentlemen did not linger over their port but quickly joined the ladies after dinner. Colonel Swanson and the duchess sat with their heads together on a settee at the far end of the room. Fiona tried to ignore them and couldn't. As soon as she was able, she escaped to her bedchamber.

However, sleep did not come. She finally gave up and waited by the window, pulling her legs up on the window seat and wrapping her arms around them. She gazed out onto the back garden, which was bathed in a silvery light. There was a ring around the moon, the sign of a change of weather.

Close to midnight she heard a scratch on her door.

That had to be Tad. If he had returned, that meant Holburn had also.

She rose from her bed and crossed to the room

without pausing to cover her night dress. She opened the door a crack but instead of Tad, Holburn shouldered his way in. He'd removed his coat and smelled of the fresh night air. He shut the door.

Both surprised and relieved, Fiona opened her mouth to greet him, but before words could be spoken, he brought his lips down on hers.

He kissed her hard, held her tight. His mouth tasted of brandy.

Holburn broke the kiss. "Don't speak. Don't think. I'm tired of words, Fee, and I can't stand my thoughts."

"Then what do you want?" she asked, desperate to do what she could to help him.

"*You*," he answered, shutting the door by leaning back on it. "You are the *one* good thing in my life. The *only* good thing." And with those words, he kissed her again.

Chapter Fourteen

*F*rom the moment Fiona had met Holburn, even when she'd first caught a glimpse of him in that ballroom, he'd taken hold over her imagination, and now her life.

He'd lived in her dreams, figured in her fantasies, and was now her reality.

All of her concerns and fears she channeled into their kiss. *I'm here for you,* she said with her lips. She pressed her body closer. *You can trust me. I will never betray you.*

And he answered back.

The world ceased to exist beyond this place, this time in his arms. Nothing else mattered. He was here . . . with her . . . wanting her.

His hand began unfastening the pearl buttons of her night dress.

Fiona let him, because it *was* him.

When his hand cupped her breast, she tensed but offered no protest. Her heart filled her throat. It grew hard to breathe. Blood pounded in her ears.

She covered his hand with her own, holding him against her. His arm came around her waist. His lips brushed her neck.

Fiona leaned on him, needing his support, his strength. If she could she'd step inside him, let him surround her—and all the while she was so very, very frightened.

He pulled his hand from beneath hers and brought his fingertips to her cheek.

It was then she realized she was crying.

"Fee, what is it—" he started but she couldn't let him finish. She didn't dare let him know. She cut him off by lifting herself up on her toes and kissing with all the yearning need in her soul, but he'd have none of it.

He pulled her arms away, turning her so he could see her face in the moonlight.

Fiona stood as if turned to stone, so aware of her braid hanging over one shoulder, her night dress unbuttoned, her skin and the curve of her breasts open to him. He used his thumb to brush away her tears and yet more flowed.

She was a fool. She had nothing to offer him. Nothing to give. He had to see that. He had to know she'd been damaged. Destroyed for any decent *loving* man.

He kissed her tears. "Is it me, Fee?" he said against her skin.

Fiona couldn't speak. She shook her head and realized her whole body was shaking. She felt such a fool.

"No one will harm you," he whispered fiercely. "Not ever again."

Did he think she feared Irishmen? It was good if he did. She didn't want him to know the truth. Then she'd have to remember it and she wanted to forget. Oh, she wanted to forget.

"Shush now," he whispered as if he could hear her disquieted thoughts. "Please, Fee, trust me. Whatever it was, let it go or give it to me. Let me take your pain. I can protect you."

"You can't. No one can."

Holburn laughed softly. "Don't you understand, Fee. You and me—we can face anything together." His voice trailed off as he lifted her up in strong arms, cradling her as one would a baby. Rocking, holding, keeping her, right there in the silvery light with all the shadows, all the darkness, all the meanness kept at bay.

He was so gentle, so kind, that he broke her heart.

It split wide open and all the anger and hate and loathing, all the sadness and loss, every bit of it spilled out.

She was embarrassed that she sobbed like a child. Not wanting the pain but afraid to live without it.

But he held her. He didn't let go.

And there wrapped in his arms, she felt the person she had become, the one who struggled, who didn't trust, who *couldn't* trust, that Fiona died.

What had kept her apart from the world melted. Vanished. Disappeared completely and leaving her whole . . . *born anew.*

"You came to heal me," she said, her words filled with wonder.

"Ah, Fee, you heal me," he whispered against her hair. "In the midst of all the lies, you are there to keep me sane."

Her tears dried. The sadness that had been so much a part of her life was now gone.

She listened to the steady, strong rhythm of his heart and knew it beat for her.

He looked down at her, his eyes lost in shadows. When he walked toward the bed, she made no protest.

Gently, he laid her on the mattress. His hand smoothed back her hair as one would a child's. From the moment she'd met him, her body had instinctively been drawn toward him. Now both her head and her heart said this man was like no other.

But he surprised her. "Sleep, Fee," he said quietly. "It will all be as it should." He started to straighten and she realized he was going to leave. "I shouldn't have come here," he started but she cut him off by grabbing the material of his shirt, curling her hands in it, and, rising up to her knees, holding him with a kiss.

This wasn't like the others they had shared. In this kiss she said all that she'd not yet found words for. She knew she loved him.

She knew he loved her, too.

His arms came around her. The kiss deepened. Their tongues met and if there was a way to drink each other's souls, they would have done it. She wasn't going to let him go. Not now. Not ever.

Perhaps there could never be anything lasting between them. He was a duke and she a seamstress. She'd never consent to be a man's paid companion. There was too much pride in her.

But there could be something pure, something outside the bonds of society, something just for the two of them.

This time, he didn't pull away. She felt the length and strength of his arousal. He wanted her.

Memories of her rape teased the edges of her mind, but love had made her strong. She didn't

want to be a victim of this fear any longer. She
wanted to be free of it. The moment to face all demons had come.

She tugged on his shirt, pulling it up and then
over his head. She tossed it aside.

His muscles were hard and well formed. This
man was not the soldiers who had attacked her.
Their skin had been pasty and their expressions
ugly. Their expressions had been ugly and mean.
They'd wanted to hurt her.

In contrast, Holburn's eyes were so filled with
care and concern, she felt humbled before him.

She gathered her night dress and lifted it up over
her head.

Holburn released his breath with a sigh of appreciation. "You're beautiful," he said. "Perfect."

It was the praise she needed to hear. He kissed
her lips, her nose, her cheeks, her hair. His arms
drew her to him. Her breasts flattened against his
chest and she reveled in the feeling of his skin
against hers.

They slowly sank down onto the feather mattress. He took a moment then to pull off his boots
and remove his breeches. His hands were clumsy.
She understood how he felt.

Her fear was that she'd feel revulsion at the sight
of his arousal.

She didn't.

He was beautiful. *Completely.*

The duke curved his body protectively around her. Fiona didn't know what to do next, but he did. She gave herself over to him as best as she could, focusing on the ceiling and reminding herself this was right, this was good.

His hands cupped her breasts. Her body responded to him as it always did. When he circled her bare nipple with his thumb, she gasped in pleasure. His lips against her neck curved into a smile.

"It's not so bad, is it?" he said.

Had he realized her fear? "No," she whispered.

"Now, you touch me."

His soft command caught her off guard. She didn't know what to do.

"You can't do anything wrong, Fee. Lovemaking is supposed to have a bit of bungling. Sometimes, that's when the best things happen."

Fiona heaved a big sigh. It would be so easy to stay curled up against him, but her body was beginning to want more. The next move, whether it was clumsy or proper or whatever, was up to her.

Tentatively, she rubbed her palm over his breast. She was surprised when his skin responded to her touch.

In fact, a glance told her that all of him responded to that gentle, cautious caress. Even his toes.

"Go on," he urged.

Fiona kissed his neck the way he'd kissed hers. He drew in his breath, his quiet laughter one of joy. She nibbled her way up to his ear, enjoying the texture of his whiskers, loving the masculine, night air smell of his skin.

With growing boldness, she ran her hand down his arm, along his ribs. He was solid, hard where she was soft and it was as it should be. Her hand traveled over the plane of his stomach. Here the muscles rippled beneath her fingertips as if he was tickled. She couldn't resist circling his belly button with her finger.

This time, he laughed aloud and caught her hand. "You minx," he whispered. "Now you know my weakness."

A sense of power as old as time gave Fiona courage. He was ticklish. The discovery took away her last trace of timidity.

She'd not thought hard about the mysteries between a man and a woman since her rape. In a general way, she'd understood what should be done. The rape had cruelly taught her realities—or so she had thought.

Now she realized there was more to the joining of a man and a woman. She'd not imagined humor could be part of it, or kindness and yet here it was.

She wondered what else she didn't know.

Deliberately, she ran her hand down the length of his erection and was surprised by its baby-smooth softness.

"You are a wicked one, Fee," Holburn said. He lay still, his eyes closed and a huge smile across his face.

"Am I, Your Grace?" she asked, the coyness coming from some secret feminine side of her she'd forgotten had once existed. She'd been the belle of the kirk, the reigning princess at the country dances.

"You are," he answered, his voice warm with desire as he reached for her hand and pressed it to him. She held him now, felt the power in him. He turned on his side to face her. "And my name is Nick. I want you to call me that, Fee. Let there be no titles between us. Not here. Never here."

"Nick," she murmured and he pressed his lips to her forehead while also showing her what he liked, and how he wanted to be touched.

Their lips found each other. They kissed deep and they kissed hard. His hand smoothed over her hip and down between her thighs . . . and then rising up so that he could caress and tease her as intimately as she did him.

Pure, keen feeling shot through her.

Fiona had not anticipated this. His clever fingers knew what drove her. She had to reach up and grasp his shoulders, overcome by what he was doing. He leaned her back on the bed, rising up over her, slipping his fingers inside her.

This was nothing like her rape. The attack had been brutal and mean. It had been designed to punish her for her brother's sins.

But Nick was teaching her that intimacy was to be yearned for, craved even. She didn't want this to ever stop.

Her breath was coming out in soft gasps and silly moues of delight. It was as if she couldn't keep her pleasure to herself. He kissed her neck, her cheek—and then he spread her legs, cradling his hips between them and opened her with one smooth thrust.

He filled her, holding himself so her body could adjust and accommodate his size. Fiona lifted her legs and wrapped them around him. He went deeper and she could have purred her contentment.

"You feel good, Fee. So good," he whispered in her ear.

"You feel good, too," she had to answer and he laughed. His laughter went through him even to where they were joined.

Then, Nick leveraged his body against hers, taking his weight in his arms. He began moving with a sure steady pace.

Fiona felt as if the secret of the universe was being handed to her. This was why men and women joined. *This* was what they wanted.

And *this* made life suddenly worthwhile.

She didn't know what she was doing. She responded on instinct, allowing him to set the pace. He encouraged her with soothing, loving words. She reveled in the feeling of his body surrounding hers. She curled her fingers in his hair, surprised herself by nipping his ear, and rejoiced in at last having all barriers removed between them.

Suddenly it all changed. One moment she moved in perfect harmony with him. In the next, it was as if she rode up a high, steep hill. She had to ride. She wanted to reach the pinnacle—and then she was there.

The sensation was so sharp, so poignantly incredible, she felt as if her very soul was being shattered.

Nick knew what was happening to her. He gathered her tighter in his arms, driving himself to the hilt inside her.

She needed him. She could not exist through this without him. She held him tight, needing him for ballast in a world that seemed to have exploded.

And once it did, a feeling of completeness, of peace in a guise she'd never imagined radiated throughout her being.

So this was the purpose to making love. This

was why ballads were sung, stories told, and poems written. She'd never felt so whole or close to another person in her life. It was truly as if they had melded into one.

Nick watched her, concern in his eyes. "You needn't worry," she said, reaching to push back his hair that had fallen over his brow. "That was the most incredible, most wonderful discovery of my life."

A fierce joy crossed his face.

"Is it always like that?" she dared to ask.

"Yes," he said. "And over time, it can grow even better."

Fiona widened her eyes at such a statement. Right now, she was so languid with bliss she didn't believe she'd ever be able to move again. Certainly she didn't want to leave this bed.

"Stay with me," he urged her. "I'm going to join you."

She smiled and hugged him with her legs as he drove deeper—and then he released his seed deep within her. She could feel the force of it. Hot, vital, alive. This was what was meant when a man and woman became one.

At last, the world made sense.

Her purpose in this life was to be with this man. Every step she'd taken, every incident, setback, twist of fate . . . had all been leading her here. No wonder she'd fallen into his arms when they met at the Swan. She had unknowingly been searching for him.

He collapsed with a deep, satisfied sigh.

Fiona smiled. She liked the weight of him upon her. She stroked his hair, enjoying its silky feel. "Mine," she murmured.

He lifted his head, propping it up with one hand to give her a lazy smile in return. "Yours," he answered.

"Thank you."

Nick shook his head. "No, thank you. That was special, Fee. It's never been like that for me. Ever. You and I were meant for each other."

Her heart gave a leap. "As if it was destiny," she said.

"It was," he eagerly agreed. "And this coupling . . . Fee, it has never been this way with anyone. There is magic between us. Power."

She laughed. A part of her thought he talked nonsense. Another part wanted to believe.

He sensed her doubt. "I make no joke. You are mine. You were meant to be mine." He reached for the bedcovers and threw them over their nakedness. Their legs were entwined; their bodies still fitted together. "I'm not letting go of you."

Fiona snuggled close, relishing his heat. She rubbed her nose against his chest. "Good, because I could spend the rest of my life right here."

"I wouldn't complain," he said.

She lay content for a moment, but then her earlier concern intruded. "Have you forgiven the Spaniard?"

He went still. "Why do you ask?"

"Because I think you wanted to."

Nick carried her hand to his lips and kissed the back of her fingers. "Don't worry about him," he ordered quietly.

She raised her head. "I think there is something I must tell you."

"What?" he asked, his voice cautious, and she knew she had to tell him.

The story of her parents' deaths—her father for defying the king's soldiers, her mother of a broken heart—poured out of her. She told him about Gordon and losing touch with her brother.

She told him of the day the soldiers took her away. She held nothing back.

He listened, his expression changing from concern to outrage. An angry muscle tightened in his jaw. She placed her hand upon it. "Please, don't be this way."

"What way, Fee? I'm furious over what they did to you."

"It was war, Nick. My brother was a rebel. They didn't do it to me but to him."

He came up to sit with his back against the headboard. "How can you forgive them?"

"Because you've taught me that it is more important to love," she said. "I no longer care about what they did . . . but you must know because someday, my path will cross with one of them. Or someone will know my story." She placed her palm against his chest. "I love you, Nick. I will always love you. But you must know, I'm not worthy of you."

"Fee, what happened was not your fault. Don't you understand that? I would never blame you for what was done."

"I still bear the shame."

He turned her around to face him. "You have no shame. You are strong and resilient. You are a survivor, Fee, and you should be proud of that. As to wagging tongues, let me be your guardian. They'll not say a word when you stand beside me."

She pressed her fingers over his lips. "Don't speak that way. You are the most generous, noble man I have ever met. And I believe you are right. Destiny brought us together and I shall always be thankful of these moments. But I must protect you from yourself."

Nick took her hand, lacing her fingers with his own. "Do you trust me?"

"With my life," she assured him.

"Then stop thinking, Fee. Live for right now and right here. The future will take care of itself."

She knew he said that because he didn't understand how quickly life could change . . . but that was fine. She wanted to live in *this* moment. She never wanted dawn to come. Then, in the light of day, he'd realize she was right. He'd know he could do far better than herself.

In fact, she would be doing him a service by making the decision for them and leaving on the morrow. To stay longer would lead to sharper heartbreak. She'd write to him, let him know where she was, and pray that there would be a place for her in his life, albeit a small unimportant one.

Nick shook his head. "You are thinking too much again. How shall I persuade you to stop?" He took her by both arms. "Fee, together, we can face anything."

"I want to believe that—"

"Then *believe*," he said, cutting off her protest.

He really thought it would be so simple. Fiona knew differently. She'd lived in London's streets, waited on the *ton*. She'd heard them in unguarded moments—and then she realized, it didn't matter.

But right now, all she wanted to do was celebrate being in love.

Fiona reached up and kissed him. Laughing, he

fell back on the bed, bringing her with him in a tangle of arms and legs and kisses and hugs that grew more intent in purpose with each passing moment.

This time, she knew what to expect.

This time, making love to him was better than the last.

Fiona's first thought when she woke the next morning was, now, I am his mistress.

She had crossed the line. Willingly.

Her heart and her body belonged to Dominic Lynsted and she felt no remorse . . . or told herself she didn't until she reached across the mattress for him and realized he wasn't there.

He'd left her already.

Once again, she was alone. Panic threatened to choke her.

She clutched her pillow, forcing herself to be calm, and focused on Nick's promises. He'd asked her to trust him . . . and she would. *She must.* She'd already gone too far to turn back now.

Her months as a seamstress had taught her a bit about the life of a mistress. Or at least the luxuries of being one. The wife was the one who had to make an accounting for every item of clothing and every household expense no matter how insignificant. The mistress bought what she wished. She answered to no one, sometimes not even to her patron.

Like Grace, the women who became mistresses knew how to live by their wits and make the most of their charms. They also understood how to move on to another protector when the current man in their lives lost interest.

Fiona frowned at the ceiling. She didn't know if she could survive if Nick turned away from her—

She immediately rejected the direction of her thoughts. She *would* survive. Loss had become a part of her life and she'd already survived much worse. Last night, she'd felt fully alive. She'd not allow her fears to rob her of this joy.

There was a scratching at the door. Tad wanted to be let in.

Fiona sat up and then froze, realizing that over the past night she'd exercised muscles she hadn't even known existed. Pushing her tangle of hair back from her face, she ignored those sore muscles and found her night dress. She slipped into it before going over to the door to let Tad in.

A cold draft across the floor made her bare toes curl in the carpet. The level of the light leaking into the room from behind the closed curtains made her realize the day was later than when she usually woke and she wondered what had happened to

Sarah. Fiona was growing spoiled. She liked having the maid stoke the fire before she rose and the dozens of other things Sarah did for her.

Once Fiona opened the door, the big wolfhound happily padded into her room, stopped, and sniffed the air. Fiona crossed her arms, knowing Tad sensed Holburn had been here—but then the dog did the silliest thing. He turned his head, looked right at Fiona and gave her a big wolfish grin of approval.

"So you like it here?" Fiona said to him softly.

Tad walked over to her and nudged her hand with his nose.

She stooped down and put her arms around him. "I believe Holburn will let you stay here although I won't be able to." As his mistress, she would be an outsider. She would live somewhere else while he divided his time between his real life and herself.

Fiona pressed her face against Tad's fur, hugging him tightly. She'd grown to like Gillian and Aunt Agatha and all the others. She didn't want to think of how their opinions would change once they learned of her and Holburn. Or had they suspected it would? His fib about her being his ward was complete nonsense.

A knock on the door warned her it was about to open. Sarah entered the room. "There you are, miss,"

Sarah's sunny voice said. "It's almost luncheon, so I didn't know if I should bother with a tray of hot chocolate or not and then decided to prepare it anyway."

Fiona held her breath as the maid carried the tray to the desk by the window. Could she tell that Holburn had been here? If Sarah did, she gave no sign.

"His Grace told me to let you sleep," Sarah said as she opened the draperies. "It's cold and damp outside. A good morning for a snooze."

"That was kind of him to let me sleep," Fiona said, standing.

"Would you like to bathe this morning?" Sarah asked, her expression betraying nothing but her usually good humor.

"Yes, that would be nice."

"Very well. I shall make preparations."

Fiona held her breath until the maid left and then almost collapsed where she stood. Tad watched her with interest.

"I don't know if I can be sophisticated about all this," she told him. "There's no way she couldn't have known. The servants gossip. Holburn's valet had to know he didn't sleep in his bed last night."

Tad poked his nose at her hand for another pet as if telling her to stop worrying.

An hour and half later, Fiona was bathed,

dressed, and had enjoyed a stimulating cup of chocolate before she went downstairs to face everyone. A footman met her at the bottom of the stairs to inform her the family had already gathered in the dining room for the mid day meal.

That was unusual. Breakfast and luncheon were informal events with food being put out on the sideboard and the family members eating when they wished. Then around half past six, they would gather for the formal evening meal.

Fiona didn't know why the routine would be upset. She couldn't remember Gillian or anyone else telling her about this change.

Realizing she was likely the last one to join the table, she hurried down the hall toward the sounds of conversation and laughter.

They had not yet started eating and today, the children were included. Fiona glanced around the busy room full of Nick's relatives and waited for Williams the footman to pull a chair out for her. All in all, there were some fifteen people gathered for this holiday season. Nick stood at the head of the table, pouring glasses of wine, which he proudly distributed.

The room went quiet as everyone realized she stood in the doorway. Their expressions looked expectant as if they had all been waiting for her.

A huge welcoming smile crossed Nick's face.

For a second, Fiona forgot where she was or that they had an audience. A woman could drown in a smile like that, especially when it was just for her. He held out a hand and all her reservations fled her mind.

"Fee, at last you join us. Your maid said you would not be long. Come and sit by me," he ordered. He turned his attention back to the glasses that Larson and a maid helped distribute. "Does everyone have one?"

"I don't," said six-year-old Davey, one of Holburn's many cousins, and the adults all laughed.

"Raise your mug of milk," Aunt Agatha instructed.

The duchess was at the other end of the table from her son. Colonel Swanson, her "cavalier," as Gillian called him, was seated beside her. A frown formed on the duchess's face as Fiona walked to stand beside her son. "What is this about, Dominic? Why have you ordered us all here and interrupted our other plans?"

"I have an announcement to make." Nick drew Fiona closer to his side. "But first, let me ask one question."

Puzzled eyebrows raised with interest and necks craned for a better look. Fiona didn't know what to expect. Certainly he wasn't going to announce that she was his mistress.

Dominic took her hands in his. With everyone in the room as witnesses, he said, "Fiona Lachlan, would you honor me with your hand in marriage?"

He'd proposed marriage to her.

Her fondest wish was being granted to her. Holburn didn't want her for a mistress. He wanted her for a wife.

But as she opened her mouth to shout a glad *yes* at the top of her lungs, his mother stood and said, "*No.* No, no, no, no, *no.*"

Chapter Fifteen

*E*veryone in the room, even the servants, turned with stunned surprise at the dowager's outburst.

But her attention was on Nick. "You shall not marry *that* woman. You don't *need* to marry."

"I will marry her." He spoke to his mother but he meant the words for Fee, who had gone deathly pale. He knew his love's character well enough by now to understand that his mother's words had hit their target. Fee silently agreed with his mother. She did believe herself unworthy. That was the reason he'd gathered everyone. He wanted Fee to know how proud he was to ask her to be his wife.

Why, he wouldn't be surprised if Fee had assumed he had thought to make her his mistress instead of offering marriage. Always self-effacing, always attempting to do what was right—that was his Fee.

And his mother's rudeness went beyond all bounds.

He'd understood her reasons for putting on airs. He witnessed the petty slights his uncles and others like them had delivered to his mother over the years. And yet, she'd never learned the gift of grace. She was as bullish as his uncles and he'd spent a lifetime appeasing both parties—but not any longer.

Beware innocence.

The Oracle's words whispered in his head as his mother announced in ringing tones, "She is not good enough for you."

"On the contrary, Mother, I pray I will be good enough for her." He turned to Fiona. She was shaking. He could feel it in her hands but she still held her head high and didn't disgrace herself by returning his mother's comments in kind.

He spoke from his heart. "Your courage has won me, my lady. I am humbled by your sense of honor, your beauty, and your grace. I'd dare not offer anything to you less than my best. Fee, I'm not a perfect man. I've blundered and made a fool of myself a thousand times. I'm also managing to make a ham-handed mess of this proposal. But I know one thing to be true, I *need* you in my life. I *want* you by my side. Please say you will be my duchess, and I'll do all I can to be worthy of you."

His throat had tightened as he spoke and there was a suspicious burning in his eyes.

Dead silence met his words. Fee had listened to him with somber eyes. She was so lovely, so precious to him, he didn't know what he'd do if she refused him.

Nick wasn't the only one anxious for her response. His mother radiated tension and everyone around the table seemed to have a stake in her answer. Even the children appeared involved.

Fee lowered her head as if unable to look at him. "I'm humbled by your offer, Your Grace—"

His heart fell. She was going to refuse him.

"—I could never find another man for whom I have so much affection and so much respect. Yes, I will marry you, Dominic Lynsted. I will be your wife."

Nick wasn't certain he'd heard correctly. "Did you say yes?"

"Of course she did," his mother declared. "Who wouldn't want to be a duchess?"

But Nick and Fee ignored her. Fee smiled at

him. "Yes, I said yes. Yes, yes, *yes*." This last over-
rode his mother's "no's."

Nick wrapped his arms around her and kissed
her with all the happiness that now filled his soul.
He'd never imagined such complete and utter joy
existed. He didn't deserve an angel like Fee, and
now he would be her husband. He would be
bound to her for all eternity.

His mother carried on like an angry hen at her
end of the table but his blessed relatives gave out
a cheer and drowned her out—until she threw
her wine glass on the floor.

The room went silent. Nick braced himself for
one of her tantrums. She usually wasn't public
with them . . . but he was never certain when her
anger would spill over.

Addressing everyone at the table, his mother
said, "Very well. I see how it is. You all side against
me. Colonel Swanson warned me but I told him
he was wrong." Her nose was turning red, her
eyes pinched into angry slits. "I should have listened to him. Come, Colonel, I am no longer hungry. As for the rest of you, I shall leave you all to
your happiness." She said this last word as if it
were a disease. "I hope you roast in it."

Turning on her heel, she left the dining room.
Colonel Swanson quickly fell into step behind her.

Nick wondered if the colonel had ever witnessed

one of his mother's tantrums. Or perhaps he didn't care? A good number of men would put up with anything if they smelled money.

However, the second his mother was gone, glasses were raised and toasts made. It was as if she hadn't even spoken, and Nick forced himself to relax.

There followed several suggestions concerning the wedding. It was decided unanimously that Nick and Fee should marry in three days' time on Christmas Day, right here at Huntleigh.

Nick listened to Gillian, Aunt Agatha, and the other women start to make plans. He'd leave it all up to them. Whatever Fee wanted. For his part, he would send a man immediately to secure a special marriage license. This would allow him to marry without waiting several weeks for the posting of the banns.

Every time he looked at Fee, he couldn't believe his good fortune. He held her hand, even through dinner, receiving teasing from all his cousins, but he couldn't help himself. For the first time in his life, Nick was genuinely happy.

Later, after an overlong meal that left everyone sated with food and drink, Nick and Fee went out for fresh air and an afternoon ride. Tad accompanied them, diving in and out of the hedgerows, scaring up birds.

The grooms had all heard of the marriage proposal when his mother had ordered up her coach. They lined up to wish them well. Nick thanked them, and said he'd be sending down two kegs this Christmas along with the staff's dinner to be certain everyone was extra merry in honor of the wedding.

Fee smiled but didn't make a comment. In fact, she seemed a bit withdrawn.

He waited until they were away from the house to say, "You mustn't let Mother's nonsense bother you."

She was silent a moment and then said carefully, "How could I not? I don't wish to be the source of strain between you."

He almost laughed at that thought. "You aren't. There are many strains between my mother and myself."

She lifted an eyebrow in doubt and he knew he had to explain. He let out his breath slowly before saying, "Mother is difficult. I don't want to hide the fact from you, Fee. You know she was a former dancer and I know she was made to feel inferior for it. Of course, that should mean she would be more compassionate toward you. After all, you have the lineage to be a duchess. But that isn't the sort of person she is. She's wears the title like a sign around her neck. But she isn't alone. There are many of us like that. I take pride in being a duke, although I haven't always been wise to my responsibilities."

"I understand wanting to hold on to what is yours," Fee had the good grace to admit.

"It's a bit more than that," Nick emphasized "She's overly concerned about money. She always gambled but lately, she has been over the top in her losses. Several months ago, she attempted to arrange a marriage for me in return for a commission. Fortunately, I discovered her scheme and stopped it. I can't decide if this Colonel Swanson is good for her or bad."

"Is he greedy?"

"I hardly know him, but yes, he strikes me as the greedy type. But then so is Mother. Wouldn't like attract like?" He shook his head in answer to his own question. "That was silly for me to say. Look at us. I'm a failure in so many ways and you are strong and resilient."

"I don't see you as a failure," Fee said. "Nor do any of those people back at Huntleigh, including the servants. Nick, you aren't perfect, but neither am I. What is important is that you always try to do what is best. I've never seen you do anything less than that."

They rode over the wooden bridge leading to the

knoll. Nick listened to the horses' steps before saying, "Remember the Oracle of Delphi's curse?"

She discounted his concerns. "Do you mean the 'beware innocence' prediction? Nick, have you ever stopped to consider that such a warning is too open to be of value?"

But he refused to be mollified. "I did at one time. I ignored it completely until evidence proved to the contrary."

Fee shook her head in disbelief. "You are not the first gambler to be superstitious. Any other would welcome such good fortune."

"I haven't considered it a blessing. It seems a man should be able to determine his own fate."

She reined her horse to a stop. "Perhaps you are carrying this too far?"

"I wish I was. I was not joking when I said I've tested the Oracle in many different ways. I only win at cards. If I invest in a ship, buy shares in a company, or any number of other endeavors, I lose all I put into it."

She cocked her head in doubt, looking so beautiful in the wintry afternoon light, and said in her practical Scottish manner, "Perhaps you are just not good at choosing your investments. Or have partners who aren't wise."

Fee made it sound so logical.

"What if I have to understand the curse in order to finally be free of it?"

"I don't want you to tempt fate, my love," she said, "but I also wouldn't base my future on superstition. That would naïve." She smiled, the expression brighter to his spirits than the sun, and changed the subject. "Race you to the top of the knoll."

Before he could answer, she was off. He hesitated, praying she was right and no harm would come to her because of him.

Of course, she was right. He could spend a lifetime in worry and doubt, or seize this moment and the love she offered.

The Oracle could be damned.

Nick heeled the horse and went after her. He caught up with her and won their race. Her forfeit was a kiss . . . and then another one.

He marveled at how she could change his mood with her solid advice and clear thinking.

Evening came early this time of year and it was past dusk when they finished their ride. As they walked arm-in-arm up the path from the stables, Fee pulled up short. She looked up at the house.

"So, what happens now with your mother?" she

asked. "I dislike thinking of her alone in London."

"She'll pout for a while, spend money, and then be fine," he said. "Let us not forget she has her friend Colonel Swanson to keep her company." He turned her around to face him. "Fee, Mother may accept you or, and I abhor saying this, she may continue her tiff. She's capable of it. Much will depend on Colonel Swanson."

"Why is that?"

"She's had few male friends over the years and she seems particularly attached to this one. Either way, I don't care. Let her stew in her own vinegar until she comes to her senses. I will not have her show disrespect to my wife. I've taken very good care of her over the years, including changing my will to see to her beyond this life. Don't search for logic in her behavior. Sometimes she doesn't have any. I'm her son so I can say Daisy Lynsted is selfish. It's as simple as that and I'm not being cruel. Occasionally she will show a maternal instinct but not often. And when she does, I'm usually suspicious."

Of course Fee saw right through him. "I think there is a part of you that wants to please her."

"I *can't* please her. At best I placate her, but my patience is wearing thin. But if she wants me to choose between the two of you, I choose you. I'm in love, Fee. And the wonder of it is, you love me in return."

The family had always treated Fiona with kindness and respect, but this evening she had a sense of belonging she'd not felt anywhere else, including back in Scotland.

Aunt Agatha ordered her over to sit by her and listen to the children perform. Nick was on the far side of the room, enjoying himself with Gillian and one of their cousins, Carter Lowrie, son of the earl of Netherfeld, who had only arrived that afternoon. His parents would join them on the morrow. Carter had brought a friend with him, a Captain Jack Moffat who seemed to have his eye on Gillian.

That night, Nick walked Fiona to her room and left her there with a chaste kiss on the cheek.

For a second, Fiona was confused. "Your Grace," she said. He turned to her, no more than six feet between them. "Is all good between us?"

He came back to her, his smile reassuring. "Shortly, you shall be my wife. I can wait, Fee. The anticipation will make it all the better."

Fiona thanked him for his thoughtfulness with a searing kiss.

"Thank you," she whispered, and slipped inside her room where she slept very well indeed, surrounded by the realization that this man cared for what she thought and what she felt more than his own needs.

The next day was an exciting one for the residents of Huntleigh. Snow lightly covered the ground. Nick, the other young men, and the children set off in search of their Yule log.

When they returned, the women were called upon to judge a sliding contest. A puddle had turned to ice on the front drive. The test was to see which team, the men or the children, could have the most "slides" before someone fell.

The children won.

A private messenger arrived just as the women were herding everyone back into the house with the promise of something warm to drink. Gillian had been clever enough to think of wassail and the servants had set it up along with bread, cheese, and meats for those who had enjoyed the snow.

Nick met the messenger instead of letting him hand the letter to a servant; however, he had a few words with the man.

Fiona wished she could hear what was being said between the two of them. Nor was she the only one curious. Once the messenger had left, Carter was the one who asked, "What is that?" He nodded to the letter.

"For Gillian," Nick answered curtly. When he

went inside, he placed the letter on the hallway table.

Later, when Fiona was going upstairs to her room, she found Gillian in the hall reading the note. Her friend didn't appear pleased.

"Is everything all right?" Fiona asked.

Gillian looked up with a start and then ripped the letter into fourths, which she tucked in her pocket. "Yes, it is fine. That was from my husband, Wright. He's ordering me to return home. He sends the letter once a week and I ignore it. Where are you going?" she asked, changing the subject, and Fiona let her curiosity go. She liked Gillian too much to pry.

Later, before dinner, the children painted the Yule log and added bits of string and lace. Gillian had made one of her holly bundles as a finishing touch. The men shared a pint, pouring a bit of it on the log as a blessing.

It had been a day full of fun and family. Fiona couldn't remember when she had laughed so hard or enjoyed herself so much. That night, when Nick walked her to her room, he suggested an early morning ride.

"There will be more relatives coming in," he assured her.

Fiona tried not to think of all the people she was meeting. She was growing nervous about the wedding. Everyone in the family was kind and generous but she was not looking forward to having all eyes on her. A ride was an excellent suggestion to break the tension.

The next morning, they met at the back door at half past eight. Other than the servants, the house was quiet. Even Tad seemed to prefer a spot before the hearth in the sitting room to going out of doors. It was a reluctant dog who joined them.

Nick and Fiona took their ride in their usual direction. The horses that had been saddled for them were young and had tremendous energy. The ground was just the right hardness to make riding easy.

Fiona was pleased her seat was returning. She sailed over several walls and hedgerows, keeping up every stride of the way with Nick.

They had reached the knoll and were starting to trot back when they heard someone shout, "*Holburn.*" Both of them turned at once.

A rider was coming toward them yelling at them to run. It was the Spaniard.

At the same moment that Fiona recognized who the rider was, a shot rang out.

A heart beat later, Nick's body jerked on his horse and she knew he'd been hit.

Chapter Sixteen

*N*ick felt the bullet go through his arm and out again. If it hadn't been for Andres's shout, he wouldn't have turned at the last moment, and the ball could have proven fatal.

Instead, it made him angry.

He looked over across the hillside in the direction where the shot had been fired and saw movement behind a huge boulder. The shooter knew he had missed his mark and now scrambled to make an escape. Nick couldn't identify him because of the hat pulled over his face.

But if the bastard thought he was going to put a bullet in Nick and run, he was wrong.

"Stay here," Nick said to Fee. He kicked his horse

up the hill, hoping to gain on the man before he hit a knot of trees and shrubs that would make chase by horse impossible. The man probably had a horse waiting for him somewhere around there.

Andres came riding up beside him . . . as did Fee. *So much for obedience,* Nick thought wryly and focused his attention on capturing his shooter.

In the end, with the three of them giving chase, the man didn't stand a chance.

Nick pushed his horse to cut off the man's escape route, forcing him to surrender. Andres slid off his horse and pulled the hat off the man's head to reveal Colonel Swanson.

For a moment, Nick felt as if someone had punched him in the gut. He didn't want to believe what the implications of the man's presence meant.

Andres had no such problem. "So, you could not afford more Irish men?" he charged.

The colonel's back went ramrod straight as he glared at the Spaniard with disdain. Andres didn't care. He looked to Nick. "This is the man who has been trying to kill you. I followed your uncles to London like you asked but decided they are not the killers. They had no visitors and when I asked questions, none of the servants had seen or heard of any Irishmen."

"You asked the barón to follow your uncles?" Fee said, sounding confused.

"I did," Nick answered. "I rode out after him that day and asked for the favor."

"But I thought you were angry with him?" Fee said.

"It was a trick," Nick answered. "I wanted people to think I had washed my hands of Andres. I didn't know who it would flush out, but, of course, I suspected my uncles. It was imperative I link them to the Irishmen. Only then would I know we were safe."

"But *when* did you talk to the barón?" Fee wanted to know.

"After Mother arrived, later in the afternoon, I went for a ride. I had wanted Ramigio taken to the village inn just so I could talk to him."

She nodded, now understanding.

Nick turned to the Spaniard. "When did you suspect Swanson?" he wanted to know.

"Now for my story," the Spaniard said, taking over the center of attention. "I follow your uncles and decide they are not the ones who want to shoot you. So I ask myself, who would do such a thing? I have no answer."

"Then how did you know that Swanson was here?" Nick asked.

"I did not," Andres answered. "I came back to report to you. The grooms at the stable told me you were out riding and I thought you would prefer a report in private, so I followed. I arrived in time to catch sight of this man positioning his rifle. It was luck, Holburn. *Suerte.*"

"If you hadn't called out when you did," Fee said, "that bullet would have killed the duke."

Andres lowered his eyes with false modesty. He knew he'd repaid his debt of honor to Nick and was going to bask in it. He might even believe the scales between them had tipped in his favor, and they had.

Nick took charge. "Fee, I think it best you return to the house. Andres and I will take the good colonel to the village."

"I am going with you," Fee answered. "I want to hear his story and I'm also a witness," she reminded him. "The magistrate will want to see me. I am not going to sit home and wait while the two of you have the excitement."

Her stout refusal made him smile until she gave a soft cry of alarm. "You are bleeding."

Nick looked down and saw the wet spread of blood on the sleeve of his black riding coat. He'd been so furious with Swanson, he'd not thought about his wound. "It's nothing," he assured her. "I barely feel it."

"Let me see," she said and ordered him to dismount so she could do a bit of doctoring.

"You don't want to take me to the magistrate,

Your Grace," Colonel Swanson said, breaking his silence at last. "You will not be happy with what might follow."

Nick knew exactly what he threatened. A great weight came down on his shoulders. "You hired the Irishmen, didn't you? This isn't your first attempt on my life."

Colonel Swanson stared off into the distance, his lips pressed tight. He didn't need to answer. Nick knew in his soul this was true. He also knew someone had helped him with the plot, a person who had intimate knowledge of Nick's life.

Beware innocence.

His poor, silly, greedy mother.

Fee understood, too. Her hands that were busy tying a torn portion of her petticoat into a make-shift bandage paused momentarily. She didn't look up at him but the connection between them was so powerful, he knew what she was thinking. She continued what she was doing, and for that he silently thanked her.

Knotting the bandage, she said, "There, you are ready to go. Be careful. It looks clean but one never knows."

"*Una mujer maravillosa*," Andres said. "She doesn't flinch at a gunshot wound. Not one sign of vapors."

"Scottish women are made of stern stuff, barón," she answered.

"*Si*," he agreed. "If I was the colonel, I would be quaking in my boots."

The colonel shot him a look of irritation and Andres laughed, taking the reins of Fee's horse and ordering the colonel to mount up. For a second, the colonel appeared ready to defy the order, but then Andres produced a small pistol from his riding jacket. It added merit to his command. The colonel mounted.

Nick climbed onto his horse. His arm didn't bother him. It might tomorrow but today he was fine and heartily glad of it. He took Fee's hand and lifted her into the saddle in front of him.

"Should we let someone at the house know where we are going?" she asked.

"I'll send a messenger from the Black Bird," Nick answered. The Black Bird was the village inn. The magistrate, Sir Clarence, was usually in its public room.

They set off at a brisk pace and reached the village in less than an hour. Two local lads came running up to walk their horses. Nick gave each a half guinea and then escorted the colonel into the inn, which was doing a brisk business with the holiday almost upon them.

Mr. Jones, the innkeeper, came hurrying up to greet them. "Your Grace, what an honor!" he said bowing deeply. "And it is good to see you again,

Colonel. I'm glad you returned. May I offer Your Grace a table?"

Apparently, Colonel Swanson had not traveled far when he'd left Huntleigh.

Nick saw Sir Clarence standing by the end of the bar. He was having a pint with some friends. Nick could call him over, but decided the wisest course was to first know exactly how far the culpability went.

He smiled at Innkeeper Jones. "Yes, we'd like a table. And will you ask my mother to join us?" He watched Colonel Swanson as he said this. The man didn't flinch.

Perhaps Nick was wrong . . . except Mr. Jones said, "Certainly. I will have one of my daughters go up to her room with a message."

The color drained from the colonel's face. He had apparently not been expecting Nick's mother to be there. The whole story was made clear fifteen minutes later when his mother came down to join them at their table.

She had not anticipated seeing the colonel between Andres and Nick. Her step faltered. She forced herself to go forward but a wariness appeared in her eyes. Apparently she was willing to brazen it out.

The men rose as she approached. "How good to

see you, Dominic," she said, offering her cheek to him for a kiss.

He didn't move. Fee had not stood. Nick could tell by the anger in her brown eyes that she had pieced together the story.

Realizing her son wasn't going to give her any sort of welcoming sign, his mother took her seat. "What brings you to the village?" Before Nick could answer, she caught the attention of a passing serving girl. "A sherry."

The girl hurried away.

The colonel's jaw had gone tight with anger. Nick wondered why. "I thought you had returned to London, Mother," he said.

"I am but I decided to linger a day here." She hadn't yet met Swanson's eye. She knew he was angry. Now she let her lashes sweep low before shyly raising them and saying to Nick, "I know I was rude at the house. The announcement of your marriage was so abrupt. You can forgive a mother for being momentarily confused by such a sudden decision on your part, can't you?"

"I can forgive many things," Nick said. "What I can't understand is why a mother would plot to murder her only child?"

His mother's eyes rolled in shock. "Murder?" she said as if horrified at the thought. "Where do you collect such ideas?" she demanded. "Or is this Swanson's idea? Harry, what have you been doing?"

She'd never been a convincing actress.

The colonel didn't think so either. "Give it up, Daisy. I told you to return to London. I was trying to protect you. You chose not to listen to me. The fact that you are here tells him all he needs to know."

"I didn't want to return without knowing you were safe," she said to her lover. "I couldn't leave without you."

The colonel leaned back in his chair, his frustration clear.

"I know how you feel," Nick commiserated with him. "My mother always does as she pleases. However, *you* are the one that chose *her*."

"Perhaps I haven't," Swanson muttered. "And perhaps you wouldn't like what I have to say, Your Grace, especially with the magistrate close at hand. Your mother has been a foolish woman, but it is your family name that will be on everyone's lips."

Before Nick could reach across the table and choke the life out of the man, the serving girl returned with the sherry. While everyone waited until the girl was gone, his mother reached for the glass and all but drained it.

She spoke first. "It wasn't all my idea, Dominic. Harry persuaded me."

The colonel snorted his disbelief. "She came to me with the idea. I was to be paid well."

"You mean you aren't my mother's escort?" Nick asked, uncertain.

"Ours was a business relationship, Your Grace," the colonel answered.

Across the table, both Fee and Andres's mouths had dropped open. Nick sat back, shocked himself. He looked to his mother. In a low voice that could not be overheard, he asked, "Why, Mother? I've always taken care of you."

She pushed her empty sherry glass a few inches across the table. Her lower lip quivered. "You wouldn't cover my losses. You refused." She played with the stem of her glass, not meeting his eye.

"What would you gain from my death?" Nick wondered.

"The money you put in trust for me. I would have that," she answered. "I was very angry, Dominic. Very angry," she said, as if that justified her actions. "I haven't been so angry since your father was alive. He was always telling me I couldn't do what I wanted to do. He became unfair about it."

"Would you have murdered him, too, Mother?" Nick asked.

Her smiled turned brittle. "He made me angry," she repeated and suddenly Nick realized she could have. He sat back, his mind reeling with the thought.

His mother threw her hands over her face and burst out into loud, noisy tears. "Now look at what you've done. You've made me think about something I don't wish to think about." She dropped her hands. "Where is Rocky? I need Rocky."

She started to pull away from the table. Nick reached for her wrist. She tried to yank it away from him and then realized people around the public room were staring. Her manner changed. She turned serene. "I threw the ink blotter at him. You know, the brass one that you have on your desk."

Nick still used it. The blotter was a good solid piece of metal.

"He refused to pay my debts," his mother said. "Told me we should both quit gambling. I threw the blotter at him in a fit of temper. It was very bad of me. It hit him right here." His mother indicated a point on her brow. "And he fell. His head hit his desk. I heard him grunt and then he was quiet."

She was playing with her sherry glass again. Glancing up at Nick as if she were a reluctant child, she said, "I was very good after that. Brandt paid my debts and I was good. But then, I wanted to play again. I won, Dominic. For a long time I won and then I just started losing."

Nick let go of her wrist. He sat back in his chair, stunned by the confession and realizing for the first time that his mother was not completely well.

"Do you still wish to call over the magistrate?" Colonel Swanson asked.

Nick could have murdered him to wipe the smirk off his face. Instead, Andres leaned across the table. "*Bastardo*, you'd best shut your mouth."

Beware innocence. His mother had stopped playing with the glass. She'd folded her hands on the table, as patient as a school child.

And then he realized he was a duke. Sir Clarence would listen to him. He could make a case that Colonel Swanson had taken advantage of his mother.

As for her . . . he'd give her living quarters and a staff, but she'd not be let close to anyone. For the rest of her life, he'd have her watched. Cared for, but watched. Sir Clarence could help him with those arrangements, too.

As to Colonel Swanson, Nick would recommend he be transported to a penal colony in New South Wales.

"Yes, Andres. Please ask the magistrate to join us," Nick said and had the pleasure of watching Colonel Swanson lose his swagger.

"Whatever happens to me will happen to your mother," the colonel threatened.

"I doubt that," Nick answered, and he was right. Sir Clarence was very amenable to Nick's ideas.

It was a somber threesome that left the inn. A light snow was beginning to fall. It made the air smell clean, but Nick didn't feel that way inside. He was relieved no one spoke on the way back to the house. He had no need of words right now.

At Huntleigh, the family knew nothing about what had transpired and Nick wasn't going to tell them. He had a new secret to keep now.

He introduced Andres as a close and valued friend. The handsome Spaniard was an immediate attraction to the young women of their company and served to deflect any notice of the hole in Nick's riding coat.

His duties done, Nick was anxious to escape to his rooms. He felt strangely detached from all the gaiety. However, before he could leave the hall and escape upstairs, he felt a tug on his coat.

Six-year-old Emma stood by his side, her eyes dancing with mischief and two front teeth missing from her smile. "Look where you are," she said.

"Where am I?" Nick forced himself to be pleasant.

"Under the mistletoe," Emma said, laughing. Her other cousins and siblings her age giggled around her. "Cousin Gillian put it up. She says we are now ready for Christmastide."

"Ah, good," Nick answered and would have excused himself but Emma wasn't done.

"You have to give Miss Lachlan a kiss," she prompted him.

Suddenly, Nick couldn't stand here and continue to pretend all was fine. It wasn't. It might never be again.

"I will," he managed to say to the girl. "Later." He then went upstairs, escaping to his rooms without further comment.

Once alone, he ordered Gannon to fetch a bottle of brandy. Upon his return with the bottle and a glass on a tray, Gannon said, "Lady Wright wondered if you would be joining them for dinner."

"Tell her no," Nick answered and poured himself a healthy draught. As he started to raise the glass to his lips, he said, "And you are done for the night, Gannon. I won't be needing you."

The valet bowed out, and finally, Nick was alone.

He drained the glass.

Fiona had a hard time following the conversations over dinner. Her mind and thoughts were with Nick . . .

His chair sat empty.

Occasionally, someone would ask her if he was feeling well. She didn't know what to answer. She was thankful for Andres's presence. The handsome Spaniard had no loss of words for dinner conversation.

Gillian sought her out after dinner. She hooked her arm in Fiona's as they walked into the sitting room. "I know you have much to think about for tomorrow, what with the plan to marry Christmas morning, but I wondered if you wished to help deliver the charity baskets. It might settle your nerves to keep busy."

At last, Fiona allowed the fear she had been holding inside to express itself. "I don't know if we are going to be married," she whispered. It felt so good to speak her fear out loud.

Pulling Fiona off to the side and away from everyone else, Gillian said, "Please, you must be strong."

"What if he is having second thoughts?" Fiona allowed herself to say. That Nick would go off on his own, that he would shut her out, hurt. "What if he has doubts about this marriage?"

"He's not that sort of man," Gillian said. "I don't know what happened today but I sense something did." She paused as if waiting for more information. Fiona studied the floor. She'd not betray Nick's confidence.

Gillian took Fiona's hand. "If Holburn wished to cry off, he'd do so."

"Things have happened between us very quickly," Fiona answered. "Perhaps too quickly."

"No, if ever there were two people who are well matched, it is the two of you. From the moment I first met you, I knew you were good for him. I've never seen him this happy—"

"He's *not* happy now," Fiona asserted.

"I don't believe it has anything to do with you," Gillian answered. "Holburn has spent his life alone. He's never understood that there are so many of us willing to help him. It's pride and perhaps being under Brandt and Maven's thumbs growing up. They are relentless. And certainly Duchess Daisy lacks interest in anyone other than herself."

If only Gillian knew.

"But there is something else brewing, too?" Gillian continued. "Perhaps you are a bit intimidated by the thought of being a duchess."

That was true, too. "I haven't the slightest clue what to do," Fiona confessed. Life had been so busy, she'd not had time to reflect on what it would all mean. She'd witnessed this afternoon the power behind the title. That Nick had been able to maneuver matters concerning the dowager and Colonel Swanson exactly to his liking was impressive, and daunting. "I haven't really stopped to consider what having the title means." *Other than that it would make her Nick's wife.*

"It's whatever you wish it to mean," Gillian assured her. "The cottagers will grow to admire you as much as those of us in the family do. So please say you will join us tomorrow?"

"Of course I will." How could she refuse?

Gillian smiled her pleasure. "And don't worry," she said, giving Fiona's hand a final squeeze. "Holburn is probably just tired."

Fiona nodded. Gillian started to excuse herself to have a word with Cook before retiring, but Fiona stopped her. "What of you?" she asked. "Why do you live under this roof instead of your husband's?"

The smile remained on Gillian's face, but her eyes grew guarded. "Or do you mean why do I offer advice when my own marriage is obviously not well?"

Heat rushed to Fiona's face. "I didn't mean to sound rude. I'm curious, that's all. In two days, I may marry and what do you know that I don't?"

"Wright isn't like Holburn," Gillian said. "And sometimes we make a mistake in the man we choose to love."

"I don't want to make that mistake," Fiona said.

"You haven't," Gillian assured her.

But Fiona wasn't so certain. She wanted to quiz

Gillian about Wright. She wanted to know why such a vibrant, intelligent, beautiful woman chose to live apart from the man she'd taken in marriage.

"Trust Holburn," Gillian counseled as if reading Fiona's mind. "I wanted to trust Wright." She turned away then, her frown warning Fiona that Gillian felt she'd already said too much.

People retired rather early this evening. The younger crowd of Carter and the cousins his age stayed up around the fire. Fiona headed toward her room. She lingered in the hall, watching Nick's door and wishing he'd come out and share with her what he was thinking.

She didn't like it when people withdrew. She'd always been one to confront problems. She'd learned shutting herself off from others never resolved anything.

Sarah helped her undress and Fiona knew she was tired. However, at midnight, she was still tossing and turning in her bed.

The scene between Nick and his mother disturbed her. A woman didn't arrange for the murder of her child. She couldn't imagine how Nick must feel, and hated that he had not looked to her for comfort.

In the middle of the night, Gillian's reassuring words held no meaning. Suddenly, the marriage that had seemed to be her fondest dream was filled with foreboding.

Fiona and Nick barely knew each other. What if the magic, the haze of love around them disappeared? Then what sort of man would she be married to?

In fact, the later the hour and the more she thought about his reaction to the day's events, the crankier she became. Her earlier understanding and patience made her feel foolish.

And what sort of man always turned to brandy to deal with the challenges in his life rather than the love she had to offer?

At last, she could take it no more. She rose from her bed, put a robe over her night dress, and headed out the hallway door. She was tired of guessing what he thought. The time had come to speak to him.

Chapter Seventeen

*N*ick sat in a leather upholstered chair by the fire. The brandy decanter on the table next to him was still half full. Drink wasn't an answer for what he was feeling.

Instead, he stared at the flames in the hearth. He wanted to remember every detail, every nuance of his father's death.

He'd always been suspicious. He'd noticed the change in his mother's behavior, but had lacked the courage to confront her. He could have gone to his uncles, who were his guardians . . . except that he'd lost one parent. He hadn't wanted to lose another.

It wasn't until he'd grown much older that he

truly noticed his mother's oddities—the stacks of possessions, the overwhelming insecurity—and he placed the blame for those on his uncles or her background.

Nor was any one thing that alarming. He could remember nothing that would have branded her the murderer of her own husband—

Nick caught himself. His father's death had been an accident. She could have thrown the blotter toward another portion of the anatomy and his father would be alive, and his own life would have been much different . . .

The door to his bedroom opened. He frowned. What the devil was the time? Gannon should have gone to his bed hours ago, or was it morning already?

A figure dressed in white slipped into his room. He recognized her immediately. *Fee.* She moved toward his bed.

"Nick?"

"I'm here," he said from the chair and she gave a little start as if he'd scared her.

"I wasn't expecting you to still be up," she said. "Not without a candle."

"I have the light from the hearth." He set aside his empty glass. She had her hair down around her shoulders. He liked it when she wore it loose and liked her dressed in white. She was the most beautiful woman he'd ever known . . . and he was so unworthy of her. "Why are you here?" he asked, the question sounding brusque because of the pent-up emotion in his throat.

Her Scottish stubbornness came out. "I came because I'm worried about you," she said. There was a beat of silence and then she added, "You don't seem pleased to see me. Have you had a change of heart?"

"Change of heart?" he wondered confused.

"About the marriage."

Nick was shocked at the direction of her thoughts. "I *haven't*. I *wouldn't*."

She came around to stand before him. "Then what has upset you?"

He didn't think he could tell her.

"Please," she said. "What I heard this afternoon filled me with revulsion. I can understand why you would feel betrayed. She's a terrible person."

"She's my mother. I don't think of her as terrible."

Fee didn't soften. "We can't help who births us." She knelt in front of him. "Her actions were wrong. But you were compassionate to both your mother and the colonel. However, I don't understand your behavior. Why are you closing yourself off from me?"

"Closing myself off?" He was puzzled. "What makes you believe that?"

"You weren't at dinner," she said.

"I did need to be alone. Fee, I'd just learned that my mother had a hand in my father's death. That everything I thought I knew about her was wrong."

"But that doesn't mean you shut me out . . . or does it?"

He was too startled to speak. He'd not realized that was what he had done. It took him a moment to consider the matter.

Unfortunately, she misunderstood his silence.

Fee turned away from him. "I don't know if we should marry." Her voice was tight with emotion. It tore at his heart. "I was raised to want to marry well. Being a duchess would have made my mother proud. But life has taught me to consider more than the superficial. Dominic Lynsted, I love you and that means that I don't just love your title, I love *you*, the man. You could be a footman or blacksmith or a tinker, and I'd still love you. You've won my heart with your kindness and your humor and your gentleness. I hadn't expected to find those traits in a man."

A tear escaped her eye. She wiped it away with the sleeve of her robe, the gesture defiant. "The other night, you set yourself up as my protector. You promised that nothing could harm me when I was with you. Well, it works the other way also. I'm here to keep you safe. Your battles are *my* battles. I stand beside you, Nick, but I can't if you won't confide in me."

She looked so damn beautiful, like some determined, avenging angel. The firelight had even caught the red in her hair and made it appear a halo.

"It's not you," he said. "My mother killed my father. I needed time to understand the matter. I don't know if what I arranged for her is justice. She's not right in the head. She can't be. And yet, there is a steely coldness about her. I don't seem to know anything any longer, Fee, except I can't lose you out of this, too."

The words just flowed out of him.

Fee sank back down to his feet as if her legs had gone out from underneath her. She took his hands and pressed a kiss in his palm. "As long as she can't harm you, I'm satisfied."

"I don't deserve you," he said.

She didn't miss a beat. "You don't when you pull away from me the way you did this evening. I refuse a marriage that is a sham. You are important to me, Nick—the breath of my soul. Don't ever treat me again the way you did tonight."

"I won't," he promised and her response was a smile so full of grace, he felt transformed.

"An hour earlier, life was very bleak. Now, it's worth living again."

Fee laughed. "That's what we do for each other—we make life worth living. Before you, I had never thought I'd feel whole again. You are my love. My rock. Never again will you be alone."

She understood him so clearly.

His answer was to kiss her. He lingered on the kiss, deepening it, letting it warm them both, and then lifting her into his lap.

She was so lovely. He undid the belt of her robe. She was naked beneath her night dress. "I should wait," he murmured. She had to know he wanted her. He was hard, harder than he'd ever been before.

Fee did know. She moved closer to the tightness in his breeches. "We could wait," she agreed. "But I don't think I can."

Her bald admission made him tilt back his head and laugh. Was there any sound more freeing than laughter?

"You are my life," he said. "You stumbled into it, changed it all around, and I'm blessed to have you in my arms."

"Well, now that you have me here," she said, her lilting Scot's accent more alluring than a siren's song, "don't you think you ought to do something with me?"

Nick had plenty of ideas for her and he was

happy to demonstrate what they were. He unbuttoned his breeches, and took her right there.

To his never-ending pleasure, Fee's lust matched his own.

When they'd finished and she was resting in his arms, he held her and counted his blessings—that all began and ended with his Fee. After that, he carried her to the bed and made good and proper love to her.

Fiona was surprised to wake the following morning in her bed. The doubts that had sent her to Nick had been given a good drubbing. All that was left was a certainty that she was meant to be with this man.

God had brought them together. Nick could believe in Fate but she knew differently, and couldn't wait for the ceremony Christmas Day to make their union official.

Sarah arrived with hot water for bathing, reminding Fiona that she had agreed to help with the charity baskets.

Within an hour, Fiona was downstairs having her breakfast. Nick was still in bed, which was good. His would be a healing sleep, the same sort of sleep she'd had after the night he'd exorcised her demons.

Most of the women in the family were up. They gathered in the kitchen and worked together packing the charity Christmas baskets. There was bacon and a ham in each along with a loaf of bread, a jar of jam, and some of Cook's meat pies.

After an early luncheon, the women divided into groups and set out making deliveries. The Reverend Mosley and his wife also helped.

Fiona liked the reverend. He had kind eyes and a hearty voice. He would be the one officiating at their wedding ceremony and she was pleased.

"Christmas is a popular time to wed," the reverend said. "Makes it easy for a man to remember his wedding day." He said the last with a wink and the women laughed.

It took most of the day to deliver the baskets. Fiona watched Gillian carefully, almost overwhelmed by the amount of organization it took for the whole project.

"You have me shaking with terror," she said to her friend. "I could never organize all of this as well as you do."

"Nonsense," Gillian said. "You will be a perfectly wonderful duchess."

By the time they returned to the house, the men had chopped the enormous Yule log. A section would be burned this evening and every evening over the next twelve days until the log was used up. The family tradition was that the cinders of the log would be distributed around the grounds as a protection from the devil.

"We've been doing it for hundreds of years," Nick assured her.

"And has it worked?" Fiona teased him.

"Yes," he said. "The devil is gone. But the Yule log had some help." He gave her hand a squeeze so that she knew he considered her the blessing.

No one else in the family understood, but they did.

He smiled.

She smiled.

He pulled her out into the hall, away from the others gathered around the Receiving Room hearth. "I had some unexpected news today," he confided.

Fiona's first thought was of his mother and the colonel. "Nothing has happened there, has it?"

"No, they are being well taken care of," he answered. "No, my news is good. A messenger came from my banker. It turns out that an investment I made several years ago in a Scottish lead mine has paid handsomely. Fee, my profit is a hundred times more than what I invested with more to be received in the future."

"The curse is broken," she said, happy for him.

"Or perhaps there wasn't ever a curse, as you

had suggested. Perhaps my superstitions had the better of me."

"What is past doesn't matter," she answered. "We will only look toward the future."

"Uh-oh," Emma's loud voice said. "Look at where you are standing. Your Grace and Miss Lachlan, you are under the mistletoe."

"The what?" Fiona asked and looked up in the direction the child pointed and realized she stood under a branch of mistletoe tied with one of Gillian's ribbons.

Before she could blink, Nick kissed her while the relatives hooted and clapped.

That night, Fee slept untroubled until Gillian woke her the next morning.

"I didn't know if you had a dress to wear," Gillian said.

Fiona said, "I was thinking of wearing the yellow muslin."

"I don't know how you will feel about this but I have my wedding dress," Gillian offered. "We are about the same size. It wasn't a lucky dress for me but perhaps it will be for you. Would you like to try it on?"

"Yes," Fiona said without hesitation. "I'm not superstitious."

Gillian went to the room to fetch her dress. "It's

perfect," Fiona said when she saw it. The dress was a snowy white muslin with pin tucks and rows of pearls across the bodice.

"I thought I could do some holly leaves for your hair," Gillian suggested.

Fiona laughed. "I adore your holly bouquets," she said.

"They will really stand out with your hair color," Gillian answered before saying, "And Aunt Agatha wants to know if you would like to borrow her red cape. It's warm and will go with my holly bouquets."

"I deeply appreciate her offer," Fiona said. She sat on the bed, feeling like the luckiest woman in the world. "I am so blessed to be marrying into such a generous family."

"No, we are the ones who are pleased," Gillian said. "For the longest time, Holburn was such a distant figure. When he was a boy, he was closer to all of us. Then, when his father died and he inherited the title, everything changed. His uncles were like a wall between him and the rest of the family."

"Do you not like the uncles?" Fiona asked.

Gillian shrugged. "They are who they are. I don't see them often. That whole side of the family is rather puritanical. While we always enjoyed our

Yule log, they'd frown at us as if we were druids."
She scrunched her nose. "Come to think of it, I'm
glad they aren't here. Now let's dress you."

The hours until half past ten when they had to
leave for the church flew by in a haste of primping
and laughter.

The marriage ceremony would take place after
the Christmas service. Nick would travel separately
to the church and sit several pews ahead. He was
not to look at his bride until after the service.

Of course, that didn't happen. Fiona could feel
his gaze on her the moment she walked proudly
into the church. The women of the Lynsted family
had gone to great lengths to see that she was a
true Christmas bride. Gillian had gone holly mad
and had even made a huge bouquet of holly for
Fiona to carry.

The church was small and intimate. A host of
servants and parish members who wished to witness the wedding filled the pews along with the
family, so the church was very crowded.

Reverend Mosley knew what people wanted.
His service was not unduly fast, but it did move at
a good clip. At last, he called Nick and Fiona to
the altar rail along with their witnesses Andres
and Gillian.

Fiona could not believe this was happening
to her. Nick looked amazingly handsome in a

midnight-blue velvet jacket, white breeches, and white figured waist coat. Her gloved hand trembled as she placed it in his.

There had been a time when she'd listened to the vows spoken at her friends' marriages and dreamed of the day it would be her turn to be the bride. At no time had those words taken on the meaning as they did this Christmas day when she was asked to promise herself to Dominic Lynsted, Duke of Holburn.

At one point when she was speaking, she sensed a movement at the window. A shadow seemed to move there, and she thought of her parents.

Tears filled her eyes . . . and from deep within, she experienced a feeling of peace.

They were happy for her.

And then it was his turn to make his vows. He spoke with quiet assurance and when the time came to offer a ring, she was surprised when he placed a heavy gold band on her finger. He sealed his actions by lifting her hand to his lips and kissing the band.

At last, Reverend Mosley raised his hand over their heads and pronounced them man and wife. If the skies had opened and angels had started singing, this moment could not be more momentous.

Back at the house, all was ready for the wedding breakfast. Some wagster in the family had placed mistletoe over the chairs at the head of the table where Nick and Fiona were to sit. At different moments during the breakfast, everyone would start clanging on their glasses with their silverware and demanding a kiss. Usually the glass clanging was started by the giggling children although Carter and Andres led it several times.

Fiona also noticed that Andres was paying marked attention to Gillian.

After dinner, Fiona and Nick went down to the stables where the servants were having their Christmas celebration. There was a merry band of musicians and everyone stomped their feet until Nick and Fiona led a dance.

At last, they could return to the house where the family was still celebrating with games and good cheer. Both she and Nick had decided not to linger. The time had come when they wanted to be alone. He tucked her hand in the crook of his arm. "Come. Let's go upstairs."

However, his invitation to her set off a round of catcalls and suggestions in the family.

The cousins rose from their seats and Fiona could see they were in the mood for a country custom of teasing and mocking the newlywed couple to their bed. Sometimes, overzealous family members would even try to help the bride and groom disrobe.

Nick must have had the same fear. "Run," he said. He didn't have to tell Fiona twice. They took off up the stairs while the younger family members chased them all the way to the bedroom door, which Nick slammed shut in their laughing faces.

At last, Nick and Fee were alone. "Husband and wife," he said. She smiled.

A table had been set up with enough food and drink for them to live a few days inside the room and her clothing now filled his wardrobe.

Fiona went to where she had instructed Sarah to hide her gift for her husband. From under the pillows on the bed, she pulled out a swath of green and blue plaid that had kept her warm and her dreams alive for the past year—her family's tartan.

She faced Nick. "In Scotland, it is the custom for the groom to pin a plaid to his bride. I thought we'd do it in reverse. This, my husband, is the honor of family." She placed it around his shoulders. She rested her hands on his shoulders. "I pray that we have many strong children who will take pride in their father and their heritage."

Nick ran his fingers lightly over the material as if it were more valuable than silk. It was. "It's the only thing I own," she told him, "that is truly mine."

"No, there is something that is truly yours," he answered. "You have my heart."

He held out his arms and gathered her close. "You have seduced me, Fee. Mind, body, and soul. From this day forward, we are one."

And so they were.

Later, holding her lover, her friend, her husband in her arms, Fiona realized that all the roads of her life had led her to this moment, to this man.

She was blessed.

Very blessed indeed.

Celebrate the World of
CATHY MAXWELL—
a world of
love, laughter, and adventure!

**Here's a sneak peek
at tales you may have missed . . .**

In the Highlander's Bed

The survival of his clan depended upon his kidnapping the heiress ... but what to do with her once he had her?

Gordon Lachlan had a choice. He could have beat Constance Cameron or kissed her into submission. He chose the latter—*except* he hadn't anticipated he would have a reaction to this kiss.

When she leaned into him, her breasts flattening against his chest, his hands had no choice but to come down to her waist and pull her closer.

Nor was he satisfied with pressing their mouths together.

Since they were going through the exercise, the very least he could do was show this young woman how to kiss. He ran his tongue along the line of her pressed lips. The sensation tickled and her lips parted.

Gordon took full control. He breathed her, tasted her, enjoyed her.

His men had gone silent. It crossed Gordon's mind that they probably wondered what had come over him. A part of him wondered too. He only meant to subdue her.

But another part of him, the *hard* part, knew he had another motive as well. It was more than just bending her to his will. He'd wanted to know how she'd feel against him.

Here was the edge of desire. One step more and they'd be lost.

But Gordon knew better than to take that step. He held both her hands in his left while his mouth explored hers. Her initial surprise was followed by a searching exploration. Constance had a bright, inquisitive mind. He could tell she'd not been kissed often, but she was a quick learner.

However, someone should have warned her that the curious always paid a price. She paid hers now when he broke off the kiss and stepped away to reveal that he'd tied her hands together with the rope.

His men noticed before her kissed-muddled brain could grasp what had happened. They burst into cheers so loud and so raucous, Gordon almost felt sorry for her.

Almost.

And he was just thankful it was dark enough for Thomas and the others to not notice how tight his breeches were. He was ramming hard.

"You have no one to blame for this but yourself," he said. "You should have been a more willing captive."

"You tricked me," she accused.

"I *kissed* you," he clarified. "There was no trick in that." He leaned closer to say, "But it is a lusty temperament you have, Miss Constance Cameron. There's a fire in you."

He anticipated another attack, expected her to attempt to kick him. Instead, tears welled in her eyes. She looked away, blinking, not wanting him to notice. But he had, and he felt a complete scoundrel.

He hardened his heart. "Mount up," he ordered the lads.

Thomas roared his delight. "You appear the one ready to mount up," he said, and Robbie and Brian laughed.

Apparently the tightness in his breeches had not gone unnoticed.

Gordon frowned. "Save your clever remarks for the English."

Thomas laughed and did as told. Constance was still looking away. The moon's light caught the path of one tear that had escaped down her cheek. Gordon realized she stared in the direction of Edinburgh. He refused to feel guilty.

Instead, he climbed into his own saddle, reached down, grabbed Constance by her waist and pulled her up onto the saddle in front of him.

She arched her back, ready to fight.

"Have done, lass," he said. "No matter what you do, I shall come after you. You are *mine*. At least until Colster hands over the sword. A wise woman would conserve her strength." He couldn't help a tight smile as he said, "The better to tear me apart limb from limb later."

Her struggle stopped. The tear was gone now, dried by the wind. "This isn't a game, is it?" she said quietly.

"Who said it was?"

Her jaw tightened. "That was my first kiss."

He sat back, not knowing what to say.

"A first kiss should mean something," she whispered.

Dear God, had he ever been that innocent? He couldn't remember.

"Kisses rarely do," he answered, and kicking his horse forward, he set off for Ben Dunmore, the mountain camp where his clan waited.

Bedding the Heiress

She'd set the scene for seduction—moonlight on a balcony, the scent of roses in the air—but even the best laid plans can go astray . . .

*F*rancesca Dunroy waited for Lord Penthorpe, the most disreputable rake in London, in the darkness of the terrace outside her father's library, the only relatively private place in a house bursting with guests, laughter, and music. She'd sent him a note, imploring His Lordship to meet her. He was late. He was making her cool her heels, knowing, as she did, that with one word he could ruin her.

For the hundredth time she wondered *why* she had trusted him, and knew the answer—because her father would never have approved of him.

Two days ago, thinking herself safe because it was the middle of the afternoon, she had disguised herself in boy's clothes and, with the help of her maid and a footman, snuck out of her house without alarm. She'd anticipated a lark, an adventure.

Instead, she'd met disaster.

Penthorpe had not wanted some innocent meeting. He'd wanted to elope. When she'd refused to leave with him, he'd attempted rape.

Only her quick wits and a well-aimed kick had protected her virtue, but in the struggle she'd lost her late mother's necklace.

Apparently, during the struggle with Penthorpe, the chain had broken. Francesca hadn't discovered its loss until she'd returned home.

She had to have it back. Not only was it her most cherished possession, it was also proof that she had been in Penthorpe's private rooms.

The door in the library opened.

Penthorpe had come.

The door closed.

She sensed his progress through the library. She heard the faint movement of his steps across the room's thick Indian carpet. He didn't walk out to the terrace immediately but paused in front of the fire.

Her heart pounded. She stepped back into the

shadows. Her original plan had been to firmly demand the pearl, threatening to have the servants toss him out if he refused.

Now, she realized such a plan wouldn't work. He knew she wouldn't call the footmen because then her father would learn the truth.

Francesca was surprised to realize that, in spite of her anger at her father for betraying her mother's memory and marrying so quickly, she didn't want to disappoint him with her own foolishness. Nor did she want anyone else to know how stupidly she had behaved over a rake.

No, she was going to have to cajole the necklace from Penthorpe. She must appeal to his vanity, to make him believe she'd had a change of heart. She would have to seduce him into giving her the pearl. It was the only way that would work.

There was a footfall. He was coming toward the terrace door.

A cloud covered the moon. His shadow darkened the door. Framed as he was against the hearth light from the other room, he appeared taller and larger than she remembered.

He stepped out onto the stone terrace and moved toward the balustrade. He was dressed in black relieved only by the snowy white of his neck cloth. Tension radiated from him. He braced the railing with both hands, acting as if something weighed heavily on his mind. Perhaps he repented what had happened between them—?

Her moment had arrived. *God give her strength.*

She moved forward, her kid dancing slippers making barely a whisper of sound—and yet, he'd heard her.

He started to turn.

Quickly, she slipped her arms through his and around his waist to hold him in place. Pressing her breasts against his back, she whispered, "At last you've come"—even as she realized his shoulders really were broader than she remembered.

And it hadn't been her imagination. He *was* taller. And more muscled . . . and even smelled differently.

This man *wasn't* Penthorpe.

The realization so stunned Francesca, she couldn't think fast enough to untangle her arms before he turned, taking *her* in *his* arms.

His face a shadow, he said, "If I'd known you were waiting for me, lass, I'd have been here sooner." His rolling Scot's brogue confirmed her worst fear.

Before she could issue protest or apology, his lips came down over hers.

And now here's a preview
of the next tale
of the Holburn Series—

Gillian's story . . .

"*A*re you challenging me to a duel?" Wright asked.

"I am," Andres answered.

Gillian's tears evaporated, replaced by stunned horror.

"Swords?" Wright suggested, without missing a beat. "I'm afraid it must be done now. I don't have time to waste. I wish to be back on the road as quickly as possible."

"Then you may leave now," Andres said amicably.

"Not without my *wife*," Wright answered quietly.

Andres shrugged. "Swords are fine."

"No, you *mustn't*," Gillian said to Andres.

"I do it for you, *amor*," he said quietly in his Spanish-accented English. "I love you, Gillian. From the moment I saw you, I knew I was to be with you. Do not worry. All will be well. There isn't an Englishman who is a better swordsman than I."

He loved her. He'd said it aloud. She'd never had anyone say those words to her before—and he'd said them in front of her husband.

But right now was *not* the time for her to be distracted. What if Wright ran him through? What then? Did all men think themselves immortal?

Gillian turned away from him and walked over to where her husband now stood preparing for the duel.

"Wright, you must not fight. Not over me."

Her husband folded his well-cut coat and placed it on a stump by the stable door that was used as a stool or a mounting block. "I take care of what is mine, Gillian."

She made an impatient sound. "Don't claim this is about me. Never me. I matter little to you."

A spark of fire came to his eyes. "Obviously you matter a great deal or I wouldn't be here."

She shook her head. "Wright, our marriage was a sham. It was one of convenience. You married me because of my *father's* political influence."

He released an impatient sigh. "Gillian, this is an old argument between us. So what if those were considerations when I asked for your hand? You could have refused. Why didn't you?"

Now it was her turn to take a step back. She could never tell him the truth—that from the moment she'd first laid eyes on him, she'd tumbled in love with him. He'd think her even more provincial than he already did.

However, that heady, earnest young love had long since died. Her heart was now as hard as a metal shield against him.

"We all make mistakes, Wright," she said, proud at how imperial and cold she sounded.

A flicker of emotion she could not name seemed to pass through his eyes. He looked away and it was gone. The man she knew as her husband returned. "Yes," he drawled, "apparently we all do."

"I hope he runs you through," she said. Turning, she walked away.

A few moments later, the men faced each other, swords in hand.

Gillian crossed her arms. A part of her didn't believe this was going to happen. Men didn't fight over her. Especially her husband.

"First blood wins," Wright said calmly.

"As you wish," Andres answered, without any sign of emotion.

And then they raised their swords.

Wright was a bruising swordsman. Gillian had heard him described that way by an officer who had served with him on the Pennisula. For the first time, she realized her husband had killed men.

She didn't know Andres's experience, but she knew his heart. He would fight to the death for her.

There was the slide of steel on steel, then both men drew their arms back, preparing to fight—

Gillian found her voice. *"No."* She rushed forward, even daring to step between them. They pulled their weapons back just in time, but Gillian was not concerned with her own safety.

"This is nonsense," she informed them. "I'm not worth fighting over."

"We disagree," Andres said.

Wright was quiet, wary, and impatient. Both men were anxious to continue their duel . . . and Gillian knew what she had to do.

Her husband would not give up. Not with his pride at stake.

And Andres . . . Andres so much wanted to be her champion. His love, his loyalty, pierced her soul.

She had only one option. "I'll return to London with you, Wright. You've won. Have a coach readied. We'll leave as soon as I pack."

She did not wait for a response, but started walking toward the house.

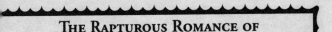

At Avon Books, we know your passion for romance—once you finish one of our novels, you find yourself wanting more.

May we tempt you with . . .

- **Excerpts** from our upcoming releases.
- Entertaining **extras**, including authors' personal photo albums and book lists.
- Behind-the-scenes **scoop** on your favorite characters and series.
- **Sweepstakes** for the chance to win free books, romantic getaways, and other fun prizes.
- Writing **tips** from our authors and editors.
- **Blog** with our authors and find out why they love to write romance.
- **Exclusive content** that's not contained within the pages of our novels.

Join us at
www.avonbooks.com

AVON

An Imprint of HarperCollins*Publishers*
www.avonromance.com